I0580328

THE AMBASSADOR'S WIFE

ROBERTA GATELY

Copyright © 2024 Roberta Gately

The right of Roberta Gately to be identified as the Author of the Work has been asserted by her in accordance with the Copyright, Designs and Patents Act 1988.

First published in 2024 by Bloodhound Books.

Apart from any use permitted under UK copyright law, this publication may only be reproduced, stored, or transmitted, in any form, or by any means, with prior permission in writing of the publisher or, in the case of reprographic production, in accordance with the terms of licences issued by the Copyright Licensing Agency.
All characters in this publication are fictitious and any resemblance to real persons, living or dead, is purely coincidental.

www.bloodhoundbooks.com

Print ISBN: 978-1-916978-72-0

With love and gratitude for my literal better half—my twin sister, Susie, who has looked out for me since the day we were born. Can't imagine life without her. xoxo

The lenses on his sunglasses fogged up as soon as he stepped from the cooled to perfection air of the car into the heat and humidity of the jungle. He paused to wipe his glasses clean noticing as he did the languid, lazy air, even the birds too hot to take flight. A trickle of sweat ran along the back of his neck. He loosened his tie and tugged at his collar, but it did nothing to alleviate the soupy miasma that hovered out here over the countryside.

Bangkok had been hot, make no mistake, but at least there he had air-conditioning and ice-cold drinks to ease the misery. Out here in the middle of nowhere, there were none of Bangkok's luxuries, although really they were necessities—electricity, running water, paved roads—all required for a civilized life. But none available out here. Even the trees offered no relief, and instead served as a backdrop for the veil of mist that seemed suspended from the branches.

The man blinked away the sweat that clouded his vision and looked around. A small circle—all men, and all in suits— stood with their eyes planted firmly on the poor soul who was busy with a crowbar and hammer trying to pry open a heavy wooden crate. The worker wore a tee-shirt and khakis, his feet in plastic sandals. He worked smoothly, only the fine sheen of sweat that coated his face and saturated his shirt, proof that he too, was feeling the effects of the sweltering sun.

The heat was unforgiving and unrelenting—no breeze to lessen the impact. The man took an envelope from his pocket and began to fan himself, the flimsy waft of sodden air not much relief. Jesus, why the hell were suits required for this sort of thing anyway? He stuffed the envelope back into his pocket, slipped his arms from his jacket, and exhaled noisily. The other men followed—throwing off jackets and loosening ties. They barely noticed as he leaned closer to the box and swatted away the flurry of flies and insects that had seemed to gather to watch.

He leaned in for a closer look, but the workman still hadn't been able to loosen the nails that held the crate locked up tight. The worker paused to wipe away the beads of sweat that ran along his forehead. And then he restarted, all eyes trained on him once again. Suddenly, a crack sounded—the unmistakable sound of splitting wood. The heat forgotten, the men moved in closer.

The worker pried open a corner with his crowbar and as a small gap opened in the crate, the putrid scent of rot spiraled out and burned the eyes of the onlookers. In unison, they stepped back as countless flies and insects swarmed in. The worker pulled and banged and finally ripped one long board away, and then another.

The men leaned in and heaved a collective gasp.

"The ambassador's wife," one said, his voice almost a whisper.

CHAPTER ONE

Ambassador? I remember thinking. *Ambassador's wife?* How was that even possible?

The truth of it was, I was invisible by the time I met John Fielding, the kind of invisible that happens to a woman of a certain age when she fades into the background of life. Women will know what I mean—if you don't have children in tow or a man on your arm, it's as though you don't exist at all. And though I detested that invisibility, I would come to crave it in the months ahead.

But I didn't know that then. I knew only that I was ordinary. There was almost nothing remarkable about me—at five feet five, I was of average height, and at one hundred and twenty-five pounds, I was of average weight. I might describe my hair as light brown with flecks of gold, but if I was honest, it was probably a mousy brown. My eyes, though, labeled *brown* on my driver's license, were really a kind of golden honeyed brown. I had creamy skin that never needed makeup, full lips that might have been plumped artificially but weren't, and a nose so pert, I seemed always to be smiling.

I suppose my tendency to see myself as ordinary came from

my mother who named me Nora Rose, a name that conjures up an older, maybe hunched woman well past her prime. My last name was Buckbee which only added to the cringeworthiness of my name. *Nora Rose Buckbee.* Can you even imagine?

I attended a local junior college where I was promised a stepping stone to an exciting legal career. The ad showed a young woman dressed in a tight skirt and Jimmy Choos running up the stairs to a courthouse, files and binders in hand—and really, who wouldn't have believed the sky was the limit? That bit of questionable education led to my job as an administrative assistant, a fancy term for a secretary who's expected to do more than the other secretaries, but for less money, at a law firm in Boston. Among the lawyers all jockeying for recognition and position among their peers, I wasn't even on their radar beyond the messages I passed or the briefs and depositions I copied and filed. It was where my invisibility first became apparent.

Is it any wonder I fell for George? The love of my life, I used to call him, though he wasn't—I just liked the way it sounded. George was a car salesman, the tritest of clichés, and a devilishly handsome charmer who had only to flash a smile and women would fall at his feet. But, at least for the first year or two of our five together, he was as smitten with me as I was with him. Until the day, prodded by my best friend and roommate, Kelly, I gave him the age-old ultimatum: Marry me or else. George took the 'or else,' and I was back on the market at thirty-two, and I'd been there ever since.

Bars were out. I hated the crush of people and preferred to stay at home and watch reruns of *The Bachelor.* Online dating? I was too lazy to make the effort and too fussy to take the chance. But I hadn't lost all hope, and I hadn't really given up on men either. At thirty-five, I was younger than both Jennifer Aniston and Angelina Jolie, and my honey brown eyes sparkled with the right eyeliner. And thirty-five wasn't hopelessly over the hill, just perilously close. I could, after all, still have babies though that window was narrowing by the minute.

My parents, who'd just celebrated forty-four years of wedded bliss, still wished the same for me. It had worked out for my older sister, Susie, who already had seventeen years of marriage and four children under her belt. So, there I was, looking for something, someone, to help me shake off a lifetime of ordinary. I considered changing jobs, but where could I go where I wouldn't have to start at the bottom, a place I was still trying to work my way out of? I considered going back to school but the thought of studying and taking exams again seemed like a giant leap backwards. As for my apartment, Kelly and I had another six months on our lease, and I had a limited—make that zero—budget for exotic travel and adventure.

And then, my mother called. "Nicole's getting married, dear. Isn't she the last of your group?"

I held my breath and counted to ten. I knew she just wanted me to be happy, but she made it feel like a contest, and I was in last place. "Actually, Mom, Kelly and I are both still single."

"Oh, that's right. Well, maybe you'll meet someone nice at the wedding."

I made a face and sighed. Every man at the wedding would be married, gay, or divorced and angry. No thanks. "Hmm," I murmured to avoid an argument.

"All right then, sweetheart. I'll call you Sunday."

I hung up the phone and had a good, long look in the mirror. There had to be something I could do aside from buying a dress for yet another friend's wedding. I unclipped my hair and let it fall to my shoulders. I could start with that—my hair. I knew that no matter what I did, no matter how badly it might turn out, it would eventually grow out. There was a kind of security in that, so I took the plunge, and the following Saturday I sat in the salon chair, my fingers gripping the armrest, while the colorist painted on the sunny hue. She covered my head in foil and then plastic wrap and set a timer. I'd taken slightly less care with the last meal I'd cooked, and nervously, I chewed on my nails and calculated the cost of a wig.

Once she'd finally rinsed, trimmed and styled me, she spun my chair around so I could get a good look at myself under the harsh fluorescent lights. I held my breath, opened my eyes, and... miracle of miracles, I looked good. Actually, I looked better than good. I couldn't help but smile. I exhaled loudly. The blood supply returned to my poor stiff fingers as I ran them through my hair. I was meant to be a blonde. At least that's what the hairdresser said, and I knew she was right.

"Reese Witherspoon," she proclaimed. "That's who you look like." She tucked a stray strand behind my ear.

"I kind of do, don't I?" I said hesitantly, remembering my mother's warning about pretty girls. "Those girls have nothing else on their minds. And you can't spend a lifetime looking into mirrors." But I was new to this kind of pretty, and buoyed by my sexy new look, I stopped at Macy's on the way home and bought the perfect little black dress that hugged me in all the right places. And, despite my mother's admonitions, I smiled at my own reflection—Reese Witherspoon, look out.

As if change had only been waiting for me to step up and embrace it, Kelly's cousin, Ally, who had a glamorous job at the State Department, invited us to Washington, D.C. for a long weekend in a city filled with men and endless possibilities. As if that weren't promising enough, there was a State Department party on Saturday. I wasn't sure what the event was for, but Ally had invited us as her guests. And that was all that mattered.

DC, it turned out, was everything that Boston was not— young and alive and still awake well into the wee hours. On the appointed evening, we primped and preened and slid into Ally's tiny car and drove—at least in my mind—the yellow brick road to the party somewhere near the Capitol.

Though there was traffic aplenty and even pockets of back-ups, the closer we drew to the Beltway, even that seemed magical. It wasn't like gridlock in Boston where drivers shouted obscenities and saluted one another with raised middle fingers. In DC, it was almost symphony-like, drivers crawling through intersections, darting through quickly changing signals, all the while their headlights dancing like tiny swarms of fireflies.

Once we arrived and stepped into the ballroom, the magic continued. Chandeliers glowed above us, and the hum of conversation and the tinkle of cocktail glasses swirled around us as we made our way through the crush of people milling about. I took a glass of wine from one of the roving waiters, and stood and watched, and took it all in. The party, Ally had said before she'd disappeared into the crowd, was to celebrate a deputy assistant to an assistant under secretary of one department or another getting promoted to deputy, but I wasn't sure I understood. I mean, isn't a deputy an assistant so a deputy assistant is an assistant's assistant? No wonder nothing ever gets done in government. Probably, no one knows whose job it really is. But anyway, I wasn't here to worry about that. I was here to have fun so when the music started—my head turned along with everyone else's toward the source of the soft jazz. And there, on a small stage, a jazz quartet played. I nudged Kelly and we moved closer to the music, instinctively tapping our feet and bobbing our heads to the rhythm. Kelly was busy scanning the room for prospects, and it wasn't long before she disappeared too.

I reached for a second glass of wine and turned to watch the partygoers, men and women who probably all knew each other, angling to impress one another, all air kisses and smiles. I forced myself to smile too. No one likes to see a woman standing alone pouting. I spied Kelly through the crowd, chatting up a man whose back was all I could see. I stretched and tried to get a better look, but the crowd shifted, blocking my view. I gripped my evening bag. Maybe I'd look for the Ladies' Room. On the way, I could get a better look at Kelly and her mystery man and the rest of the people here. I couldn't be the only one standing by myself, the proverbial wallflower.

"Excuse me." A decidedly deep voice interrupted my thoughts.

I turned, and in that instant everything around me seemed to come to a full stop. The music faded, the conversation died, the world stopped rotating.

"My name is John, John Fielding," he said, sticking out his hand. "A beautiful woman standing alone in DC is as rare as an honest politician, and I must say you look as out of place as I feel. Okay if I join you?" He raised a brow conspiratorially, and his eyes, a shimmery blue, twinkled. His beard, just a touch over the fuzzy needs a shave look, almost hid his dimples, but they flashed when he smiled. His hair, a deep brown, was trimmed just right. His shoulders strained at the seams of his charcoal suit, the buttons undone, his tie loosened. He was the perfect combination of rugged and yet, somehow, still polished.

I felt my jaw drop open, and my knees went weak, and I do mean weak. I tucked my bag under my arm, transferred my glass to my left hand and held out my hand. His grip was strong, and my skin tingled where he touched me. When he released my hand, I sighed—and quickly composed myself. "I'm Nora Buckbee," I said, avoiding the overwhelming urge to pat my hair or smooth my dress. "Do I really look out of place?" I laughed and tried to sound sophisticated as though I attended these State Department events all the time.

"Maybe out of place is a poor choice of words. Different, but somehow familiar at the same time. Understand?"

My nose crinkled at that, and I shook my head.

He smiled. "You look familiar to me, as though I know you from somewhere, but I can't quite place you."

This time, I smiled and silently thanked Reese Witherspoon. "And different?" I asked.

"As though you're new to this, as though you're as perplexed by all this hoopla as much as I am." His eyes scanned the crowd.

Relieved, I nodded. "You don't work here either?"

"Actually, I do, but I don't really know anyone in DC. I'm usually assigned to the field."

"The field?"

"Foreign offices. I'm just back from the Afghanistan border."

"Really?" I said, unable to keep the gee-whiz tone from my voice. "I'm impressed."

He smiled, his eyes dancing in the tiny shards of light spilling from the chandelier. "Don't be. That stuff always sounds like a bigger deal than it is."

"What did you do there?"

"A little of this—a little of that. But what about you? You live here, in DC?"

I shook my head. "Boston. I'm just visiting, actually."

"Boston, huh? Beacon Hill? I had a roommate once who grew up there."

I shook my head. "I live in South Boston."

"Ahh, *Southie*. Ever run into Whitey Bulger?"

If anyone else had said that I would have groaned and rolled my eyes, but instead, I threw my head back and laughed, as though I'd never heard that line before. "He was on the run long before I got there, but the legend lives on, if you know what I mean." What the hell *did* I mean? What the hell was I talking about? My mouth was speaking before checking with my brain. I took a deep breath.

"So, what do you do in Boston?" he asked, locking his eyes firmly onto mine. I could feel myself swimming in them, his irises pulling me in, the sparkle holding me.

And it was that sparkle that convinced me that he was feeling something too. I hesitated, almost afraid to speak, afraid I'd ruin this moment and break this spell. I didn't want to be boring Nora, the invisible woman. I wanted to be the woman he'd seen—a confident, pretty woman who could stand alone at a party full of strangers. And that, I decided, was the beauty of being in a new place. I could just reinvent myself, and so I did. "I'm a legal assistant at Bain and Worth, a torts and malpractice firm in Boston." That much was true, technically at least, but I didn't stop there. Even to my ears, I sounded as though I was delivering a resume, an embellished one at that. I was so caught up in my story that I made myself sound more important than I was. And I chose the image of that old television ad—the harried assistant running to court, arms full of binders, head full of legal strategy, a woman of substance. He listened intently, nodding every now and then, and so I went on and on. And, why not, I thought. I'd probably never see this gorgeous prince of a man again, so why couldn't I just be Cinderella in Jimmy Choo knock-offs for this one night?

"I went to law school," he said when I finally stopped talking. "But I've never practiced, not even for a minute. I've been here at State since I graduated."

I felt a rush of heat on my cheeks. If he was a lawyer, he'd know my story was a lot of baloney. It was too late to take it back now. "All that work in school, and you didn't want to practice law?"

He shook his head. "Too dull—interrogatories, depositions, briefs, endless case reviews. No thanks. By the time I discovered I hated it, I'd put in too much time to just quit, so I graduated, took the bar, and then looked for something else."

All my white lies—for nothing. I began to laugh, a little at first, and then so hard my sides hurt. "Sorry," I finally said, deciding to come clean. "I feel your pain. It is boring as hell, isn't it? It's not nearly so exciting as I tried to make it seem. But it's a job, so I can't really complain." I shrugged and finished my wine, my eyes searching for the roving waiters. I was definitely going to need another glass.

He brushed a strand of hair from my face, my skin sizzling where he touched, his hand lingering for a minute longer than necessary. I sighed. I could imagine him tearing off my dress and taking me right there on the floor. He smoothed my stray hair and took a slow deep breath, seeming to catch himself. He'd been thinking the same thing. I was certain. I could see it in his eyes and the way his shoulders stiffened as if to hold himself in check. He stepped back the tiniest bit and cleared his throat, but that hint of magic remained.

Suddenly, the music stopped, fluorescent overhead lights flickered and buzzed before throwing the room into full light. I blinked at the unexpected brightness and watched as everyone moved to the center of the room. A tall, thin man took the microphone and tapped it, sending a shrill whistle through the room. He adjusted his eyeglasses and peered at the crowd, his eyes finally resting on John who nodded politely.

"Glad to see you all tonight," he said. "I know we're here to celebrate, but before this party really gets started, I wanted to remind you that we're here to recognize one of our own, so let's get on with it." A round of polite applause interrupted him, and he held up his hand in acknowledgment. "This man has been a tireless advocate for the State Department. He has never turned down an assignment. He has faced equal amounts of both danger and boredom, and he's done it with great enthusiasm and vigor. He's an asset to whatever mission he's assigned. And, tonight, we are proud to see him promoted to a richly deserved position—Assistant Deputy Under Secretary for Political and Foreign Affairs."

The room broke into cheers and hoots and wild applause, and I watched stunned as the man on stage pointed toward John.

"John Fielding," the man on stage said. "Come up and take a bow."

John squeezed my hand and leaned into me. "Promise you won't move," he whispered. "I'll be right back." And with that, he was gone—almost swallowed by the crowd of well-wishers until a shadowy figure of a man reached out and grabbed his arm. John shook his head and pulled away abruptly before disappearing back into the crowd. The man, a scowl on his lips, raked his hand through his hair, his eyes riveted then on the stage. Moments later John emerged and stepped up to the podium where he embraced the speaker and took hold of the microphone.

"Thanks for the kind words, Ron. I just want to thank everyone for arranging this little get-together tonight. Any excuse to drink, right?" He raised his glass in a mock toast to the crowd, and a cheer rose up. "But seriously, thank you all. I really do appreciate this." He smiled and looked over the crowd. "I see more than a few empty glasses out there. Let's have a round on the State Department." Another cheer erupted, and the lights were once again dimmed leaving only the speckles of light from the chandeliers.

I stood desperately sifting through my remarks to John. Had I actually mentioned how absurd the title of assistant deputy to the assistant deputy sounded, or had I just thought it? I needed another glass of wine so I headed toward the bar, my eyes scanning the room for any sign of Kelly. Instead, I spotted the man who'd stopped John. He was shoving his cellphone into his pocket, his eyes boring into the crowd. He said something to a young woman, and she shrugged, a puzzled look on her face. When he turned my way, I ducked and elbowed my way through the partygoers. When I made it to the bar, I found myself wedged in behind a crush of people with the same idea. I turned back. I'd likely find more success searching out the roving waiters, but there was no sign of them either.

I was just about ready to give up when I felt a hand on my shoulder and a rush of hot breath in my ear.

"I thought I'd lost you," John whispered.

My heart fluttered, and I turned.

He tilted my chin up and kissed me, a slow lingering kiss, and I melted into him as though I'd known and loved him forever. I heard muffled voices, a whistle and a smattering of applause, and I pulled away, embarrassed. John wrapped his arms around me and kissed the top of my head. "We're stars," he whispered.

And that was how it all began.

CHAPTER TWO

Six months later, after a whirlwind courtship, and a series of almost meteoric promotions for John, he was named ambassador to Thailand, and we were married in the rectory at St. Brigid's. My parents, John's tiny Russian-speaking mother, and Kelly, crowded into the cluttered space. I wore a sand-colored cocktail dress with three-quarter sleeves and tiny seed pearls sewn into the bodice that I'd bought on sale at Macy's. John wore a three-piece suit and a rakish smile that took my breath away. When the priest asked if I took John as my husband, I choked back my tears of joy. "Yes," I whispered. And though it was true that I still knew so little about the details of his life, I loved him and what else did I really need to know?

John squeezed my hand and slipped a simple gold band onto my finger. My fingers trembled as I slipped an identical band onto his. Through a fog, I heard the priest say, "I now pronounce you man and wife."

My heart fluttered. John pulled me close and kissed me. "Mrs. Fielding," he whispered.

Our honeymoon had to be delayed. "There's too much to do," John had said. "In DC, we both have to go through some protocol training, and I have a slew of meetings before we leave, but maybe we can stop in Paris on the way to Bangkok."

Wedding—Paris—Bangkok. My life had certainly changed, and I felt it. At the State Department, a curving labyrinth of corridors and wide hallways, people walked with their eyes to the floor as if avoiding everyone—like the law firm only times a million. I fought my insecurities and remembered I was Nora Buckbee no more. I was Mrs. Fielding now—the wife of the next ambassador to Thailand. I smiled giddily through it all. As they learned who I was, people began to notice me. They smiled and nodded and looked me in the eye. I was one of them—an insider. And, as people treated me differently, I began to see myself differently. My days of invisibility were a blurred memory.

I sat through two days of protocol training, the basics of meeting and interacting with kings and queens and presidents, and even common folks. Who knew there were so many nuances to a simple hello, or that the head was the most revered part of the body, and I should never touch someone's head? Well, the State Department knew, and they were determined that I'd know too. In Thailand, I would greet locals with my hands together as if in prayer while I bowed my head. "Would you curtsy to a princess?" a protocol staffer asked me during a particularly rigorous round of instruction. My brain tried to sift through the endless rules that had been drilled into me, but I just wasn't sure. "Yes," I said, feigning a confidence I didn't feel and scribbling Mrs. Fielding all over my notepad. I did like the way it looked.

The staffer shook her head sadly.

I fared better on the political and history part of my training. I learned that Thailand, formerly known as Siam, was a kingdom, and it was that kingdom on which the movie, *The King and I*, was based. I felt like an expert already. I mean, I'd seen that movie only about a hundred times. So, when they said there was still a king there— King—I knew I'd be okay as long as I didn't have to pronounce his name. And maybe Prince William and Princess Kate would visit. It wasn't out of the realm of possibility, right? And with that, my training was finished and we were on our way. We headed for the airport, and the first flight on our trip to Thailand.

"Paris next time. I promise," John had said. "I already have some issues to deal with in Bangkok, and I'm expected there for meetings this week."

"What about the king?"

John chuckled. "He's not coming to the airport, but we'll likely meet him soon enough. You ready?"

We flew first to San Francisco and then to Japan, changing planes one last time before heading on to Bangkok. The trip took a dizzying twenty-eight hours, and any fear of flying I might have harbored, was whittled away. We flew business class, so it was slightly more comfortable than coach, and there was even a little more wiggle room.

"Try to get some sleep," John said, planting a quick kiss on my lips. He folded his arms, stretched out his legs, drew up his blanket, and within what seemed like minutes, he was snoring softly. I tried to follow his lead and I curled up in my seat, closed my eyes, and lay wide awake, my mind racing, silently quizzing myself on the last week's lessons. Did I curtsy? No, I bowed as if in prayer. Did I serve beef? I couldn't remember, but I think I had a handbook somewhere. I fished through my carry-on, but all I found was the latest gossip magazine. I wondered if they had these in Thailand. I plucked it out and sat back to read, and probably even napped, for it seemed not so long before we were descending through the clouds, the puffy white scenery replaced by a portrait of a lush landscape—a jungle almost. I pressed my nose against the tiny window to see it all—the swaying palms, the trees that almost touched the clouds, and tiny ant sized huts that peeked through the green. As we descended further in our approach to Bangkok, the scenery changed once again, and I saw not the tiny kingdom I'd envisioned, but a vast metropolis instead. I nudged John awake, my gaze locked on the city below. Soaring skyscrapers and glistening lights dotted the streets. Could this be Paris, after all? I turned to John.

I felt more than heard the thud of the landing gear as we approached Bangkok, and instinctively, I smoothed my hair and uncrossed my legs, all the while praying I was ready for this.

"May I have your attention?" the stewardess asked, as the plane glided onto the runway. "We will be stopping shortly to allow our new ambassador to Thailand, and his wife, to depart the plane. Please remain seated during their exit. And please join me in wishing them much success in Thailand." A murmur of voices and polite applause followed.

John took my hand. "Look," he whispered as a sleek black limousine, a small American flag waving from the hood, pulled into view. I swallowed the hard lump in my throat.

John squeezed my arm. "Beautiful sight, isn't it? You're going to love it."

Okay, so it was Bangkok, just not the somewhat old-fashioned Bangkok I'd imagined. The plane taxied, not to a terminal, but to a spot in what seemed the middle of the runway. A stairway was rolled out to the plane and, as John and I exited, I noticed a small official-looking group standing on the tarmac. "Are they here to meet us?" I asked.

John nodded. "Some embassy staff, and a few local officials. Just nod when the Thais greet you, no handshakes. I'm just not sure if there are any royals among them."

And then I remembered one of my first lessons—no

touching the royals. Maybe it would all come back to me after all. I followed John down the stairs and into the sticky heat of late afternoon. It was late March, and Boston, and then DC, had still been mired in those cold gray days when it seemed winter would never end. I'd dressed for that. My new suit was made of wool, and as beads of sweat began to trickle down my back, the fabric became unbearably scratchy and damp. I resisted the urge to take off my jacket, and instead I smiled and folded my hands in greeting. The reception line was informal, the smiles genuine, the chatter comforting.

"This is the start of summer really," one young woman whispered. "You'll have staff to take you shopping when you're ready."

"Thank you," I whispered, grateful for the offer. "Is today too soon?" I asked, only half joking. I didn't catch her name, and afraid of seeming rude, I only smiled.

"I think you'll want to rest today and maybe have a look around your house. But this week, we'll do it this week if you'd like."

I bowed and placed my hands together each time a local official was introduced, and I kept a friendly smile planted on my face to stifle the long yawns I could feel coming. Damn, I was tired.

And then the limousine appeared—right there on the tarmac. The doors opened and we were ushered inside, alone again at last. I exhaled noisily and yawned.

"You'll be able to sleep at the house." John pushed a damp strand of hair behind my ear and kissed my forehead.

I squirmed in my jacket and poked at my back. "I didn't know it would be so hot," I said, reaching a hand under my jacket, and finally—blissfully—scratching my back.

"I always forget the weather stuff, but it's spring right now, probably the best time to come." He reached for me. "I'll scratch your back when we get home. In the meantime, I'll turn this on." He fiddled with some buttons and a cooling breeze filled the car.

"We forgot our luggage," I said, anxious to have my own things close by.

"Probably already there," he said. "Staff handles that stuff."

I settled into his embrace and watched through the tinted windows as we made our way out of the airport and through the streets of Bangkok, and suddenly, I was wide awake. We were driving on the wrong side of the road, and as I peered through the Plexiglas separation, I could see the driver was on the wrong side as well. I sat forward, my back rigid. I flinched every time a car came too near.

"I forgot to mention the driving system here. Sorry about that, but it really is safe. I guess I don't even notice anymore, and I'm willing to bet that soon enough, you'll be driving here, too." He pulled me back and draped his arm over my shoulder.

He was right. I needed to take a deep breath, just relax, and let myself experience Thailand. I glanced through the windows again, and saw the streets were teeming with cars, bicycles, tiny motorized rickshaws, and a few brave pedestrians all struggling to squeeze in. As crowded as they were, the streets were immaculately clean—not a speck of trash or litter anywhere in sight. Tucked in between the buildings were bustling shops and little bazaars where tiny bent women hawked trinkets and souvenirs. Signs in English were sprinkled in among signs in scrolled, whirling, fanciful script. The Thai language, I guessed, though my instructors in DC said most people in the city spoke English. Bangkok—at least what I could see—was a thriving blend of old and new, foreign and familiar. It was as strange and exciting as anything I'd imagined, and I clung tight to John's hand, and wondered how I'd ever find my way through the maze of streets and the crush of people. We drove on and John pointed out the embassy, but all I could see was a high white fence and an endless line of armed guards. "I'll bring you in this week," he said.

We continued along the boulevard, moving further into the hub of traffic and people, passing more high fences and still more armed guards. "A fair amount of embassies and official residences along here." John pointed to a row of red-tiled roofs poking above the fences and shrubs.

My eyes fixed on the guns, and a chill ran along my spine. "Is there trouble here?"

"Not really, but the US is always a target. Better to be safe. You're not worried, are you?" He pulled me close and kissed the top of my head. "The house is just up here on the same street as the embassy. Good to know if you ever get lost."

We made a wide turn into a bank of high fences topped by curved metal spikes. An armed guard stepped forward and opened the gate, waving the limousine through a long, winding driveway. I sat forward, my eyes open wide. The ambassador's house was a palatial white house, ringed by palm trees and lush greenery. Flowering shrubs provided a splash of color. Plantation shutters adorned the windows. An American flag flew from the second story. The car doors opened, and I stepped out and inhaled the sweet scents of roses and jasmine and newly budding lilies. A small group stood at the entrance. John placed his hand on my back and guided me along.

"Good to see you, John," a tall man said, extending his hand to John.

John slapped the man's back and gave him one of those quick man-hugs. "I guess this means no time off for me, huh?" He laughed and turned to me. "This is my wife, Nora. Nora, this reprobate is Dave, my old friend from many a mission."

And I stepped back. This Dave bore a striking resemblance to the mysterious man I'd seen in DC the night we'd met, the man who'd reached for and been rebuffed by John. The man's smile cut through the chiseled lines of his jaw, and he took my hand. "Nora Fielding, so good to meet the woman who tamed this old bastard."

"Nice to meet you too, Dave." I smiled and looked nervously back to John who gave no hint of the rancor that had seemed to define their odd encounter in DC. Instead, he turned and motioned to a pretty, young woman. She stepped forward.

"This is my wife, Nora."

A shadow passed over the woman's face, but disappeared so quickly, I might have only imagined it. She nodded and bowed slightly. I placed my hands together and bowed in turn. She was small—maybe five feet, but she carried herself with the grace of a much taller woman.

"I am Mae," she said, her voice a sing-songy mixture of accents. Her almond eyes flashed. "I will help you to run the house, and to manage things. So everything is perfect. You understand?"

Despite her gentle demeanor, there was a decidedly hard edge to her smile, as though she was forcing it. I nodded. "I'm Nora, and I will definitely need some help with everything. Could we start with protocol lessons?"

She laughed softly, her perfectly manicured hands fluttering to her face. "Yes. Yes, not to worry. But first things first—here is Chai."

She moved and a tiny woman, her gray hair held tight under a net, stepped forward. Her head was bowed, her hands gnarled and held together in the prayer-like greeting. When she raised her face to look at me, I folded my own hands and nodded.

"Hello. It's good to meet you." I'd already forgotten her name, but there was time enough for that.

She dropped her hands to her sides and nodded, the weariness in her eyes making her seem older than she likely was. A trickle of sweat ran along her forehead. She glanced at John and then back toward the house, impatient, I thought, to get away from the fuss. I reached out to take her hand, and suddenly remembered the rule—no touching. I snapped my own hands back and smiled again, hoping to put her at ease. "I know you probably have work to do. I won't keep you."

She nodded, the slightest tilt of her head, as she turned and disappeared back into the house.

Mae sighed heavily. "Good help is hard to find," she said. "Ahh, well, we can worry about that later. I know you've had a long trip. Are you very tired? I can show you to your room." Mae was suddenly as animated as the older lady was listless.

The yawn that I'd been holding back finally broke free, and I covered my mouth with my hand. Mae giggled. "Come," she said, turning to the house. "Let's get you settled."

John kissed my cheek. "I'm going to the embassy with Dave. Get some sleep. I'll see you for dinner."

Mae led me inside, and I stopped, my mouth agape. The entrance was grand—high ceilings, a chandelier glistening above, shiny hardwood floors beneath, sparkling rooms off to each side and a central staircase just ahead. I took a slow, deep breath. I was definitely not in Southie anymore.

Mae led me up the stairs, and along a wide corridor. An open porch, a veranda, ran along the back. She stopped and opened a door and nodded. "Here we are," she said. "This is the smaller master, but it will have to do. No one told me that the new ambassador was married."

At that moment, she seemed almost angry that she hadn't known about me. "Well, we only just got married," I said, rushing to explain. "I'm sorry you weren't informed, but this room looks perfect for us, so please don't give it another thought."

"Your suitcase is there," she said, pointing to a small table that held my luggage. And if you'd like, I can have the staff unpack for you." She went to the windows and pulled in the shutters. Immediately, a comforting darkness settled on the room. She opened another door. "This is your closet."

I peeked in. It was the size of my bedroom in Southie.

She opened another door. "And this is your bathroom."

My jaw dropped open. A sparkling white room with an oversized bathtub, separate shower, double sinks, and a reading chair greeted me. Thick cotton towels were folded into a basket. John and I had stayed at the Four Seasons when he'd come to Boston, and I'd always been impressed by the understated elegance there. But this took it a step further, a click above, and I was going to *live here*.

"I know you need to sleep, so I'll leave you now." She shut the bedroom door softly and I pulled off my clothes, hung them up quickly and crawled into the most comfortable bed in the world. I pulled the comforter over my head, and that's the last thing I remembered before drifting into a blissful sleep.

CHAPTER THREE

I woke to a splash of sunshine trickling in through the shutter's slats, and an eerie quiet that I wasn't used to. No blaring horns, no sirens, no sounds of a city waking. I rubbed my eyes and glanced at my watch. Ten p.m. No way it was still night. I'd fallen into bed just as dusk was settling on Bangkok. Damn, I hadn't changed my watch. What had they said? The time difference was eleven hours. Or was it twelve? Either way, I'd been sleeping for at least twelve, maybe thirteen, hours. It had to be eight *a.m.* John's side of the bed was rumpled, proof at least that he'd been there, though he was likely long gone. I threw back the covers and opened the shutters, a flood of light filling the room. Below, I could see a small man, his head and face obscured by a broad-brimmed hat, bend to a lush rosebush, clippers in hand. I breathed deeply, the rich scent of flowers carrying all the way to my second-floor window.

I craned my neck trying to see if John's car was still there, but it was no use. I couldn't see beyond the rows of flowers and hedges. But perhaps he was still here, and if I hurried, I might just catch him. At home, I would have thrown on a robe and just gone downstairs. But this didn't feel like home, not yet, and clothes were probably required for the ambassador's wife. I rifled through my suitcase and chose jeans and a blouse, and then I stopped cold. Were jeans okay? Damn it to hell, I should have paid attention in class instead of scribbling my new name all over everything. I pulled on my jeans and blouse and pulled open the door praying that Mae was here.

On the main floor, the French doors and windows were thrown open to a cool morning breeze. A bouquet of fresh-cut flowers had been placed on the entry table, intensifying the garden scents that wafted in. I hadn't had a look around yesterday, so I poked my head into the rooms off the entryway. To the right was a formal living room, and to the left a large library, or maybe it was an office. Either way, the furniture seemed a little ornate, right out of one of those *House Beautiful* magazines that dotted waiting rooms everywhere, but a little stuffy for me. I turned, and out of the corner of my eye, I caught something slithering along the wall. A rat? A snake? I snapped my head around to get a look and caught a quick glimpse of a tiny lizard scurrying out through the French doors. I laughed. Maybe not so stuffy after all, but still there was going to be a lot to get used to here in Bangkok.

A clatter of dishes and pans drew me through a long hallway and back to an enormous kitchen. Restaurant-sized appliances lined the wall, and in the center, a long butcher-block island was flanked by glass-fronted cabinets filled with dishes and glasses. I stepped inside and there sat the older lady I'd met when I arrived. Bent to a steaming cup of tea, she was engrossed in reading a small book. I cleared my throat and, a slight smile draping her lips, she jumped to attention.

"No, no," I said. "Please sit. Enjoy your breakfast. I'm just looking for coffee."

She stood, her gnarled fingers raised, her head bowed. I

bowed in turn, and she smiled, wider this time. One small victory.

"Hello," she said softly. "You remember me? I'm Chailai."

"And I am Nora." I paused, afraid I'd butcher her name. "Nice to meet you again, Chlyee." I could have kicked myself. Even to my untrained ears, I knew I'd mangled the pronunciation. I winced.

She giggled. "Sorry to laugh," she said, a choppy accent evident. "Chailai is difficult to say. "Just call me Chai. Think of the tea that people drink."

"Ahh, Chai. Thank you. That much I can remember and say."

"Come." She pointed to the hallway. "There is coffee in the dining room. You can sit and I will make your breakfast."

I shook my head. "I can't let you make breakfast just for me, Chai. I'll—"

Her eyes flashed. "It is my job," she said adamantly. "If you cook, I have no job." She folded her arms tight across her chest and looked away.

It was then I noticed remnants of a younger Chai—a hint of sparkle through the hazy veil of age that shadowed her eyes, a loose strand of blue-black hair poking through the gray, and a barely there blush almost hidden in the loose skin that draped her cheeks. I could feel the heat of her stare. "I-I'm sorry. I guess I didn't realize we'd have someone cooking for us. It might just take some getting used to."

Her face softened. "You'll be busy, Miss. You won't have time to cook. So, what would you like?"

And suddenly, I realized I was famished. "Could I get some eggs and toast?"

She nodded. "You like scrambled?" She led me into the dining room, a large, formal room off the main living room. A long mahogany table filled the center of the room; serving tables lined the wall. One of those held a silver coffee pot and a tray of cups and saucers. Before I could reach for the coffee, Chai had poured a cup and placed it on the table. "Sit," she said, pulling out a chair. Several newspapers sat on the sideboard, and I grabbed one. Might as well read. I sipped the coffee and read the *Bangkok Post*. No gossip, at least that I could find, no stories about Boston or DC, no word on the Red Sox spring training. And then I found my horoscope:

> You're feeling domesticated today and will enjoy being busy around the home. You might be inspired to do some cleaning or tidying up, or you could get the urge to be busy in the kitchen. It's also a good day to stock up on a few household essentials, such as cupboard ingredients, and you might even snap up a few bargains in the process.

And I laughed out loud just as Chai returned with my eggs. I inhaled my breakfast, had another cup of coffee, and returned my plates to the kitchen.

Chai's face fell when she saw me. I looked at the dishes. "I'm not supposed to bring them back, am I?"

"That is for me." She took the dishes and piled them into a deep, industrial-size sink. "You here for lunch?"

"I'm not sure. Did you see John this morning?"

"The ambassador?"

I nodded.

"He say he back for dinner, say for me to make something special." She smiled, revealing a row of crooked teeth. "Okay?"

"Okay. Is Mae in?"

Her brow furrowed and she shook her head. "Mae comes later. You go. Have a look around the house. Tell Mae if you approve."

She bent to her work, slicing, chopping, grating, her

fingertips laced with cuts and scrapes, testament to her work. I winced as she sliced perilously close to her fingers, and I knew I should just leave her alone. But the scents were intriguing, and I wanted to say something polite. "Chai, thank you for everything, and though I'm really not a cook, I'm definitely someone who likes to eat."

I was on my own, at least for now, and I spent the morning exploring my new house—the three extra bedrooms—probably for children, but for us they'd be for guests, at least for now. Another room—the other master, maybe—was locked, but it didn't matter. There were so many rooms already. I couldn't wait to tell my parents and Kelly. As long as we could have visitors, I'd be okay. The second floor was also home to what must be the family room. A couch, two cushioned reading chairs and a table flanked a cozy fireplace. A deeply tufted rug covered the floor. Bookcases lined one wall and a large stand held an oversized flat screen television. The table held an array of magazines—Thai visitor guides and current events calendars. Not a gossip magazine in sight. I sank onto the couch pulling my feet up and began to flip through the magazines when I heard the tapping of shoes on the corridor's wooden floors. I stood just as Mae entered.

Her hands together, she bowed slightly. I returned the greeting. "You slept well?" she asked.

"Too well. I only got up an hour ago."

She smiled. "You were very tired. Have you had a look around your house?"

I nodded. "But I'd love a real tour. I'm not sure what all the rooms are for. There are so many. And one is locked."

"That one's been locked. The key is lost, I'm told. But we can look at the other rooms if you'd like." She led me back through the rooms on the second floor, and tucked in a corner off the long hall, was another informal room with couches and easy chairs arranged around a table. "For unofficial meetings," she said, rearranging a cushion. "The ambassador may sometimes prefer to speak with others up here where there is greater privacy."

She continued back down the hall pointing out the three guest rooms. Ignoring the locked room, she led the way back to my bedroom, and I stopped cold. My bed was made, the comforter drawn up, the pillows fluffed. I glanced into the closet. Someone had unpacked my clothes, ironed them and hung them up. I ran my hand over my linen dress, now smooth as glass and free of the wrinkles I'd noticed this morning when I'd pulled out my jeans. I looked questioningly at Mae.

"You have staff here. Besides Chailai, there is a part-time housekeeper, a gardener, and sometimes people come from the embassy when there are big events to plan."

And then it hit me. All the pomp and circumstance, the big house, the staff—I was the *ambassador's wife.* I had responsibilities. I cursed myself—not for the first time, and surely not the last—for daydreaming during class in DC. I wanted to call Kelly, but a quick peek at my watch confirmed that it was late at home. She'd probably be sound asleep. Mae must have noticed my consternation.

"It's quite a lot to take in on your first day. But you'll get used to the way things are here, and in only weeks, you'll feel right at home."

I breathed a sigh of relief. "It is overwhelming. I think I just realized what a big deal it really is."

Mae nodded. "You aren't the first wife to feel that way, and you will do fine—just as they did."

I wondered about the others, how they'd managed, how they'd gotten used to this. "What do I need to know right now? There must be some rules of etiquette that are absolute."

"There are—the Thai national anthem is played in all

public places in the morning and again in the evening. If you are out, you must stop to show respect. And if you attend a public event or a movie, a photo of the king will be shown and the King's Anthem will be played before the show can begin. For that you must stand too."

For someone so young—she couldn't have been more than twenty-five—Mae was well versed in diplomacy, and in life, I guessed. I suddenly felt old and insecure and worried that maybe I wasn't up to the responsibilities here. I took a deep breath. "And you'll help me to remember it all?"

She fiddled with the bracelets that lined her wrist and hesitated before nodding her head ever so slightly.

CHAPTER FOUR

My first days passed in a blur of new people, new sights, new food, and very little John. "So sorry, babe, but I'm swamped. I'll make it up to you." And with a quick kiss he was out the door again. Most evenings, he was home only for a hurried dinner before he was gone again. My visions of cozy nights in front of the fire or in the garden remained only visions. I puttered around, hung our wedding portrait above the fireplace, and placed another on my bedside table, small reminders that this was our house now. But, aside from putting a bit of a personal touch around the house, there wasn't much to do, so I was grateful when Mae announced that first week, that she was taking me to the embassy for a look around.

"So, you can see where the ambassador works," she said, smiling as we passed the armed guards on our way out of the residence. I wasn't sure I'd ever get used to them.

The driver navigated along the route we'd taken the night we'd arrived. Already, I was less anxious about the whole wrong side of the road thing. I rolled down my window to get a better feel for the city, the heat of the day and the hazy air quickly seeping into the car. Mae sighed and fanned herself dramatically with a paper she'd pulled from her bag. I should have offered to close the window, but I didn't. I pretended I didn't notice and turned my attention to the road. The city's sights were much the same as those I'd seen on my arrival—crowds jostling for space, harried drivers beeping, shouting, everyone in a rush just like it would have been at home. The scents I'd expected—of exotic spices and tropical plants—instead were replaced by the smoky stench of car and factory exhaust. Bangkok was a large, bustling city after all, not so different from Boston or New York. The driver took a turn and stopped at the embassy gates. And my jaw dropped open. We were so close we could have just walked. When I asked Mae why we hadn't, she shook her head.

"People should know who you are," she said. "You should always arrive in style."

I held back the laughter that threatened my composure. It seemed like a whole lot of fuss, but I knew I had to do what was expected. After a thorough check of our documents, a trio of guards waved us inside, and as I exited the car, my gaze was instantly drawn to the building. It wasn't at all what I'd expected. The embassy, a white concrete fortress with rectangular slits masquerading as windows, resembled a prison. If it weren't for the expressionless Thai soldiers and somber U.S. Marines, guns at the ready, standing guard, and the grilles over every window, I might have been looking at any nondescript building anywhere. I'd expected something grand like the White House, but instead the embassy was more like an office complex. Once inside, the halls were filled with throngs of people—Thais and Americans—and I smiled every chance I got. An American flag and pictures of the president and secretary of state flanked the main hall. Mae led the way pointing out the different offices—defense attaché, visa specialist, public information, and on and on—too many to remember. Several hundred worked here, and it seemed at that moment, they were all scurrying this way and that along the corridors.

Finally, Mae turned back to me. She tucked an errant strand of silky coal-black hair into the smooth bun at the nape of her neck. "It's a lot to take in. Would you like to see the ambassador's office?"

I perked up. "I'd love to. Is John in, do you know?"

She shrugged her shoulders. "Hard to say for sure, but we'll see."

I followed her to the top floor and along a carpeted hall to a glassed-in reception area. She pulled the door open and nodded as a young female Marine watched us warily.

"Hello," I whispered to the Marine who relaxed and smiled in turn. I wasn't sure why I was whispering but it somehow seemed appropriate in this office.

Mae approached the desk and explained who I was. The young woman stood and stuck out her hand. "Welcome to Bangkok, Mrs. Fielding."

I shook her hand. "Thank you—" and I paused, waiting for her to tell me her name. She seemed confused, and a blank look came over her face. I leaned in closer. "I don't know your name."

She shook her head. "I'm sorry. I don't know where my head is today. I'm Kim."

I flashed my warmest smile. It hadn't been so long ago that I would have been the nervous one. "Nice to meet you, Kim. I'm Nora. Is the ambassador in?"

"You just missed him. He went to the border, I think. I'm not sure when he'll be back."

I felt my shoulders slump. I'd hoped that seeing him in his new element would help me to understand his work and forgive him for all the time he spent here. I heaved a sigh and turned to Mae.

"Well, I'm sorry we've missed him, but we'd like to see his office," she said.

Kim snapped to attention and picked up the phone, and within seconds, a tall man with unruly brown hair that fell into his eyes, and one of those immediately appealing smiles, appeared. He adjusted his loosened tie with one hand and extended the other to me. "Mrs. Fielding, good to meet you. I'm Jim Leo, the deputy chief of mission."

His handshake was warm, his grip firm, his eyes a warm mahogany. I liked him right away. He'd be perfect for Kelly, I thought as he released my hand. "I'll call you Jim if you'll call me Nora," I said in my embassy whisper.

He leaned down. "No need to whisper, Nora. The place is bugged and if you speak too softly, the powers that be will be suspicious of our meeting."

I burst out laughing, my first genuinely relaxed moment since I'd arrived in Bangkok. "Well, that's good to know," I said between my fits of laughter. "You know, just in case I have secrets."

Jim chuckled and I followed him to a double, wide mahogany door. There on a gold plaque I read *The Honorable John Fielding, Ambassador to Thailand*. My brain felt fuzzy at the sight. Jim sensed my surprise. "They tried to post a picture of him in the lobby—right under the secretary of state. That's the protocol, but he wouldn't have it. Said this post is temporary and the less people see of him, the better."

Mae giggled, not for any reason I could tell other than to get Jim's attention. He ignored her and turned, throwing open the wide doors, and I stopped dead in my tracks. This room really did look like the Oval Office that I'd seen about a million times on the nightly news—a fancy desk flanked by pictures of the secretary of state and the president, a flag in the corner, computers, telephones and trunk lines everywhere, papers and folders stacked helter-skelter on the desk, and a full bookcase lining one wall. I stepped inside reverentially and went behind the desk, and there amidst the diplomatic clutter was our wedding picture—John kissing me right after our vows. I picked it up and had a good long look. It wasn't that I was surprised that he had this right on his desk—though maybe I was a little—it was just that it seemed he was shouting to the world that he loved me. I felt a tiny shiver of happiness, and I placed the photo back on his desk. His chair was like the partners' chairs at my old law firm, but maybe better—it was leather and swiveled and rocked back. I gripped the back, the leather smooth and buttery to the touch. In front of me, along the wall facing the desk, were a matching leather couch, and a coffee table with two chairs on either side. Two closed doors, closets maybe, or entrances into other offices, were tucked, almost hidden, in the side wall. I spun around one more time. This was the office of an important man, and I understood—for the first time—how important John was. I cursed myself for my months of whining—mostly to myself or Kelly—about how busy he was. Now I knew.

"Pretty impressive, huh?"

I looked up to see Jim straightening a pile on John's desk. "It usually takes a visit to the inner sanctum for a family to realize just how much an ambassador has on his plate."

I whistled. "I can see that. I guess I thought it sounded easy—shake hands, give statements, speak to the secretary—that kind of stuff. Sounds pretty naïve." I ran my finger along the desk. "Will he be back soon?" Maybe we could have lunch or just spend even a few minutes together, I thought.

"Afraid not. He's out for the day, maybe for the night."

Jim spoke so matter-of-factly that it took me a minute to realize he'd said *for the night*. "Really?" I asked, trying not to sound surprised or hurt. Mae moved closer, inclining her head as Jim spoke.

"He didn't really say much. He had some issues to deal with, that's all. Wish I could be of more help. But—" He shrugged his shoulders.

"Will he call?" I heard my voice crack, the morning's confidence shattered. Our courtship, lightning quick as it was, was marked by his frequent unexpected trips out of the country. "I'll be traveling less in Thailand, I promise," he'd said. And I'd believed him. Every word. So much for promises.

"Can't say. Maybe. If he does, I'll tell him to call you pronto, okay?"

I nodded, afraid to speak. Why hadn't he called me? Why did I have to hear about his trip from a stranger? I took a deep breath. I had to stop. I was creating a problem where none existed. It was that old demon—insecurity—rearing its ugly head. I was Nora Buckbee once again—the invisible legal assistant—just trying to find my way. I shook off the thought, forced a broad smile, and stuck my hand out. "Thanks for showing me around, Jim."

Jim took hold of my hand in his and squeezed. "It's all good, Nora. He's a busy man."

"I know."

He patted my shoulder. "I'm sure I'll be seeing you again soon."

"Thank you, Jim," Mae said in her sing-songy voice, and I suddenly realized we'd come to the embassy because it was Jim —not John—she wanted to see. I smiled. I could relate to that.

I said my goodbyes, all the while mulling over John's busy life. I had too much time on my own hands—that was the problem. I'd known John would be busy, but I hadn't known how un-busy I'd be. And though we'd only been here barely a week, I needed responsibility, a schedule, something to do. I didn't even have to do laundry or iron my own clothes. There were people for that. Once in the car, I turned to Mae. "I need some work of my own. What can I do?"

She smiled. "I'm glad you asked. There is so much for you to do here. Of course, we are arranging some receptions and teas for you so that you can meet the other diplomatic wives, and important expats in the region." She patted her briefcase as if the party plans were right there. "And of course, you'll want to be involved in something local. Other wives have chosen to work to beautify Bangkok—they've showcased particularly attractive gardens."

I shook my head. "I love flowers, but I don't know the first thing about them. Isn't there something else?"

A crease sprouted in the center of her perfectly smooth brow. "Well, the hospital maybe. Would that interest you?"

I wrinkled my nose. "I hate to sound picky. I'm really not, but hospitals make me queasy. What about the orphans or the young girls in the sex trade here?"

The crease in her forehead spread. "No, no," she said. "Nothing political, nothing that might embarrass the government. It must be something safe. You understand."

I smiled politely and twisted my wedding ring around on my finger to distract myself. But I didn't understand. I didn't understand at all.

CHAPTER FIVE

Things were moving too fast—or maybe too slow. I guess it depended on the day. I didn't feel as though I was adjusting. I felt as though I was one of those hamsters on a spinning wheel, just trying to keep moving. It didn't help that I'd barely had any time with John aside from quick dinners and quicker kisses at bedtime. Some days, I never saw him. He was up and out of the house before I woke, and he came home in what my mother would have called the *wee hours*, long after I'd given up waiting and gone to bed.

As busy as John's days were, mine were just the opposite, and I was bored, and afraid to go out alone in this strange new place. In Boston, I was brave, the type to go anywhere—alone or with Kelly—at least that was how I saw myself—the type to maybe rescue a lost child though I never had, or to stop a crime, though I'd never done that either. Still, I never thought twice about going out alone. But here, where the streets all had strange, difficult to pronounce names—Ratchadamnoen, Lat Phrao, Vibhavadi Rangsit—I was afraid of wandering too far and finding myself hopelessly lost. And who would even notice?

With John away, it would be up to Chai or Mae, and they'd likely just assume I was with John.

I wanted to see my new city, learn how to pronounce those tongue twisting street names, just do something—anything—but I'd hardly been out of the house, and that, I suppose, was also due to Mae, who seemed intent on teaching me the inner workings of Bangkok from the cocoon of the office here. "Too hot," she'd say to my pleadings to go out. "Better to just stay in and enjoy the air-conditioning."

And it *was* hot, the oppressive air seeping into everything outside. Steam rose from the pavement leaving a fine mist on windows, and a sheen of sweat on my skin when I ventured out to the garden. And the heat seemed fodder for the bugs and the bees that were as large as any I'd ever seen. The bees, their stingers like swords, flew in frenzied patterns swooping in over the flowers, and then me, and I found myself hurrying back inside. I understood Mae's reluctance to spend time in the all-enveloping heat and bug infestation of the day, and I didn't really have much choice, so of course, I agreed. But the house was tense when Mae was there. She seemed determined to harass Chai every chance she got. The tea was too hot, the water too cold, the food too spicy, or not spicy enough. Chai tried to avoid her, and they both tried to appease me. I decided to just ignore their animosity. There was some history there that had nothing to do with me, and the last thing I needed was someone else's drama.

But by the end of the second week, it was abundantly clear that what I really needed—aside from more time with John— was a wardrobe for hot, sunny Thailand. My jeans, three work dresses, one suit and one cocktail dress just weren't enough and weren't really right for the weather here. And so, I made up my mind. I'd find a mall—alone if need be. When I asked Mae which one she'd recommend, she clapped her hands together.

"We'll go out, that's what we'll do. Might as well get used to the heat, and we can visit some of our Buddhist shrines, maybe the golden Buddha and a temple, and then we can head to the Siam Paragon. Oh, you'll love it. Everyone is there –Jimmy Choo, Prada, Louis Vuitton, Versace." Her eyes were shining at the prospect.

And though the stores sounded a little rich for me, I was desperate for an adventure, so off we went, the driver battling for space with other cars and limos, and motorcycles, the streets and even the sidewalks teeming with activity. And the heat never really touched me. I moved from my air-conditioned house to an air-conditioned car, and I was pretty sure every stop would be to an equally climate-controlled setting.

"The golden Buddha is one of the favorites of visitors to Thailand," Mae said as she settled herself beside me in the back seat. "It's not too far from where we are. It sits within the *Wat Traimit* in Chinatown. It is breathtaking. Maybe we can see the monks at prayer. And at least you'll have one touristy trip to check off your list. You can bring your friends when they come."

I nodded. A tourist, that's what I was right now, hovering somewhere between my old life and this strange new one. But first we had to get there, and I braced myself, worrying silently that the roads, with cars and drivers on the opposite side, were perfect set-ups for accidents, and I steeled myself for the inevitable crashes. It was all just one more thing to get used to. But at least the view was pretty, traditional buildings, their pagoda-like roofs daintily peeking toward the sky, were the perfect backdrop to orange-robed monks and gracefully clad women carrying parasols against the sun. And as our car crawled through the morning crush, I sat mesmerized by it all, my attention and anxiety diverted from the wrong-side, upside-down, backwards traffic.

We passed a strip of stores that might have been Times

Square —all gaudy signs and twinkling lights beckoning me in for a massage or a photo or even a tattoo. But it was the familiar Burger King sign that caught my eye, and when I craned my neck, I could just make out that it was wedged in tight between a bar offering Lucky Beer and a currency exchange. I reached for my cellphone and snapped a photo. Kelly would never believe this. I mean—Burger King in Bangkok. Would wonders never cease? A row of tailor shops filled the next block. *Get your suit made here. Best prices in Bangkok*, the signs proclaimed.

We pulled away from the frenzy of that street, and onto a sleek modern highway that wound through the city, leaving me a paltry view of trees and hedges, and tall buildings off in the distance, and not much else. When we finally pulled onto another street and into the temple's entrance, I breathed a sigh of relief that despite my inattention to the traffic, or maybe because of it, we'd somehow avoided a crash.

I gazed in awe at the main building—a gold-tipped several storied structure that seemed the center of every magical tale ever told. We took the grand staircase to the temple's entrance where Mae, flashing her embassy ID, pushed her way through the line. When we were waved inside, the line of curious tourists, waiting under a merciless sun, instantly frowned, and I cringed. Embarrassed, I turned back and mouthed *sorry* to the unhappy, perspiring crowd. When I caught up to Mae, she was standing in front of the golden Buddha, her palms together, her head bowed, and all of my self-righteous plans to announce we should go back and wait in line, evaporated. My eyes were drawn to the magnificent statue perched slightly above and back from us on an elevated platform. When I could peel my eyes away, I read the small booklet that Mae handed to me. Built in the 14th century, the Buddha weighed over five tons and was worth two hundred and fifty million dollars. The room was hushed, people reverent and quiet. Only a young monk, who sat with his bowl of alms, spoke.

"Blessing?" he asked softly, and afraid of committing any cultural blunders, I turned to Mae for approval. She nodded, and I turned back to the monk who beckoned me forward. He sat cross-legged and I bent down almost squatting to be near him. He waved a small brush dipped in water toward me before wrapping a string bracelet around my wrist. I made a silent wish for a lifetime of happiness for John and me, and I bowed my head and nodded. "Thank you," I whispered as I dropped ten dollars into the monk's bowl.

Back outside in the harsh glare of Bangkok's unrelenting sunshine, I squinted. I needed sunglasses and warm-weather clothes, so when Mae asked if I was ready for the mall, I almost raced to the waiting car. Once inside, I pressed my face to the tinted window to get a better look at Bangkok's towering buildings, sleek offices and trendy shops that lined the streets. And I noticed again how clean the streets were—no trash littering the curbs, no papers skittering along the sidewalk, no litter anywhere. It wasn't just the cleanliness that held my attention—it was the exotic faces and clothes—some of the women wore long flowing silky skirts, and the cars—small European sedans that buzzed through traffic—and it struck me again how lucky I was to be here with John.

"The Siam." Mae nudged me, and my gaze rose to the grand glass and metal five-story complex that spanned at least a block. My jaw fell open. The driver let us out in front, and I followed Mae through the mall's maze, my eyes flitting from one ritzy store to another. Mae hadn't been kidding. She led me into Prada, a hushed, serene shop with price tags that made me weak. My gaze was drawn to a slip of a dress, sophisticated but almost plain, and surely within my limited budget. I posed in front of the mirror—gripping the hanger, the dress draping elegantly over my curves. The tag read simply 30,000 *baht*. I hadn't even thought about money and conversion rates. One more thing to learn. I heaved a sigh, held up the tag, and turned to Mae.

She examined the numbers and seemed to be thinking. Finally, she nodded as if agreeing with herself. "One hundred *baht* is about three U.S. dollars." She scrunched up her face to do the math. "So, this dress, which is lovely by the way, will cost nine hundred dollars. But, just feel this," she said, holding out the fabric toward me. "Don't you just love it?"

The color drained from my face. I tucked it quickly back into the rack, afraid I'd somehow damage it and have to buy it, and then I shook my head. "That is so far out of my league. That's more than I made in a week. There must be more reasonable shops here. At least, I hope there are."

Mae giggled her signature sing-songy laugh. "Of course, you know best. But let's just wander and have some fun."

And so, we roamed through the mall, stopping every now and then to have a look in some of the other shops, and to watch the shoppers—a mix of Europeans, Thais, Chinese, Indians. A little slice of the world was here in Bangkok. I listened to the accents, and the languages and the words, and wished I could speak more than just English. I watched as the truly well-heeled made purchases and signed the receipts with barely a glance. The mall had a sixteen-cinema theater, an enormous aquarium and a Lamborghini display that I knew John would love. But I'd come to buy something to wear, and the seven hundred dollars in my bag—all the money I had in the world, not counting our wedding money which we'd deposited in a DC bank, was burning a hole in my pocket. But, I wanted, no I needed, to be frugal, since it was all I had. "Can we just find a store that sells things I can afford?" I asked.

We headed back to the first floor, and when I spied GAP

and H&M, my shoulders relaxed. I went straight to the clearance rack and chose a linen dress that looked to me a lot like the nine hundred dollar one at Prada. I held the tag out to Mae.

"*Thirteen hundred baht* is—" she paused and punched in the numbers on her iPhone. "A very reasonable thirty-nine American dollars," she declared.

Relieved, I added a pair of tailored pants, a silky blouse, a pair of slim cut jeans, two summery tops, a tee-shirt, a pair of tailored capris, and a pair of sandals. My grand total was one hundred and ninety-eight dollars, a sum that would have made me faint at home, but here, it seemed a bargain. And a lesson. I was going to need money. I don't know why I hadn't thought of that before. But my paltry seven hundred was already whittled down. I needed more than just something to do with my time, I needed a job. I needed to meet people, and for that, we needed to have a party, and so I asked Mae.

"What about having something here at the house? An open-house, maybe, so that we can meet people?"

Mae hesitated. "Well, the ambassador has indicated that he'd like all events to be held at the embassy."

"I—I—" I was embarrassed and speechless. Why hadn't he told me that? And why did Mae know if I didn't? She noticed my discomfort.

"I think he just wanted you to be comfortable, and since you are here for a short time, he didn't want to make a splash—socially. You know."

She nodded as if expecting me to nod in turn. But I was puzzled. Why was she explaining my husband's actions to me? I didn't want any cracks to appear in my façade, or my marriage, so I finally nodded. "I think he probably did tell me. There's so much going on, it's hard to remember every detail, but let's try to arrange a reception, at least. I mean, it must be expected, right?"

"I'll be going back to the embassy next week," Mae announced days later, a long pout draping her bright red lips. "The car will be reassigned to the embassy as well."

The knot in my neck tightened. "You don't work here? The car's not assigned to us?" My voice cracked. What would I do without Mae? Without the car? She was my only friend here, my guide, my connection to Thailand. And the car was my only way out. We'd only just started venturing out and planning the reception. I'd be lost, alone.

She patted my hand. "I'm disappointed, too. I've spent a lot of time here in this house." She threw her hand up as if to emphasize the whole house. "I feel as though I belong here, almost as though it's my house."

I wasn't quite sure what to say to that. I was still lost in my own drama—she was leaving me. What else mattered? "Oh?" I asked, feigning an interest I didn't really feel.

"Things were different then," she said, her voice suddenly dreamy as though she was remembering an old lover. "I had responsibilities then. The ambassador's wife had left, so I was asked to step in for ceremonial duties, and well—you know."

I shook my head. I didn't know. I didn't even know who the last ambassador was, never mind that his wife had left him, but suddenly, with that bit of gossip, I was interested. "She left?"

"Disappeared—without a trace. No one really knows why, but one day, she was gone. He waited for her to come back. He kept her things just the way she'd left them, but after a year, he left too."

"When was that?" I asked, thinking that since no one had thought to mention it, it must be ancient history.

Mae hesitated. "I suppose it was sometime last fall," she finally said.

That recently? "And no one's heard from her? Where's her husband now?"

"I've said too much," she answered. "I thought you knew. I shouldn't say anything else."

I couldn't let her off this easily. "Is that why the room is locked? It was theirs?"

"Yes," she answered distractedly, a small line creasing her brow. She glanced at her watch. "I didn't realize how late it was. I've got to go." And she reached for her purse and hurried to the door flinging it open. "I'll call," she said breezily as though we were just discussing the weather.

I shook my head. Why hadn't anyone told me?

As soon as she was gone, I raced upstairs to the locked room, my ear angled against the door, my hand on the knob. I don't know what I expected to hear, but there was only silence, everything as quiet as before. I jiggled the knob and pushed at the door but neither budged. The room and its secrets were locked tight as a drum.

CHAPTER SIX

Later that afternoon, my intentions not very honest, I texted John.

Miss you, babe, miss your touch, the heat of
your kisses. See you tonight?

I had questions to ask, and I wanted to distract him enough to tell me everything he knew about the last ambassador. I asked Chai to make a light dinner, something that we could eat upstairs in the private living room. I chilled some wine and I slipped into a bubble bath. I dressed in the short silky robe I'd bought for my honeymoon, set a small fire in the fireplace—for atmosphere only since the weather was already warm, then I arranged plates and glasses on the floor, and I waited. And waited. At six thirty, John texted me back:

On my way. Love you.

And then I made a mental list. I'd ask first about the missing wife, and then tell him that with Mae leaving, we'd need to move the reception up so I could meet people, and maybe that would lead to a job. And then, I'd need a driver's license, a car. My list was growing when John appeared. I opened my mouth to speak, but he covered my lips with his own, and rushed to open his laptop.

"Just have to send some quick emails, then I'm all yours."

He sat on the couch, his feet on the coffee table, a drink at his elbow, his computer resting on his lap, as he typed some report or other. I watched and waited and uncovered the plates that held our dinner—cold chicken and rice noodles. He reached for a piece of chicken but otherwise, he barely noticed me and my silky robe, and I wondered if the last ambassador's wife had felt this way—lonely, abandoned—and so I sprang my questions on him. "Mae said the last ambassador's wife disappeared just last year. Did you know about it?"

John sank deeper into the couch as though considering what to say, but his answers were vague. "I remember," he said, "hearing something about that. I think they just assumed she left him for another man. They kept it quiet so he could save face."

And suddenly, I was interested. A scandal? Here? "You must know more. Was it someone from the embassy? A guard, maybe?"

But John only shrugged, his eyes glazed over, his disinterest palpable. "They kept it quiet."

"Do you know their room is the master suite and it's locked?"

He sighed and pecked away at his computer. "I thought we had the master."

I shook my head. "Mae says we have the smaller one, which is fine, really it is, but can't we get a key for the locked room?"

"I guess I can ask about that."

He turned back to his work, his eyes riveted to something on the screen, and I knew it was time to leave him to his work. But I was more intrigued than ever. Somebody had to know something. I'd ask Chai, that's what I'd do.

The next morning, John and I shared a slow, sultry shower that led to an hour of intense lovemaking and later a quick breakfast of coffee and toast. He promised to have Mae work on the reception at the embassy.

"That reminds me—why not have it here? I mean, we have this great house—"

"We're not here for the long haul. The State Department would like us to stay as anonymous as possible. I'm not doing the usual big events, no interviews, no appearances. I'm just releasing statements. The plus is that it allows us to keep some semblance of privacy, and still follow the State Department's latest guidelines. I know it's a drag, but the risk of terrorist acts has increased exponentially over the last few years, and we have to be mindful and alert."

"But you're the ambassador. Doesn't that mean socializing and being interviewed and all the hoopla that goes along with that?"

His brow creased. "Normally, but this is different. I still have some other responsibilities, other projects I'm involved in. To tell you the truth, that other stuff is what takes up my time. And though being the ambassador's wife just might help you find a job if you still really want one, it could be a real negative when you want to do something worthwhile. People are going to be asking you to do them favors—get a brother or cousin a visa or a work permit for the US, or maybe a job at the embassy. The requests will be endless, and you have to be ready to just say no. It's not going to be easy, but you have to say no. Agreed?"

I nodded. "The people I'd like to work with won't be asking for favors. At least, I don't think they will."

"Perfect, then go for it."

My pulse quickened. He *did* understand. "I was thinking of doing something with orphans." The orphanage idea had especially appealed to me. I'd read in one of the local newspapers the story of one small boy—a refugee from Myanmar—living in a camp not far from Bangkok and my heart broke for the poor kid who was hungry, sick and waiting for his *lost* mother to find him. I loved that—that he described her as lost. And I knew I could help. But I knew too that John would have to approve, and when I saw his lips curl downward, I mentioned the other story I'd read. "Well, then what about the young girls who are sold into prostitution? Either of those things appeal to me. You know—something important."

He groaned. "Not the girls. We have to be sensitive to the Thai government, we can't embarrass them. They're very touchy about that subject, so stay away from that. And the orphans—I don't know."

His words were dismissive, and I felt a rush of color to my cheeks. Maybe he didn't understand. "But—"

Oblivious to my reaction, he turned to me and held out his tie. He was hopeless at adjusting his own tie. "You don't want to be my personal assistant, huh?"

"No, and if Mae won't be around, I'll need a driver's license, and a car. Can you help with that?" I adjusted his tie, smoothed the front of his shirt, my hands stopping at the feel of cold, hard metal at his waistband. My breath caught in my throat at the sight. "A gun?" I whispered.

"Old habits die hard. I always traveled with it. Guess I'm not ready to give it up. You okay with it?"

I couldn't really think of an answer, so I nodded and stood on my toes to kiss him. He lifted me into his arms and onto the bed where he hovered over me.

"I wish I could stay here all day. I want you to be happy, Nora, so let's do this. I'll ask Mae to plan something at the embassy. We'll invite expats and anyone else who seems—"

"And you won't forget to ask about a key for that room?"

"I won't."

I pulled him down to me and kissed him, a deep lingering kiss that I knew would stay with him all day.

And apparently, it did.

He came home early that evening, a driver's license application in hand and a broad smile on his face. "Party planning has begun," he announced proudly. "A week from Saturday—in the reception room at the embassy."

"Any word on the key?"

His shoulders slumped. "I forgot. Remind me tomorrow."

And the next morning, I did, but he was running out the door, his mind already on the day ahead. I felt pretty sure he'd forget again, so when I saw Chai in the kitchen, I decided to ask her.

"Morning, Chai," I said, reaching for the coffee pot. She smiled and nodded, and I took that as an invitation to sit across from her. I slid into the seat and watched as she pulled fresh vegetables from a paper sack. "I was wondering," I began, hoping my voice sounded disinterested, "do you know anything about the locked room upstairs?"

She shook her head, and pulling a knife from the holder, she began to chop a scallion, slicing again and again, so intently, I thought she'd slice right through the table.

"Chai?" I said to catch her attention. She looked up. "Do you have a spare key somewhere? It seems silly that I can't get in."

And though I thought I saw a flicker of warning in her eyes, she only shook her head. "No," she answered. "Ask Mae."

She knew something. I was certain. "I did. She doesn't have it."

Chai raised a brow and turned back to her cutting, a clear signal that I was dismissed. I went back upstairs and rattled the doorknob once again. But the door was still locked, the secrets safe inside. I'd just have to wait for John to get a key.

———

Ten days later, I shimmied into the little black dress I'd worn the night I met John. I turned this way and that admiring my own reflection when John stepped from the shower and whistled. I turned and whistled right back.

"You're sure you want to go to this?" he asked, wrapping a towel around his middle.

Slipping the towel from his waist, I wiped the dampness from his chest. I leaned against him, inhaling the scent of his skin. "Ordinarily, I'd say the hell with it, but not tonight. Tonight, we're going out."

He turned to the sink and began to shave, and I sat and watched. He'd taken to shaving almost daily since we'd arrived in Thailand. "Can't have a scruffy-faced ambassador, though I don't know why," he'd said. He ran his hand along his chin to check for smoothness, an instinctive gesture that invariably made me weak at the knees. I don't know what it is about a man shaving but, at least for me, it is one of the most sensual things a man can do. And before I knew it, my dress was off and we were rolling around on the bear-skin rug.

Half an hour later, his phone beeped, and when he picked it up, his face fell. "I have to get this. Just give me a minute," and off he walked, his arms slipping into his shirt, the phone tight against his ear.

I pulled my dress back on, reapplied my lipstick and headed downstairs, my tousled hair bouncing on my shoulders, my heels clicking on the tiled hall floor. I inhaled the sweet scent of the ever-present flowers on the entryway table and checked my reflection one last time in the mirror. I ran a comb through my hair and was just reapplying one last coat of lip gloss when John came down, his tie askew, a deep line creasing his forehead.

"What is it?" I asked.

"I can't go. I have to go to Geneva."

I could feel the acid churning in my stomach. "Now?"

"It can't be helped."

"But the reception—"

"Will still go on. It's for you anyway. You'll have fun."

"I don't want to go without you." I dropped my evening bag on the hall table remembering the last-minute trips—to Pakistan and Iraq and God knows where else—that had taken him away when we were dating. He'd promised that was over and yet here we were. Again. I heaved a long sigh more for my own satisfaction than his.

"I called Jim. He's sending a car, and he'll stand in for me. You can give everyone my regrets."

"But—"

"I know, baby," he whispered, pulling me close. "I'm sorry. I'll make it up to you."

How many times had I heard that?

The intercom sounded and John picked it up. "Car's here, sir," I heard the Marine guard say.

John pulled me close and brushed his lips against mine. "Come home soon," I whispered.

He took my hand and walked me to the waiting car, holding the door open as I slid inside. He leaned in and ran his finger along the line of my jaw and then he kissed me. "I'll be home as soon as I can."

I could only nod. No wonder the last wife ran away.

CHAPTER SEVEN

I was the first to arrive at the embassy, the guards waving me through, Jim at the gate. He stepped up, opened my door and held his hand out. "You look beautiful, Nora. How are you doing?" He planted a kiss on my cheek, took my hand in his and guided me through the main entrance and straight back to the elevator.

"I'm okay, but disappointed that John couldn't come. What about you? Is your wife coming?" I asked, looking around.

"I'm divorced," he said, laughing. "I sure hope she doesn't show up." He pressed the button for the elevator.

The reception was on the fourth floor in a large room that opened onto a veranda. Palm trees swayed in the soft evening air, and comfortable chairs were arranged around a few tables. It was an elegant, but still casual, setting—exactly what I'd hoped for. Mae was already there, positioning flowers and checking hors d'oeuvres. A bartender was busy setting up a small bar. And off in the corner, an American flag and a state department banner hung limply, a fitting metaphor for the way I felt without John here.

I tugged at Jim's sleeve to slow him down. "Thank you for standing in for John tonight. I hate that he had to leave tonight, of all nights."

Jim opened his mouth to say something, but then, as though thinking better of it, and with a sudden twitch distorting his right eye, he only nodded.

His reluctance to speak and his nervous tic made me want to ask if every ambassador traveled as much as John seemed to, but at that moment, that question of a man I barely knew seemed a huge betrayal to John, so in an almost secret language reply, I nodded as well.

Jim ran a hand over his right eye, the twitch there fading. "How about a drink to start the evening?" he asked, effectively cutting off that topic and our shared discomfort.

He led me to the bar, and I happily followed. God knows I needed a drink about then.

"What'll it be, sir?" a young man clad in a short white jacket asked.

"Scotch, neat, for me, and what will you have, Nora?"

"White wine," I answered just as Mae approached.

"It's going to be a wonderful evening," she said, kissing my cheeks in the European manner.

"You look beautiful," I whispered as Jim tipped the bartender.

She smoothed the front of her dress, a satiny red fabric embellished with tiny sparkling gemstones. It looked like one of those fancy dresses we'd seen at Prada. "Thank you. I spent far too much on this dress, but I just loved it."

I touched one of the tiny jewels and wondered how she could ever afford a dress like this. Maybe, I should ask John for a job at the embassy. "It really is stunning." I smoothed my own dress, suddenly wishing I'd bought something new for my very first event as the ambassador's wife. But Mae was oblivious to me, and I watched as she pirouetted.

"Do you really think so?" she asked, her gaze landing on Jim as he turned to us.

"Girl talk, or can I join you?" he asked as he handed me a glass of wine. "Anything for you, Mae?"

Her face lit up as she turned to him. She shook her head. "I still have some last-minute details to attend to, but thank you, Jim, for asking." Her voice was soft, sultry almost.

I took a sip of my wine and wondered if John had left yet. Maybe I could call just to say I loved him. I hadn't told him that before—

"Right, Nora?" Jim's voice broke through my reverie.

I raised a brow. "Sorry, I was daydreaming."

"The receiving line. Mae's decided we don't really need one. She and I will take you around and introduce you to people you'll need to know. Okay with you?"

Mae nodded and I followed suit, though a part of me wondered if a receiving line, silly as it sounded, might not be the best way to meet lots of people.

"Well, I'll be off then," Mae said as she turned for the veranda. "I want to do a few last checks."

"She's a great gal, isn't she?" Jim asked, his eyes following her as she walked away.

I nodded. A few guests had started to arrive, the room filling with sound and laughter. My stomach fluttered. I wished Kelly was here. She'd love this.

"Hello," a voice boomed. I turned to see the man who'd been at the house the evening we arrived, come striding toward us. He slapped Jim on the back before turning to me. "So good to see you, Nora. How's Bangkok treating you? Hell, how's that old bastard treating you?" He leaned down and kissed my cheek. "Where is he?" He turned, his eyes scanning the room.

Jim whispered something and they both nodded before turning back to me.

I forced a smile. "Hi—" I'd forgotten his name. Leo? Bob? Dennis?

He sensed my confusion. "Dave," he said.

Jim began to laugh. "Don't worry, Nora. There's not a woman alive who remembers his name."

The two of them began to trade stories and jokes, and I was clearly the outsider, not one of them, even if I was the ambassador's wife. I wandered to the veranda where a cool breeze was blowing in, rustling the palm trees. The evening sky was clear, and the stars—thousands of them, more than I'd ever seen at home—twinkled and shone above us. Mae had placed small bouquets of flowers on the tables out here and the scents lingered in the night air. I inhaled the rich exotic fragrance and sipped my wine, oblivious to everything until I felt a hand brush my back. I turned to see an older lady, a slash of pink on her lips and a glass of wine in her hand.

"I hope I didn't startle you," she said, extending her hand, her freshly manicured nails the same pink as her lips. "I'm Elizabeth Miller, and you're Nora Fielding, yes?"

I nodded.

"I'm the wife of the Canadian ambassador. I wanted to say hello and tell you how happy we are to have you here."

"Thank you, Elizabeth." I took her hand. "I'm happy to be here."

"Is the ambassador here?" she asked, glancing back into the main room.

I shook my head. "No, he was called away."

"I'm sorry to have missed him. Forgive me for asking, but I'm so curious—are you living in that house?" she whispered.

"The residence? Yes."

She moved closer, and leaned in. "Has there been any word on poor Emily?"

"Emily?"

"Somerfield—the last ambassador's wife—the one who went missing. Surely, you know?"

I shook my head. "Only that she left or disappeared. I'm not sure which. That's all." And that was all I knew, but now I had a name, and that made her more real. *Emily Somerfield.* I rolled the name around in my head trying to think what she was like.

Elizabeth sensed my inattention and cleared her throat. She rested her hand on mine. "I didn't mean to put you on the spot, but well, it certainly is a mystery, isn't it?"

I nodded, wondering again what had happened. It had to be more than an affair that drove her away. People had affairs all the time. There had to be something else. "Do you know what...?"

"Well, we can't dwell on that tonight," Elizabeth interrupted. "I wanted to give you my card and invite you to tea. Some of the ambassadors' wives get together once a month or so. We'd love for you to join us. We're so happy that you've come."

I took her card. "I'd love to. Do you do any volunteer work?"

"We do. We host fundraisers and the like, and sometimes we just get together to chat and have a drink. Being the ambassador's wife is not an easy job, is it? And no one knows that better than us. And dear Emily, too, I suppose." She smiled conspiratorially and looked over the room. "Sometimes it doesn't quite seem real, does it?"

I wasn't sure if she was talking about Emily or about being an ambassador's wife, but when she squeezed my hand, I squeezed back. She glided back into the main room, and I slid her card into my bag. Everything was going to be okay. Other women had done this before and survived—well maybe not

Emily, but maybe she was out there somewhere wondering about me.

It wasn't long before Jim found me. "Having fun?" he asked.

I nodded. "I am, but can I ask you a question?"

"Sure, ask away."

"Do you know anything about Emily Somerfield, the last wife?"

His smile drooped, and his back stiffened. "Not really. I heard she left, that's it." His voice was clipped as he repeated what was beginning to sound like the company line. "But let's not talk about her tonight. As a matter of fact, Mae's looking for you. She has some people—aid workers, I think—that she wants you to meet."

"Aid workers?"

"You know—humanitarian aid stuff. They're doing some development work in the villages up north, some vaccine programs, I think, and they work along the border with the Burmese refugees."

"Burmese?"

"Or Myanmar, as it's known now. The country was called Burma until the military overthrew the democratic government and renamed it. And though the military here in Thailand staged a coup not so long ago, it's been peaceful since then, barely a ripple—"

I stopped listening. World politics was not my strong suit. "So, there are refugees nearby?" I asked, hoping to just cut to the chase.

"Actually, there are. The border's just to the west, probably a hundred miles or so from Bangkok." He took my arm and led me back inside. "Let's just freshen up your drink and then we'll find Mae."

I stood off to the side and watched as a middle-aged woman, her eyes glazed, her cheeks flushed, her hair in need of a comb, draped her arm around Jim's shoulder. "I'm Stella," she announced to Jim, her speech slow. It was looking as though Mae might have some competition for Jim's attention.

He handed me my glass, and Stella suddenly noticed me. Her gaze lingering a moment too long on my face, and, suddenly self-conscious, I tucked a strand of hair behind my ear.

"Stella," Jim said, breaking the uncomfortable silence. "I'd like you to meet the ambassador's wife, Nora Fielding."

Stella's eyes snapped to attention. "Ambassador," she slurred, seeming suddenly to realize where she was. "Nice to meet you." She raised her glass in a silent toast and moved away.

"I'm sorry about that," Jim said, his hand reaching for mine. "She's an assistant to an assistant or something like that. A reception is a chance to cut loose, and some take that a little too literally."

I laughed uncomfortably trying to show I was a good sport, but there were probably plenty more like Stella out there. I wondered if women like her threw themselves at John when he was around. His *other life* hadn't been that long ago. But I wouldn't worry about that now. I was here to meet people and have a good time. I turned to look over the room—mostly small clusters of people talking and laughing. The clink of glasses, the tinkle of laughter, the hum of conversation all filled the air lending to the magical feel.

"Come on, let's find Mae." Jim led me through the room, where we stopped for introductions every other minute. The people were kind and welcoming, but mostly older—not that I was any kid—but these people were in their fifties, probably sliding into retirement.

"Here's my card," one woman said. "We'd love to have you join our garden club."

Another woman said her book club was "always open to new members."

I smiled my broadest smile and tried to show genuine interest without committing to anything. The truth was—I loved flowers but not the dirt that invariably came with them, and as for books, I'd only read them when I had to. I was more the gossip magazine type. Pathetic, but true. So, there I was, my eyes scanning the room for the aid workers when I spotted Mae surrounded by a group of young men who all seemed to be vying for her attention. Jim waved her over, and I watched as she made her excuses and found her way to us.

"Are you ready to meet some very interesting people?" she asked as she led me away.

We maneuvered through the crowd that had grown in the last hour. The room seemed filled to bursting. Finally, she spied the small group she'd been looking for.

"Lisa, Renée," she said, interrupting their conversation. "This is Nora, the new ambassador's wife. She's been so keen to meet you and hear about your work."

I stuck out my hand, embarrassed that we'd intruded. "It's so nice to meet you both." Lisa took my hand, and in a proper British accent—which I knew from *Downton Abbey*—she introduced herself.

"Lisa Bates," she said. "Lovely to meet you. Mae's told us you're interested in hearing about what we do."

"Very interested," I answered firmly, trying to convey a confidence I didn't quite feel.

Lisa and Renée seemed about my age. Lisa was small, with sand-colored hair that she'd pulled back into a braid. Renée was taller, stick thin, with bright red lips, coal-black hair, and a steely gaze. She wore a tight black top, skinny jeans and stilettos. She blew out a long plume of smoke and flicked her cigarette into a receptacle that I hoped was an ashtray, then stuck out her hand. "Renée François," she said in a thick French accent. "You are interested to help?" She flashed a tight smile.

I nodded.

"I'll just leave you then," Mae said as she slipped back into the crowd. We moved outside to the veranda where they gave me a quick lesson on Burma or Myanmar or whatever it was called, and the situation of the refugees. Lisa was the logistician, responsible for arranging everything to do with their refugee camp—vehicles, equipment, staff, supplies. Renée was a consultant, here on assignment for the UN.

"I am here to do an audit, you know?" Renée said. "Make sure that everything is in order, and that the donor money is well spent. Understand?"

I wasn't sure I did understand, and I could tell Renée's little speech had made Lisa uncomfortable. Still, I immediately liked them both—Lisa's warmth contrasted perfectly to Renée's no-nonsense screw-it attitude. I was mesmerized by their stories, and their enthusiasm. They talked about helping refugees from Myanmar who were stuck in a no-man's land along the border, long forgotten and abandoned by the world community. "Donations and attention have dwindled to almost nothing. People are desperate," Lisa said. She told the story of a small boy who scrounged through landfills and dumps searching for food for his family. "And his story is not so unusual."

This was exactly the kind of work I wanted to do. "Do you need help?" I asked.

"But of course, she does," Renée said, quickly lighting another cigarette and inhaling deeply. "Work with the UN is more involved, you understand? And I am not in a position to hire anyone. But she will sign you up before you have had a chance to change your mind. What can you do?"

And my happiness dissolved. "I'm not sure it's anything you need. I was a legal assistant at home, but I'll do anything, and I'm a quick learner." That last wasn't quite true, but I suddenly wanted desperately to be one of them, somebody who did work that made a difference.

Lisa smiled and handed me her card. "Come out with me next week. I'll show you some of the camps we cover. I think you'll fit right in."

And my happiness burst through once again.

I was going home with a handful of cards, but even more—I was going to do something, something that mattered.

CHAPTER EIGHT

The following morning, I rose early and googled Emily Somerfield, but it was as though the internet had been scrubbed clean. The only mention was a small press release welcoming her and the ambassador to Bangkok two years earlier. I tried searching for the ambassador—a Tim Somerfield—and found precious little. But there was a picture—an older man, with thinning, gray hair, wire-rimmed eyeglasses, and a tight-lipped Mona Lisa smile. It didn't tell me much at all. It was almost as though there was a kind of information blackout on Tim and Emily Somerfield.

I googled my name, then John's and then *Mr. and Mrs. John Fielding, Bangkok,* but it was as though we didn't exist either, as though we'd been blacked out, too. Damn. Was it this post in Bangkok? I typed in Elizabeth Miller, the Canadian ambassador's wife, and the screen came alive with thirty-two thousand results including hundreds of pictures. If there were a *Yelp* for ambassadors, the U.S. embassy in Bangkok would be out of business. Something didn't feel quite right about this. I supposed that maybe the State Department was just secretive in order to protect us, and that made sense, but then why would

Canada be so lax where its own ambassador's safety was concerned? I couldn't figure it out, and I wondered if I should insist that John or someone tell me what had happened to the last wife. Someone must know something. And besides, if Emily Somerfield could just disappear, couldn't I?

A sudden shiver ran along my spine, and I rubbed my arms and headed down for coffee. A door opened letting in a warm breeze, and I looked up to see Chai.

"Good morning," she said. "This is for you." She thrust a small package into my hands.

Wrapped in brown paper with my name scrawled across the front, there was nothing else—no postage, no return address. "Did someone bring this?" I asked, my mind still racing with conspiracy theories about the last wife. Chai shrugged and moved away. Since I'd started asking about the key and the locked room, she'd kept her distance, afraid, I supposed, of my battering her with more questions. I slipped my finger under the paper and pulled, wondering who had sent it. Maybe it was from the aid workers, or another ambassador's wife. But when I'd torn the last of the wrapping away, I held a box of Swiss chocolates and a typed note in my hand.

```
Thought you might like these. I miss
you. Love, John
```

The knot in my neck smoothed itself out. "I love you too, John," I whispered, as I pulled out my phone. Geneva was a few hours behind Thailand, and though I had no idea what the exact time difference was, it was probably still early, and John was probably still sleeping. And then it occurred to me, he'd only left for Geneva twelve hours ago. How had he gotten these here so quickly? I ran my hand over the silky fabric-covered box and smiled. Perks of being an ambassador, I thought.

I texted a quick thank you, ending with a plea for him to come home.

And then I opened the box and walked into the kitchen and offered Chai some chocolate. "Please have some. I think John sent it for both of us." I plucked a piece out for myself and popped it into my mouth before placing the box down in front of her.

She reached her hand tentatively toward the chocolates, her eyes scanning the choices, before she finally settled on one large piece wrapped in gleaming red foil.

"Thank you," she said, slipping the candy into her apron pocket.

"I'm going to leave this here," I said. "I hope you'll help yourself."

She shrugged and turned away.

So much for my peace offering.

"But how will you get there?" John asked when he called that evening, and I'd told him about the aid workers and the refugees.

"I'll get my own license and I'll rent a car. So, first question —how do I get a driver's license?"

"You can fill in the application I brought home, but that's only the first step. You can sidestep all of that though, and I can just get you a license," he said.

And because he couldn't see me, I scrunched up my face. "I don't want to be one of those people—using my connections to get what I need. I should probably just apply the old-fashioned way."

John chuckled. "It's your call, but the rigmarole involved for expats is mind-numbing. It's a series of applications—for which you'll need an interpreter to navigate the forms, and a physician to give you a statement of good health. If you meet all of the criteria, there's a one-hour film to watch, and after that, you'll receive your license in about three months. And, by the way, you're already one of *those people*. I got those chocolates to you via the diplomatic pouch—it travels between embassies or embassies and DC—with messages and secrets and sometimes peace offerings to wives."

I groaned. "Diplomatic pouch, huh? Well, I guess if I'm already using my connections, it can't hurt to use them for this one thing."

"Not if you want it anytime soon. I can just get you the license and arrange driving lessons. But—I do expect something in return."

"Come home, Mr. Ambassador, and I'll show you just how grateful I can be."

While I waited for John to come home to Bangkok, and for Lisa and Renée to call, I turned my attention to Chai and her cooking. That, I thought, might be the best way to break down the tension between us. It had to be more than my questions about the locked room that had her avoiding me.

When we'd arrived in Bangkok, I'd assumed we'd be eating Thai food—spicy soups, fried noodles, sticky rice, curried chicken—my list was endless, but aside from an occasional meal of chicken satay and rice with chilies, Chai had been serving us good old American cuisine—roast beef, turkey, mashed potatoes, nothing exotic. I was eager to fix things, and food seemed the best place to start. The next morning, I took my cup of coffee to the kitchen, sank down on the long bench across from Chai as she peeled potatoes for our dinner, and waited for her to acknowledge me. But she chopped and sliced and avoided me as if I weren't sitting right there in front of her. This was not going to be easy. "Chai?" I finally said. She nodded and held up a potato for my approval.

"Very nice," I said, trying to tread lightly, and being careful not to offend her culture or traditions. "Chai, you are such a wonderful cook, an artist really, but to tell you the truth, the ambassador and I were hoping you'd cook more of your specialties." Just as I'd done with my driver's license application, I was using John's title to help me along.

Chai wiped her wrinkled hands along the front of her dress. "Food not good?" she asked.

"The food is delicious." I patted my stomach to show my appreciation. "But we were thinking the food you make for your own family is probably even better. I've been reading about Thai food—" I rattled off my list of Thai dishes, and to my relief, she chuckled.

"You want that?"

I nodded.

"Last wife want American food only, nothing spicy," she said.

I sat straighter. "That was Emily, right? You wouldn't have a key to her room, would you?"

"Tonight, you have Thai food," she said, avoiding my questions. She turned her back to me then, and the splash of water told me she was back to work, our conversation done. I walked up behind her, placed my hand on her shoulder and my cup in the sink. "Thank you," I whispered. That night, she served me sticky rice, spicy soup and prawns. When I told her I was sure John would love a meal like this, I thought she'd faint with pleasure.

Two days later, Lisa Bates called and arranged to take me to the refugee camps the following day. I called John to tell him.

"Good for you," he said. "Nothing political though. Okay?"

The following morning, Lisa arrived in a white Range Rover, and we set off.

"We're headed to Bân, that's Thai for *home*," she said, turning onto the main road. "Not very homey, but a nice touch, I guess. It's not a quick drive. It's three hours out and three hours back if the roads are dry. Everything here depends on the weather. In the rainy season, the roads are often washed out, and the refugees are as isolated as if they were on an island."

"Is there a rainy season?" I asked. "It seems as though it's just hot, humid and sunny all the time."

Lisa laughed. "We're in the hot season right now. By June, the heat will ease up some, but the rains will start and continue through October, sometimes longer. We've had monsoons in December." She turned the AC to high. "Just until we get out of Bangkok," she said.

Before long, we left the crowded city streets behind, and headed onto a ribbon of steaming asphalt that wound through the countryside. The comforting hiss of the cool air stopped as Lisa flicked the AC off. I lowered my window and angled my face to the air. The heat didn't feel quite so intense, but the humidity out here among the tropical trees and flowers soared. The bead of perspiration that had trickled down my back turned into a river of sweat. My shirt was already soaked through, my jeans sticking to my legs. I swiped my hand across my forehead and wished I'd worn just a tee-shirt and cargo shorts like Lisa had. Already, I could see another shopping trip in my future.

Lisa noticed my discomfort. "I can turn the AC back on," she said.

I shook my head. "I should just get used to this. There's no AC in the camp is there?"

"We have a generator in the health clinic so we can have lights and a refrigerator for our medicines and vaccines. There is a small air conditioner, and sometimes, we use it. But, most often, we don't."

Two and a half hours out of Bangkok, we turned off the paved road and onto a rugged dirt path that curled through what could only be a jungle. The palm trees were still, their fronds glistening with dew. The wildflowers' scent hung heavy on the wet air. I inhaled deeply. The air here was clean, no exhaust smoke, no cigarettes, no city smells, kind of like Boston after a snowfall.

"There—can you see it?" Lisa asked. She pointed off to my right.

I sat forward and peered through the windshield and saw— nothing. "Where?" I asked, and she pointed again.

"The trees hide it pretty well until we're closer. I suppose that's why it's still here, so many years after it opened."

"Was there a war?" I asked, feeling incredibly uninformed.

"Still is. It's the longest running civil war in the world. I suppose the people of South Sudan might disagree, but it's been going on, in one form or another, since Myanmar gained independence from Britain after World War II." She paused and wiped a line of sweat from her forehead. "It's complicated. The central government—they call this country Myanmar, not Burma, by the way—is a military dictatorship, and they're fighting to maintain control over the different ethnic groups who are fighting the main government and sometimes each other. Confused yet?"

I nodded. Information overload.

Lisa smiled. "This camp shelter is home to the Rohingya people. There are smaller numbers of other groups—the Karenni, and Shan, but it's mostly Rohingya. You probably don't need to know all of that. Just know that Myanmar's military have burned and looted villages, forcing these people out and into these remote camps where life is becoming more difficult by the day. Thailand is tired of hosting thousands, probably hundreds of thousands over the years, here and in other camps throughout the country. The refugees have nowhere to go. Here at least, there is some safety."

"But don't aid workers bring attention to the situation? Doesn't your presence here make a difference?"

Lisa shrugged. "Maybe, but the truth is that for most people, there's too much going on closer to home. And I understand that. Myanmar is far away. You'd never heard of this crisis, right?"

She was right. I hadn't. Suddenly, Lisa pointed once again, and I turned toward the open window. Almost hidden under the canopy of soaring trees were row upon row of bamboo shacks nestled beneath the long leafy branches and palm fronds. Trails of smoke curled through the air and hung there, caught in the day's moisture. I could just make out a few people wandering through the village and as we wound through the final turn, I saw the Bân camp—a village almost—a shanty village. The huts, made of bamboo with plastic sheeting on rustic roofs, stood clustered together tight as teeth. There was no room between them that I could see. It seemed drawn right out of an old history book—no utility poles dotting the landscape, no satellite towers, no luxuries, just the basics—the sky above, the earth below—and not much in between. I was light years away from the world I knew. I hung my head out the window and inhaled, filling my lungs with the sweet tropical air.

Lisa parked and pulled a backpack from the back seat

before she jumped out. A crowd of children and adults surrounded her, all chattering and smiling. They all looked so delicate, so frail. Disheveled, and clad in threadbare clothes that hung loosely on thin frames, they exuded a kind of calmness, an understanding of where they were. But there was more. They looked hungry—not just for food but for something else, attention maybe. They weren't so different from me after all— they just wanted to matter too. They swarmed Lisa—reaching out and touching her, the children giggling, babies squealing, women in long, graceful skirts that swept the ground as they walked. I was spellbound. She went to the rear of the SUV and pulled open the back hatch. Three large wooden crates, the letters UNHCR stamped on the side, were stored inside. Three men hustled forward, maneuvered the crates onto their scrawny backs, and nodded to Lisa.

"What's in there?" I asked.

"Just supplies. Follow me," she directed as she turned and began to walk into the village. The men walked off in another direction, their backs straining under the weight of the crates.

I stepped from the SUV and into the shade of the camp. The trees swayed gently and although still humid, the air was noticeably cooler here than in Bangkok. The smell of cooking fires, not so different from our backyard grills at home, filled the air. I pulled my sunglasses back onto the top of my head and followed Lisa. A smaller group began to walk with me. One little girl, her almond eyes shining, her matted hair tucked behind her ears, slipped her grimy hand into mine and looked up at me, a shy smile settling on her lips.

And that one small gesture, that tiny hand, changed everything. I was in love.

CHAPTER NINE

A narrow dirt path looped through the camp, huts on either side, some elevated, all ramshackle and all covered with morning dew though it was almost afternoon. A river of mud snaked along the center of the road. My sneakers squished in the muck. The little girl clutching my hand giggled, her tiny bare feet skipping along effortlessly through the sludge. I squeezed her hand and giggled back. Her raggedy dress, though mostly threadbare, still bore tiny dots of color, evidence of its previous life as someone's party dress. But it had likely been discarded and found its way to this little girl who daintily picked up the hem as she skipped. I sighed as I watched. One man's junk truly was another's treasure.

As we walked further into the camp, we passed small sturdy structures, some bamboo, some wood, but all more solid than the huts the people here called home. Many had blue banners hanging outside, but UNHCR was the only one I recognized.

"UNHCR is the UN's refugee commission?" I half shouted to Lisa.

"That's it. You're a quick study. On your left are the school and a vocational training center."

Those buildings were the most durable. Built of aluminum, with thatched roofs, they seemed designed to withstand the heat, humidity, rain and whatever else might come. The further we walked, the more moisture dotted the trees and filled the air. Although I'd never actually seen one in real life, I was pretty sure this was a tropical rain forest.

Lisa stopped and turned to face me, her arm raised and pointing to something in the distance. "Over that way is the food distribution center," she said. "People here rely on the World Food Program's rations. It's not much—rice and beans and tea—so they supplement by growing vegetables, bartering or working at odd jobs outside the camp, though the government has been strict lately about confining people to the camp. You'll see a few tea shops where enterprising refugees sell tea and rice and sometimes sweets. It's mostly foreigners coming through who buy it, but at least it's a purchase. We can get something later. You must be hungry."

She caught sight of the little girl still gripping my hand. "She shouldn't be here," Lisa explained.

I didn't understand, but I was in no position to ask questions, not yet anyway. The little girl scowled at Lisa, but held tight to my hand, and I held tight right back, thinking everyone here—including the tiny girl still gripping my hand—shouldn't be in here. They should be in comfortable villages living quiet lives. But here they were—away from home, depending on aid groups for every little thing. They all looked thin and fragile—the result of not enough food, I supposed. I remembered all the times I'd eaten to bursting, and I swallowed the hard lump in my throat. I didn't think I could ever eat again. "Could I bring food?" I asked, picking up my pace to speak to Lisa.

She stopped altogether and I caught up. "Absolutely not. I know that sounds harsh, but there are thousands of people in this camp, and there's no way you can feed them all. We can't let you feed one or two." Her gaze rested on the small girl by my side. "Even if they are irresistible. It would cause too much trouble."

My shoulders sagged. My brain understood what she said. My heart was another matter. We continued on to the clinic, another sturdy structure, a small generator humming just beyond the doorway. A young man, his black hair slicked close to his head, greeted us.

"Allo, Miss Lisa," he said.

"The people out here speak English?" I asked.

Lisa shook her head. "I wish. The educated speak a little, the rest speak several dialects of the Rohingya language, which I'm ashamed to admit, I'll never understand." She turned to the man who had greeted us. "Allo, Nath Ko Ghy. You are well?"

He nodded and bowed slightly, and then turned to me and repeated his bow. I released my hand from the girl's grip, placed my hands together and bowed. "Hello, Nath Ko Ghy." I said his name slowly careful not to trip over the syllables. "My name is Nora." He seemed confused, and he looked to Lisa for help.

"She's American, and she's here to see if she can help us in some way."

"Ahh," he said. "Nurse?"

"No, but I'll help any way I can."

He smiled, and the little girl at my side tugged on my hand. "Can I ask you a favor?" I asked Nath. "Can you ask her name?"

He spoke in a language that could have been Chinese or even Thai. I couldn't even make sense of his inflection. The little girl's mumbled reply was as small and birdlike as she was.

"I can't make sense of what she's saying. I'm not sure she understands me, or maybe she can't hear me. The sound I'm hearing is Suu, so maybe that's her name. I'm just not sure," he said.

"Suu's a good name." I bent down to her. "Hello, Suu," I said. "My name is Nora."

Her tiny hand flew to her mouth to hide her giggles, but she was helpless, and soon we were all laughing.

"She was likely born around here," Lisa said, ruffling her hair. "Imagine a life like that." Gone was the gruffness, when she'd first spied the little girl with me.

I knelt down and pulled Suu close, running my fingers through the matted tangles of her hair. "Could I do something with the children? Bring balls or simple toys that they can share?" She leaned into me nestling her head into the crook of my shoulder.

"That's a good idea. A kind of play therapy. I like that."

I knew Lisa couldn't pay me. And she shouldn't—anything she had should go for the refugees, not me. It meant I'd have to ask John for money. But it didn't matter. This place, this little girl, were more important than my pride. Suu picked up some stones from the road and began to throw them.

Nath shook his head sternly, and she stopped.

"Looks like a few toys will help," I said.

"You know she's going to look for you now every time I drive up?" Lisa asked.

I smiled. "I hope so, and I hope I'm with you." I stood up and Suu tucked her hand back into mine as we stepped into the clinic for a look.

The clinic was tiny—a series of small rooms, each off the central one. Lisa pointed them out. "That's for vaccine visits, that's for sick visits, that's mostly what the clinic does. The UN runs a maternity ward and a small hospital, and my aid group, United for Health, runs this clinic for the other stuff—small problems that can be overlooked in a refugee camp—colds, fevers, everyday aches and pains. We do the best we can with the little we have, and our supplies are dwindling. Everyone wants to force the refugees back to Myanmar, back to misery and perhaps death. The little that we do here helps them to know they're not entirely forgotten."

"What about those crates you brought today?" I hadn't seen them since the men had carted them off and all but disappeared. "Won't they help?"

Lisa smiled. "More than you know."

I explored the small rooms and wondered how she worked here at all. Sagging burlap cots, a few wooden tables, chairs, one large filing cabinet, and a small refrigerator filled the space. In the corner, the generator kept the refrigerator and the vaccines inside, cool. Next to it sat a large trunk, a padlock hanging from the latch. "What's in there?" I asked.

"Medicine that doesn't need to be kept cool—pills for malaria, for worms, some antibiotics, aspirin, not much, but it helps."

"And you have to keep it locked up?"

"We do. Some things are too tempting to leave out in the open. Desperate people will take anything."

We stopped next at the bathroom, which was a generous description for the latrines. "They're eastern toilets," Lisa explained, smiling. "And as soon as you're outside of Bangkok, most toilets are this style, so you might as well get acquainted with them here."

She led me into a small freestanding latrine that looked, from the outside at least, like a porta-potty. But inside, all similarity ended. The toilet was a hole in the ground, and the user had to squat over it. Metal footprints on either side of the hole guided users where to put their feet. The stench was overwhelming—months or maybe years of waste lay just beneath my feet. Lisa didn't bat an eye.

"There's no paper," she continued, "so if you'll need that, keep some with you. Otherwise just use a leaf or anything else handy. For washing up, there's a water pump just over there. See it?"

I nodded.

"Don't drink from the taps, or you'll be sick for weeks. Just bring your own bottled water. Okay?"

I forced a smile and nodded again to show my understanding of the process, though I wasn't sure I'd actually remember any of it. My idea of roughing it had always been no room service after ten, but I could do this. I was certain. We spent another hour wandering through the camp, before Lisa announced it was time to go. "We've got to be back before dark. We'll eat next time."

I leaned down and gave Suu a hug. "Goodbye, Suu," I whispered. She ran her fingertips along my face, and then through my hair. Finally, she leaned in and patted my face. She mumbled something but the sound was garbled and unintelligible to me. Afraid to break the moment's spell, I didn't ask anyone for help in making sense of it.

The drive back seemed somehow longer, and I chattered the whole way peppering Lisa with questions. "How many refugees are there in the camp?"

"About ten thousand, but maybe more. The UN won't allow any newcomers to be registered, and if they're not registered, they're not counted, and that means no food rations, no huts. So, as lousy as this might seem—it's still better than it is for the hundreds, maybe thousands, who can't get registered, and who live in garbage dumps or along the roads or in jungles. We still try to help, but—"

"Can't you help?"

She shook her head sadly. "No. There's not enough money, and there's danger in those makeshift camps where people scavenge for food and shelter. It's heartbreaking, but it's also dangerous for us to go in. So, we don't. We focus on Bān and the other established camps and try to get people the help they need. It doesn't mean we forget the others; we just can't help them right now."

"Could I—?"

"I know what you're thinking, and the answer is no. We'd both be in a heap of trouble, and I don't need any more of that right now, not with the UN breathing down my neck." Without taking her eyes off the road, she seemed to sense my disappointment. "There's plenty to do at Bân. Maybe you can help me with supplies. An ambassador's wife could certainly get things moving through Customs."

I shifted in my seat, John's warning ringing in my ears. But I wanted to help, and this was different. She wasn't asking for herself, she was asking for the refugees.

"But for now, the best place to start is with the kids."

"All right. How many in the camp?"

"About a third of the refugees are kids, so—" She hesitated—probably doing the calculations in her head.

"About three thousand?" I offered.

Lisa nodded, and I dove back in with more questions. "What kind of toys can I bring? Can I bring clothes? Shoes?"

We shared a bottle of water, and Lisa shared her expertise. "No clothes, not yet, and only simple toys—soccer balls, paper, crayons. Understand?"

I nodded, eager to do whatever it took to be a part of that place, and then I sat back, finally quiet, lost in my own thoughts. Had it really only been seven months since I'd met and fallen in love with John? I marveled at how my life had taken a sharp right turn to a place I'd never imagined, and a life I could only have dreamed of. When I felt the car glide to a stop and realized that Lisa had pulled up in front of my house, I unbuckled my seatbelt, and turned to her. "Can I go back with you this week?"

A hint of a smile draped her lips. She was probably relieved to be dropping me off. I was pretty sure my incessant babbling had worn her out. I held my breath and waited for her answer.

"I'll call, maybe tomorrow," she said.

I floated on air to my front door. I'd found what I needed.

It was almost five when I let myself into the house. John wouldn't be home from Geneva for another hour or more. I couldn't wait to tell him about everything—the reception, the camp, but in the meantime, I was starving. At least that's what I would have said yesterday. Today, I'd be less dramatic. I'd say only that I was hungry. And I was. I hadn't eaten since morning, when I'd inhaled a slice of toast with my coffee. Chai had left for the day. But the refrigerator held the meal she'd prepared for our dinner—fried noodles, curried chicken, and spicy soup. All I'd have to do was heat it when John arrived home. I grabbed a fork and ate some of the noodles, the empty feeling in my stomach fading. I replaced the bowl and shut the refrigerator door, thinking how lucky I was that I could do that.

I took a quick shower and changed. John was barely through the door, his bag still in his hand, when I began to batter him with questions. "Were you able to start the paperwork for my license? Can we look for a car? I know I said I didn't want your money, but I want to volunteer with Lisa and her aid group, so I guess I'll need some. Is that okay?"

"Slow down," he said, pulling me into his arms. "Guess you had a good few days, huh?"

I told him about Suu, and the camp and the misery and the happiness in that place. "I feel as though I came home a different person. Lisa said I can do play therapy with the kids."

He covered my mouth with his own, and my endless chatter finally came to an end. I could have sworn I heard a sigh of relief through his kiss. He pulled me close, his lips searching for mine and I kissed first his lips and then the coarseness of his face and the stubble on his chin. He pulled off my shirt, undid my bra and sucked at my breasts and my nipples. I moaned with the pure pleasure of it, and when I felt a longing, a powerful surge of heat between my legs, I pulled at his belt buckle, and he quickly unzipped his pants and pulled them away. He shifted his weight and pressed himself into me, and we fell to the floor in a heap, my breath catching in my throat as he tugged my pants away, his fingers and then his tongue exploring my center. Finally, I arched my body to meet his, and then I felt—bliss. That's the only way to describe it. Just bliss.

It was much later, after another round of exquisitely unhurried lovemaking, and a quick dinner of Swiss chocolate and wine, that I remembered to tell him about the reception and the refugee camp, and the people I'd met. John sat smiling, occasionally nodding while I went on and on about Suu and Ɓān. And then I remembered the last wife and decided to see if he knew anything.

"Her name was Emily," I said, looking for a reaction. But he only shrugged.

"And she is—?" he asked, his brow wrinkled.

"The missing wife, the one who lived here in that room that's locked, which reminds me, since no one can find a key, will you just ask for a locksmith?"

"I will. I'll get your license this week too, and we'll ask someone—maybe Mae—to give you some lessons. After that, maybe we can just rent a car. And, as for money—we have a joint account, Nora. Just withdraw anything you need. It's your money, too. I couldn't have come here and done this without you."

At that moment, I didn't think I'd ever loved him more.

CHAPTER TEN

I rose early the next morning, but John was already up and gone. I wasn't the least little bit aggravated. I knew what it was now to be excited about something, to jump out of bed with enthusiasm, ready to seize the day. I spent my day on the internet researching Bān and the troubles in Myanmar. Funny how seeing a place and the people involved can make facts and figures, which I'd found mind-numbing not so long ago, come alive. Suddenly, the civil war in Burma or Myanmar, or whatever they called it, was the most interesting thing in the world. The military government, who'd renamed the country Myanmar, ran the place like a dictatorship, spinning stories that any problems were those created by disgruntled refugees, not the government. The Thai government too, just as Lisa had said, was tired of hosting the refugees, placing those refugees in danger of being sent back or just kicked out of Thailand to make their own way somewhere else. There was increased crime along the border, and Thai authorities were afraid that it would spread into the cities and beyond. The entire state of affairs seemed complex and confusing, but one thing was certain—the problems in Myanmar and along the border were a big, fat mess.

I was riveted to the internet when I heard a loud bang. I shot from my seat unsure what to do. And then I heard footsteps, and then voices, and I sighed with relief. It was John's voice. He was talking with another man. They were dragging something up the stairs, and by their groans and the scuffing, thumping sounds, I guessed that it must be something heavy.

"Jesus, get that end, will you?" I heard John ask.

The other man mumbled something unintelligible right before I heard a loud crash. I raced to the stairs just as they heaved a heavy wooden crate around the corner and down the hall. I followed the commotion as they hauled it into one of our spare bedrooms where they were trying to position the very large and very bulky crate with the UNHCR logo on the side. I wondered if it belonged to Lisa. She'd said I could help with supplies, and maybe this was what she meant. It seemed a waste of energy though if I'd just be hauling it back downstairs to take to Bân. So intent were they on their work, they didn't even notice me standing there. I cleared my throat, and John jumped.

"Hey, sorry for the ruckus. I thought you were out." He straightened up and leaned in to kiss my cheek. "You know Jim."

I turned and smiled. "Nice to see you again."

"You too, Nora. This looks all set now." He kicked the trunk. "So, I'm gonna run. I'll see you later?"

John nodded and walked him down the stairs and to the door, and that gave me time to examine the crate which seemed identical to the ones Lisa had brought to Bân, even down to the sturdy nails that kept it closed. I ran my hand along the side and nudged it with my foot. It was immovable and solid, a kind of mini bank vault. I scratched my head. What was in there? John returned and nuzzled the back of my neck. I kissed him quickly on the cheek, and then patted the top of the trunk. "Is this for Bân?"

His brow wrinkled. "Bân? No."

"It looks just like the supply crates that Lisa brought there. So, if it's not for Bân, what's in it? And why is it here?"

And then there was silence almost as if he was thinking what to say. I gazed again at the crate which took up most of the small closet, and my own secret worries bubbled to the surface. He was never home, he seemed always to be traveling, and now this—whatever it was. "So, what's in there?" I asked again.

"It's Mae's, not mine. Jim said the last ambassador let her keep stuff here, so when she asked him—" He shrugged. "It just seemed like a small favor, no big deal. And we have so much room here." He took my arm and turned me toward him, and away from the crate.

"A UNHCR crate?"

"We have some at the embassy. Once they're empty, they make pretty good storage containers, don't you think?"

"It's locked up pretty tight though, isn't it?" I reached down and pointed at one of the nails.

"It is, and it's heavy as hell, but she told Jim it was shoes and clothes, and we'll never even notice it tucked in here." He nudged it with his foot and then he turned his attention back to me, tilting my chin up and kissing me, and my questions faded away. "As long as I'm home in the middle of the day—" He traced my lips with his finger. "How about...?"

He ran his finger along my throat to my breasts. I felt dizzy with desire. "I love you," I whispered into his ear, grateful for the time to explore his body and the pleasures of married life once again.

Later, after John had gone back to work, I went downstairs for a bite to eat, and as I turned the corner to the kitchen, I heard my name mentioned—not in a friendly way, but as though someone were spitting it out in anger. My cheeks grew warm, and I stopped and listened. The speaker was Mae, her usual sing-songy voice replaced instead by a low hissing tone.

"But the last wife—" Chai began.

The floorboard under my feet gave a resounding squeak, and suddenly all was quiet. I took a deep breath, and moved toward the kitchen, not sure what to say. But I needn't have worried. Mae poked her head through the kitchen door.

"There you are," she said, forcing a light tone and walking toward me.

"Is everything okay?" I asked.

"Of course, I was just telling Chai I wanted to check on my trunk." The line of her mouth was tight, her arms crossed, her eyes darting back to the kitchen. She forced a smile. "Isn't that right, Chai?" she called over her shoulder.

Chai mumbled a noncommittal and unintelligible reply, and I thought it was probably best to just separate them. I brought Mae upstairs and away from whatever the quarrel had involved and showed her the closet where John had placed it. She nodded and ran her finger along the smooth wood. "Thank you for letting me stow it here. I have so many nice things, and nowhere really to keep them. But this won't be for long. I promise."

We headed back down the hallway when I stopped in front of the locked room, and instinctively, jiggled the knob. So much had been going on, I'd forgotten to ask John if a locksmith had been arranged. I turned to Mae. "Can't we just get a new key?"

"Ahh, that," she said, touching the locked door. "We've put in a bid—"

"A bid?"

"Because this is an official residence, so the State Department has to send out bids and approve a locksmith."

"You're not serious."

Mae nodded. "I am. I wish we could get in, but—" She held

her hands up in surrender. "But I do have some good news for you." She pulled a paper from her bag and held it out. "Your driver's license."

I snatched it from her hand to have a look, and I felt all of my questions about her argument with Chai melt away. It looked a bit like my Massachusetts driver's license—a plastic encased card with my picture, my name—Mrs. Nora Fielding— my birth date and Asian lettering that could have said almost anything. In the top left-hand corner was a picture of Thailand's flag and the words *Kingdom of Thailand*. I had a Thai driver's license. I could go anywhere—including Bān—on my own. I hugged Mae. "Thank you," I said as I ran my finger over the card. "This is my passport to freedom."

Mae nodded and smiled. "The ambassador said you'd be very happy. He said you were eager to get to Bān on your own. So, things worked out with Lisa?"

I smiled and told her about the camp, the little girl, and my plans to do something for the kids there.

"Very good news," she said softly, too softly as if she were speaking to herself.

I cleared my throat.

She stood straighter. "Well, then, this is perfect timing. The ambassador arranged a rental car and asked if I might take you for your first lesson today. Would you like to have a lesson?"

"Would I? Give me five minutes." I raced upstairs to put on sandals and grab my bag. Maybe I could talk her into a quick run to the mall so I could pick up some toys. Once outside, Mae pointed proudly to the car, a small Toyota that looked the same as any Toyota at home. She pulled open what I thought of as the front passenger door and slid into the driver's seat.

"Sit on the passenger side, and just watch me closely. Everything is a little different here because everything's opposite to what you're used to. So, sit tight; we'll drive to a construction site and—"

"Construction?" I was suddenly nervous.

Mae laughed. It's only an empty lot right now, but it's paved. An old road was closed on the other side of town to make way for a new highway, but there's been no work yet. It's just a long stretch of nothing. I taught my cousin to drive there."

I watched closely as Mae started the car. Aside from the position of the driver's seat, everything inside was the same. The ignition was on the right—same as home, the shift and other buttons were in the center console—same as home, and that was where the similarities ended. Though I'd been a passenger almost too many times to count since arriving in Thailand, I never really paid attention to the road or the craziness of maneuvering a car on the wrong damn side. But now I did. My eyes were glued to Mae and the oncoming traffic. I winced as she pulled out, and into the wrong lane. I had to stop thinking that way—it wasn't the wrong lane here where people drove on the left-hand side of the street.

When we turned onto the long stretch of deserted road, Mae pulled over and exited the car. "Now you." She opened the passenger door. "Slide over, and don't be nervous. You already know how to drive. Today, you're just going to get the feel of sitting on the right and driving on the left."

I slid over and once Mae was belted in, I put the car in *drive*, and maneuvered along the old road. Debris dotted the ground, and, forgetting everything I'd just been told, I moved around it the way I would have at home.

"Okay," Mae said, "you just drove on the wrong side. Try again."

And over the next two hours, I tried again and again, sometimes getting it right, sometimes not. Finally, as the afternoon slid into early evening, Mae's patience wearing thin, she announced my lessons were over for the day. The knot in my neck eased as I loosened my grip on the steering wheel and opened the door, ready to reclaim the passenger seat for the ride home.

"Where are you going?" she asked.

"You're driving back, right?" I put one leg outside of the car.

"You do it," she said, a testiness in her voice I hadn't noticed before. I suppose teaching me to drive wasn't really part of her job description.

I flinched at the suggestion and her sudden change in mood. "I don't think I'm ready."

"So, just drive halfway. Then, when we get to the streets where traffic will be heavy, I'll drive."

"I don't know. You really think I can do it?" As soon as the words were out of my mouth, I cringed. Of course, I could do it, but it was too late—Mae had noticed. She rolled her eyes, just as I pulled my leg back in, and shut the door. I inhaled a deep, calming breath, and pulled out into the street—on the wrong side—right where I was supposed to be. I maneuvered though light traffic, keeping to the left, and at my first intersection, I stopped and tried to figure out how to make my right-hand turn from my left-hand lane.

"Same as you'd make a left-hand turn from the right-hand lane at home," Mae said, reading my mind.

I made the turn, slowly but successfully, and I exhaled as she directed me to pull over. "Traffic will be heavy. I'll drive from here."

We stopped at a supermarket on the way home. Though we had food delivered every week, and I had only to write on Chai's list what I wanted, I had no idea what it cost or where she got it. I wanted to see for myself what was available in supermarkets here. The store was like a Whole Foods at home— clean, pricey, and filled with high-brow foods, half of which I couldn't identify. I wandered through the bakery, the produce section, the butcher shop, until I found what I was looking for—the candy aisle. I scanned every package, but they didn't have what I was craving—Twizzlers—those red licorice sticks. I settled on some Cadbury chocolate bars and a bottle of wine and climbed back into the car. I'd just ask Kelly or my mom to send me a care package.

"I'm glad we stopped here," Mae said as she climbed back into the car. "I wanted to mention that I'm concerned about Chai's food account. I think she's spending too much, probably stealing for her family, but whatever the reason, we can't tolerate that. I think it's best to just fire her."

I sat rigid. Perhaps this was what the argument had been about. I'd already figured out they didn't like each other, but this felt like sabotage. "I don't think she's stealing. I think she's figuring out what to cook for us. I've made some adjustments to the menu, so any problems with the cost are all mine." I crossed my arms and shook my head. "And the ambassador's," I added for good measure. "We'll cover any discrepancies."

Mae scowled and turned the key in the ignition.

And that was the end of that conversation.

At home, I broke off a piece of chocolate, poured a glass of wine, and pulled out my phone. I'd learned the country code for calling the US and the steps necessary to make a call from my new international cellphone that John had given me when we'd arrived. I looked at my watch—six p.m. here. Boston was eleven hours behind Thailand. I tried to do the math and figure out the time at home, but I wasn't sure if daylight savings time had begun at home. Was it five a.m., or was it six? Math was never my strong suit, and I couldn't be sure of the time in Boston, so I checked my phone to see what day it was. I never knew the day anymore. Without a job and television shows to cue me, every day might as well have been Friday, but my phone said it was

Tuesday, making five a.m. or six a.m. or whatever it was, too early or too late to call Kelly. She'd either still be asleep or just running out the door to work.

I'd just have to wait for Twizzlers. And then John came home, and I forgot all about the Twizzlers.

CHAPTER ELEVEN

The next morning, I heard John roll over and groan as he pulled back the covers and got out of bed. I turned and reached for him. "Don't go yet. Stay. Just for a while."

He sat back down and pulled me close. "I wish I could, but I've got some important meetings today. And—I meant to tell you this last night, before you seduced me—the meetings are in Kuala Lumpur."

Suddenly wide awake, I sat up. "Shit, John. Where's that?"

"Not too far. Indonesia. I'll only be gone a day or two."

"Can I come?"

He tilted my chin. "I wish you could, but it's all business. No wives, no socializing, nothing."

My face crumpled into a pout. I folded my arms across my chest. I knew I probably looked like a petulant kid, but I didn't care. I felt like a petulant kid. "I don't understand why you have to travel so much. You're away more than you're home."

His brow furrowed, and he shook his head. "I love you, Nora. You don't really think I want to go, do you?" He kissed my forehead and stood up, naked and beautiful, the muscles in his back taut.

I scrambled to the edge of the bed and caressed his back. "I love you too," I whispered, running my finger along the small of his back. He turned and lowered me back onto the bed before lifting himself on top of me, his lips on mine, his hips swaying, our bodies moving in that now familiar rhythm that my body craved, the pleasure almost too perfect to maintain. And then I could bear it no more and I cried out with the pure ecstasy of our lovemaking. These were the moments when I could hardly believe my good fortune—my new life, my husband, this house. All of it.

An hour later, John sprinted down the stairs, and out the front door. I threw on my robe and stood out on the veranda to watch him go, but the swaying palm trees and the high gate blocked my view. I went back inside to hear the ping of my cellphone, and I smiled. John—it had to be. He wasn't going after all. I reached for my phone and saw Lisa's name. Well, if it couldn't be John—Lisa was definitely my second choice.

"Hey, Nora," she said. "Sorry to call at the last minute, but Renée and I are heading out to B̂ān. Interested?"

"You'll pick me up?" I asked, heading to the shower.

"Ten minutes. Be out front. Renée's in one of her moods, but if you come, it'll take some of the pressure off of me."

I washed quickly, pulled on a tee-shirt and jeans, pulled my wet hair back into a messy bun, and bounded down the stairs and right into Chai. For about a millisecond, I considered asking her about the food bills, but just as quickly, I dismissed that thought. Despite her sometimes sullen manner, she struck me as hardworking and honest. I might not be the best judge of character, but I didn't think she'd throw it all away for a few dollars. And, besides, Mae seemed to have it in for her, and I wasn't entirely sure why. I'd just have to ask John about managing the bills myself. I'd done it in Southie. I could do it here. But not today. I'd just made sweet love with my husband,

and I was headed to Bân, and that put everything—John's damn trips, the locked room, the missing wife, and Mae's problems with Chai—on the back burner.

"Morning, Chai. I'm going out for the day. Is there any coffee? I thought I might be able to have a quick cup."

She nodded and I followed her to the kitchen where I spied a pan filled with sizzling eggs. I gulped down a cup. "Sorry about the eggs," I said, letting myself out and running for the gate. A guard jumped to attention.

"Everything all right, ma'am?" he asked.

"Meeting friends and I don't want to be late." He pulled open the gate, and I stepped onto the main street just as Lisa and Renée pulled up. I slid into the back seat, and finally exhaled.

"Bonjour," Renée exclaimed breezily as she pulled out into traffic.

Lisa turned to me, a pained smile on her lips. "Glad you could make it. I told Renée how taken you were with the camp and little Suu."

Traffic was especially heavy this morning, and Renée shouted something in French. The only word I recognized was "idiots." She lit a cigarette, opened her window, and the city's noise surrounded us. The acrid scent of car exhaust wafted in, mingling with her cigarette smoke. In the back seat, I coughed, and I could see Renée scowl. Damn, I was aggravating everyone today.

I sat forward, eager to make amends, the smoke almost in my face. "Thanks, Renée, for letting me come today. I'm excited to help at Bân."

"That is good you are interested to help. The ambassador's wife can have a lot of influence for refugees. *Oui?*"

She waved her hand toward me, the hand with the damn

cigarette, and I coughed again. I cleared my throat. "I'm not sure I have any influence, but I really do want to help." I was quiet for the rest of the ride. I didn't want to provoke Renée any more than I already had. As we neared the camp, I leaned on the open window and gazed out, taking time to really notice the foliage and the scents and the scenery. The last few miles of unpaved road absorbed me. It was the path from one world to another—from city to jungle, from an abundance of everything to an abundance of nothing. The ease with which Lisa and Renée managed to move between these two worlds both fascinated and yet somehow, repelled me. I couldn't imagine how you could become so used to suffering that you could work at Bān by day, and then show up at the embassy for a party at night. It made no sense to me, but I knew I had a lot to learn, and I reminded myself that they did this work for a living. So far, I was just a tourist.

When Renée made the final turn into the camp, my heart beat a little faster, and when I stepped out of the car and was surrounded by refugees, just as Lisa had been the first time I came, I knew I was just where I belonged. My eyes scanned the crowd, and when I spied little Suu running toward me, I broke free of the people near me, and ran to her. "Suu," I said, bending to lift her into my arms.

Her tiny little arms circled my neck, and she smiled.

"Hello," I said.

She touched my face and said something that I didn't understand and then she giggled, her sweet laugh rippling through the air. I put her down, and she promptly tucked her hand into mine.

"Come on," Renée said. "I'm hungry. Let's get something to eat."

Lisa turned, a sly smile on her lips. "I'd love to, but I have to do an inventory at the clinic, and I wanted to show Nora the spot I thought might be good for a play area."

Renée shrugged and trudged off.

"You don't mind, do you?" I asked, catching up to Renée. "I'd really like to get started on that. Maybe we can get something later?"

"Of course, I don't mind. And yes—we should get something later. A drink, maybe. *Oui?*" She lit another cigarette and tramped away, her stylish boots barely touching the ground.

I looked at my own feet. In my haste to get ready, I'd slipped into flip-flops, not the sneakers I'd worn last time. The mud seeped into my sandals and between my toes, just as beads of sweat began to trickle down my back. Suu looked at my feet, and laughed, and suddenly it didn't matter—not the sweat or the mud or the heat. None of it. With Suu beside me, I trailed Lisa back to the clinic, this time trying to memorize the route so that I could start to make my own way through the camp.

Lisa tramped behind the clinic to a small clearing. "I thought this might be a good spot. It's central to everything so all the kids can find their way here. What do you think?"

I looked around, and tried to imagine a play area, maybe a place to kick balls, or draw pictures, or just sit and read. But the space was so empty—of everything—it was hard to picture it as a bustling playground. "It looks pretty desolate, doesn't it?" I finally asked.

Lisa smiled. "Exactly. That's what makes it the perfect spot. You can make it the play area of your dreams."

"Is there money?" I asked, wondering how much a playhouse, chairs, and everything else would cost.

She shook her head. "There's hardly money for medicine. Use your imagination and your influence. You can do it, Nora. Just give it some thought. There are no deadlines here."

But there were deadlines—at least in my mind there were. These kids had been without everything long enough. I'd just have to figure something out.

I spent the day, Suu at my heels, plotting out the space and the things I'd need to transform this space into a play area. In the early afternoon, Lisa appeared and handed me a bottle of water and a bowl of noodles. I sat on the ground and shared both with Suu who ate voraciously. I finally just pushed the bowl to her and nodded. This little girl needed that food more than me.

It was almost two when Renée strode back into view. "So, let's get moving." She tapped her watch. "I want to get to Cheap Charlie's."

"Is that a store?" I asked, wishing I'd thought to bring money.

"It is a bar, a fabulous bar, though it is a bit of a dive. Mostly expats, handsome men with women on their minds, understand? Maybe your husband goes there?"

I shook my head. "I don't think so. We just got here, and he's a little busy. He's away right now," I said, trying to emphasize the *busy*.

"Where is he?" Renée asked, showing what I thought was a little too much interest. I shrugged. "I'm not sure."

She laughed. "You are the perfect wife then, No questions, no curiosity. So different from the French. We want to know everything."

I pursed my lips to help me keep my mouth shut. *Bitch*, I wanted to say, but I needed Bân, and I couldn't afford to alienate someone who worked with the UN. We left the camp and drove back to Bangkok in silence. I wasn't sure I wanted to go to a stupid bar, but it was probably better than going home to an empty house.

"Where is this Cheap Charlie's?" I asked as we drove into downtown Bangkok and along a familiar street.

"It is off Sukhumvit on Suk 11," Lisa answered. "Not so far from your house or the embassy. That's why Renée likes it—lots of important men go there."

The road was dotted with small shops and smaller stalls selling a little bit of everything—clothes, food, toys, fabrics, trinkets—and I tried to pay attention to where we were so I could find my way back, but the roads were too wide, the intersections too narrow, and I gave up. "How do you find your way?" I asked Renée. "It seems so confusing to me and those street names—Phattanakan, Pridi Banomyong." I shook my head. "I can't even pronounce them. How do you know where you're going?"

"Ahh, the street grid helps. The streets, at least what I've seen, that run off a main street—say Sukhumvit, which is where we're going, anyway—the streets that run off Sukhumvit are Sukhumvit 1, 2 and so on. Understand? People just shorten that to Suk 1 or 2 or whatever. We're headed to Cheap Charlie's which is on Suk 11."

Still confused, I smiled. "I guess if I can figure out the main streets, that system will make finding my way around much easier when I'm driving by myself."

"First you must get your license," Renée chimed in. "And that will take forever."

"But I already have it," I said cheerily.

"You have it?" she snapped. "It took me three months to get mine. I wish I'd known your ambassador."

"Oh, stop giving her a hard time," Lisa said. "You'd marry an ambassador in a minute, if you could."

Renée's scowl softened. "Ahh, that is true enough." And she laughed, a harsh guttural laugh, but still—a laugh.

Lisa leaned back. "Cheap Charlie's is only two kilometers

or so from the embassy and your house, over on Wireless Road. Maybe Renée will meet her own ambassador tonight, *oui?*"

Renée laughed and turned onto a side street, and into a tiny slip of a parking spot. "Here we are." She pointed to an alley, and above the alley's entry, I saw a string of lights. She led us though the entry into the bar which really was in an alley, an outside alley to boot. I squinted through the shadows to get a better look. The bar was rustic, made of wooden logs and surrounded by stools. Clutter, not liquor bottles, lined the back of the bar. License plates from what appeared to be all fifty US states, artifacts from everywhere, and still more unrecognizable junk strewn along and above the bar. So far, I wasn't sure what the attraction was.

"Wine?" Lisa asked.

I nodded, and she stepped up to the bar and ordered.

"Lots of Americans tonight," Renée said, her gaze following the clusters of men.

"How can you tell they're Americans and not Europeans?"

"The Americans are the ones with the young Thai women hanging off of them. Disgusting I think, but—" She looked at me and shrugged.

I looked away. I wasn't sure why, but she was purposely trying to get under my skin.

Finally, Lisa appeared and passed us each a glass of wine. "I don't know a soul," she said. "What about you, Nora? See anyone from the embassy?"

I looked around. "I've only met one or two of John's friends, and I don't see either." They were probably off in Kuala Lumpur with John, but I wasn't going to offer that information in front of Renée.

We stayed and sipped wine and watched Renée flirt with the American men she despised. "Shall I tell them who you are?" she asked. "It might help me in my quest to find my own ambassador."

"Please don't," I said. "It really does sound like a bigger deal than it is." And I realized those were the exact words John had used to describe his own title the night we met.

CHAPTER TWELVE

The next day, courtesy of the diplomatic pouch, I received another plain brown wrapped package from John with the same note inside:

    Thought you might like these. I miss
    you. Love, John

And just like last time—there was no signature, just his typed name. I wondered if it was the same note; if he'd picked it up from the hall table and taken it with him. This time, my gift was a beautiful silk shawl. I draped it over my shoulders and admired my reflection in the hall mirror. At least he was thinking of me.

Once I moved the package, I spied a letter underneath, and picked it up. The envelope was smooth to the touch, and when I turned it over, I saw it was an embossed letter from the office of the British Ambassador addressed to me.

This was the stuff I'd dreamed about when I heard that John would be named an ambassador, the stuff of fairy tales. I trailed my finger along the gold lettering and wondered if it was an invitation to a royal event. Maybe the king or Prince William or even Prince Harry was coming to Bangkok. I'd have it framed, that's what I'd do.

But first, I had to open it. I slid my finger under the seal, opened the note inside and read. I was invited to a luncheon with the ambassadors' wives from France, Denmark, Canada, Japan, and a host of other countries. This was my first invitation to the inner circle, and I struggled to remember my already forgotten protocol lessons. What should I wear? And bring? At home, I would've picked up a bottle of wine, but somehow, I thought that probably wasn't the correct thing to do as an ambassador's wife.

But John was still away, so I turned again to the person who'd been my teacher from the start, and dialed Mae.

"Hello, Nora," she said in her familiar sing-songy voice. "How are things going?"

I filled her in on my visits to Bān and the invitation to the British embassy. "I need help," I whined. "I don't have a clue what to wear or bring."

Mae suggested I wear the linen dress I'd bought at the mall and as for a hostess gift, she offered to send flowers the morning of the luncheon. "After the luncheon, just send a note on official stationery. I left some in the desk on the second floor. I've been to one of those luncheons, so I know you'll have a good time."

"You've been? Could I bring you as a guest, do you think?"

"Oh no," she said. "That wouldn't be proper at all. I went as the ambassador's representative after his wife had left. I used to fill in at functions and events when a woman was needed."

And then I understood her sometimes animosity. She hadn't known that a wife was coming, and that her days as the alternate wife were done. And maybe that explained her dislike of Chai, too, a way to keep her hand in how the house was run. And I'd shown up and ruined it all.

The morning of the event, I wiggled into my dress, slipped on a pair of heels, and fussed with my hair until it was time to go. I'd decided to walk to the embassy since it was less than a mile away. With armed guards always on duty, there was no slipping out the door and down the street. Instead, I ran a gauntlet of stern faces, machine guns, and stiff backs until I passed the final Marine on duty. "Morning, ma'am," he said with a friendly nod. "Need a ride?"

"No, I'm just heading to the British embassy for lunch."

He smiled in reply and pulled open the side gate. "Have a good day, ma'am."

I waved as I stepped onto busy Wireless Road and joined the harried pedestrians already filling the narrow sidewalks. I joined a mixture of Asian and European faces, though as one of the latter, I was definitely in the minority, and for the first time in my life, I felt a tiny bit of insecurity for being so obviously different. I tried to catch the eyes of passersby to offer a smile or hello, but people seemed intent on avoiding one another until one tiny bent man, a large straw hat on his head, nodded at me and tipped his hat. I smiled and turned to watch him go, wondering if maybe he was my gardener, and that was the reason for his greeting. I picked up my pace, my feet beginning to burn in my too tight heels, and a trickle of sweat running along my neck. Too late, I wished I'd driven.

It wasn't long before I spied the Union Jack waving high above a compound that looked much like the American embassy or my own house. High white fences topped with steel spikes ringed the building, and it wasn't until I showed my invitation and ID that I was granted entry through the heavily guarded gate. Once inside, I stopped and stared. The embassy, a beautiful old colonial building with elegant columns at the entrance and flags waving at the portico, stood amidst lush gardens and ponds. I could see another building, an apartment or office complex maybe, off to the side. An odd structure housing a series of levels, some with balconies, and bamboo slats everywhere, it seemed out of place alongside the embassy. I stood and looked around, unsure where exactly I was headed, and to which building. I pulled my invitation from my bag and was having a quick look when I felt a tap on my shoulder. I turned to see the woman I'd met at the reception we'd held at the U.S. embassy. She'd been the first to share what little she knew about the last wife's disappearance. She'd given me her card which I'd promptly lost and at this minute, I couldn't remember her name or her country. Damn. Was she the British ambassador's wife?

I held out my hand and smiled. "So good to see you."

"You too, Nora. I'd intended to call you, but—well, you know how busy things are." She gripped my hand with both of hers and leaned in to give me an air kiss. "Shall we?" she asked, nodding toward the entrance.

I nodded and followed her to the entrance where she asked for directions to the luncheon, while I gazed at the portrait of the king. I wondered if I could take pictures with my iPhone, but I hadn't asked Mae about it, so I kept my phone tucked into my bag, and decided instead to memorize every detail of the day. We trailed a staffer down a carpeted hallway to a large room where a group of women were already busy chatting. A woman dressed in a silk suit broke away and greeted us.

"Thank you so much for joining us," she said in a lilting British accent. "I'm Sophie," she said, "and you—"

"I'm Nora Fielding, the wife of the U.S. ambassador." A little thrill shot through my veins at the ease with which I announced John's title. She planted an air kiss near my cheek and smiled before turning to my companion.

"Elizabeth Miller, Canada," she replied.

Of course.

Sophie turned and introduced us to the other women. They were from Japan, Australia, France, New Zealand and a few countries I'd never even heard of. Kyoko, Anna, Dianne and Grace and the others greeted us warmly. Over lunch—a cucumber salad followed by a spicy soup and then some kind of shrimp or prawn in tissue thin pastry—we talked. Well, they talked. I listened. These women were already acquainted, and some had known each other for years. They'd been at this whole embassy thing for a long time. They laughed about some tiny restaurant off an alley in Paris, crab cakes in Nairobi, music in Greece, and shopping in Dubai. I had never felt more out of place in my life, and I sat quietly and fidgeted with my food.

"And what about you?" Elizabeth Miller asked, trying to draw me into the conversation. "Where were you assigned before Bangkok?"

I squirmed a little in my seat. I hated being the center of attention. I slipped my shoes off under the table and wiggled my toes. At least my feet could be comfortable. "This is our first assignment," I said. "John and I came right after our wedding." A series of oohs and ahhs filled the room, and our hostess insisted on a champagne toast. She summoned the server and within minutes, I was being toasted and congratulated. And then, the room went silent as they waited for me to say something, but I was at a disadvantage. I had nothing in common with these women, so as nice as they were, I prayed for the afternoon to end. "Thank you for this warm welcome," I finally said, raising my glass and drinking down the contents in one gulp. An observant waiter quickly refilled my glass, which I promptly set back down. Last thing I needed was to be tipsy in front of this sophisticated group.

They began to chat again about the vagaries of shopping and dining in Russia or Nepal, and my eyes, and then my ears, glazed over. When talk turned to local affairs and work they were involved in, I perked up, my fingers gripping my glass of champagne.

"A garden," the Japanese ambassador's wife said. "I think we should choose local gardens and work to beautify them."

"Oh, I agree," Elizabeth added. A few more voiced agreement, and Lillian turned to me.

"And you, dear?" she asked.

"I have a brown thumb, I'm afraid," I said, begging off. "And I'm so busy with the refugees," I lied. "I'm not sure I have the time."

A hushed quiet fell over the room. "The refugees?" someone finally asked.

"From Myanmar. At Bân." The silence deepened. "You've heard of them, right?" A few nodded. "Well, that's where I've been working, volunteering really."

"Didn't Emily Somerfield spend time there?" one of them asked.

The room grew silent. A clock ticked somewhere. I fidgeted in my seat.

"Did you know her?" another wife whose name I'd already forgotten asked.

I shook my head and took a slow sip of my champagne and considered my position. They were obviously looking for gossip, and I had none, but they must know something. I set my glass down and pounced. "Did you?" I asked.

No one spoke. It almost seemed that no one breathed until finally Elizabeth cleared her throat. "I met her a few times. I think we all did." She glanced around the room, her gaze settling on Sophie, our hostess. "I think you probably knew her best," Elizabeth said.

Sophie smiled nervously and paused. "I guess none of us really knew her. She was quiet—reserved almost. Of course, she was much younger than the ambassador; she was his second wife, I believe, though perhaps she was the third. Anyway, there was some gossip associated with that. You know the kind —she broke up his earlier marriage—that sort of thing. And, maybe because of that, she kept her distance from the rest of us. She attended events only when she had to. And we could sense that something was wrong, that she didn't quite belong." She looked around the table, and there was a low murmur of support.

I wondered if they thought I *belonged.*

"She was beautiful though," another wife said. "So, we were surprised when we heard that she was volunteering at that refugee camp. I mean, she just didn't seem very selfless, if you know what I mean."

"Self-absorbed was more her style," another woman added.

"And then she just disappeared?" I asked. "That's so hard to believe these days—with all of our technology—that someone can just vanish." I crossed my fingers and hoped they'd just keep talking.

"Well, there are rumors aplenty about that—she ran away with another man, she took all of Tim's money, even one that she's living in that camp. I mean, really. The strangest rumor is her husband never wanted her to be found."

"Really?"

Elizabeth nodded solemnly. "That woman, Mae—is that her name—the one who was at your reception? She stepped right into Emily's role once she was gone, even came to one or two of our luncheons. There was even speculation—" She paused and glanced around as if to make sure she had everyone's attention. "That Mae was somehow behind Emily's disappearance, that she spent a little too much time with the ambassador. But of course—it's only gossip."

"Mae?" A chill ran along my spine before settling over the room. I ran my finger around the rim of my glass.

"That was nonsense though, don't you agree? To think that an employee could seduce an ambassador?" another wife asked.

More uncomfortable murmurs followed, and I watched as they seemed to fidget with their forks and glasses, all the while watching one another, and me, intently. These women were like record-keepers or court stenographers—taking down every word, every nuance, in their collective memories to be mulled over later when they were alone.

"Well," Elizabeth finally said, breaking the icy silence, "tell us about Bān. Your husband doesn't mind? You know—with all the inherent political difficulties, and the potential gossip, associated with all of that."

"He encouraged me," I said as I picked up my glass and threw back a long swallow of champagne. I could feel the first sweet stirrings of the alcohol spinning in my brain. I sat in silence through the rest of the luncheon and wished I were in Bān or Cheap Charlie's with Lisa and Renée. But I wasn't, so I drank the champagne and just listened. When the women talked about their husbands, it was clear that those men were home most every night, and I felt a pang of envy, and another tiny twinge of doubt about where John spent his time.

"Do your husbands often have to travel out of Thailand?" I asked, my tongue loosened by the alcohol.

Sophie laughed. "Well, mine's often away," she said, her fingers raised in air quotes. "But out of the country? No. And yours? Does he travel?"

I nodded, and wished I'd kept my mouth shut. Thank God, I hadn't asked if their husbands carried guns, though I guessed I already knew the answer to that question.

"The American ambassador always carries a heavier workload," Elizabeth said, coming to my rescue.

I smiled and agreed. "He is a busy man," I added, not sure if I was convincing them or myself. He'd been gone almost a week on a trip that he'd promised would be for a day or two. And, aside from the souvenir he'd sent, I'd had no word—no calls, no texts, nothing. I'd tried texting but had no replies. Calling his cell was out. I didn't want to interrupt any important meetings. I wondered if the last ambassador had traveled so much and if that had anything to do with his wife's leaving.

I turned my attention back to the ladies' chatter just in time to hear one wife exclaim over another's newly slim figure. My eyes glazed over, and I took a long swallow of my champagne, praying that it would get me through the afternoon.

As the luncheon drew to a close, a photographer arrived to take our photo. We stood arm in arm, seeming like lifelong friends. And we smiled broadly as the photographer snapped away. "Just lovely," Sophie said as he left with a promise to send us each a photo.

By the time our luncheon was over, I was feeling woozy. I teetered on my high heels and returned the air kisses I received in place of simple goodbyes. When Elizabeth offered to have her driver drop me off, I accepted, relieved not to have to navigate the busy street in my slightly inebriated state.

When I finally arrived home, I fell onto my bed, and plotted a way back to Bân, and a way into the locked room. In Southie, I would have just broken the lock but here, I had to be a good wife. Or at least seem to be.

CHAPTER THIRTEEN

In the morning, though my head was still spinning from yesterday's champagne, I phoned Lisa, but my call went right to voicemail. I knew my surest route to Bân was on my own so I called Mae and asked if I could impose on her and have another driving lesson, and maybe a quick shopping trip. With any luck, I could draw her out, and maybe, if she was feeling generous, she'd tell me what she really knew about Emily. Either way, the less I had to rely on others, the better, and that rental car was just sitting there. Mae kindly obliged, though I was sure I detected a bit of hurt pride in her voice.

Still, she arrived with a smile, though it might have been forced, and took me back to the old, deserted road, my eyes on the drab scenery that I hadn't even noticed the last time we'd driven through. The neighborhood—no more than a shantytown—was so different from my own street and the other streets I'd seen since I arrived, that I was riveted to the sights and sounds. Barefoot, dirt-smudged children ran in and out of traffic, dogs pursuing them in some kind of desperate childhood game of tag. Older women, some who resembled Chai so closely I sat forward to get a better look, swept the sidewalks with bamboo brooms. Young women, dressed in long traditional skirts and faded blouses, carried wailing babies on their hips, and tiny smidgens of hope in their eyes. The open-air markets, with shelves almost empty, were crowded with customers and shopkeepers haggling—some with raised fists—over prices. I watched as one older man, his stick thin arm raised in protest, his shirt ragged, spit on the floor of one stall before being pushed roughly away.

These streets weren't so different from the paths that wound through Bān, though here, young girls with too much makeup and too tight skirts paraded along the street, their eyes darting to the men in passing cars, and I swiveled to watch. These were the girls, the ones who'd been pulled into the sex trade, and my jaw fell open as one negotiated with an older European driver before jumping into his car. I wanted to memorize his plate number and turn him in, but here in Bangkok that would likely make me the problem, not him.

I was lost in thought when Mae pulled off the main road, and onto our deserted practice road. The quiet and emptiness there, such a deep contrast to the frenzied streets we'd just passed, had me wondering if she'd ever brought Emily out here for a driving lesson. If someone disappeared out here, they might never be found. A sudden chill filled the car. I turned the air-conditioning off, but the chill lingered, and I shivered.

"Ready?" Mae asked, motioning me into the driver's seat.

I hesitated and forced myself to put Emily and the streets we'd just passed on the back burner of my mind as I slid over. Within the hour, I was feeling pretty confident, or maybe I was just eager to get the hell out of there. "I think I'm all set, Mae. Thank you for taking me again. I know it's an imposition. Do you mind if I drive back? I'd like to go to some of the shops on Sukhumvit, and then find my way home."

Mae nodded and programmed the dashboard GPS for Sukhumvit Road.

"I can get directions in English, right?" I asked Mae.

"Yes," she answered. "You can."

"In two kilometers," the device began, "turn right and then turn left."

"Two kilometers! Damn. I have no idea what that means."

"A kilometer is almost two thirds of a mile. Just try to do quick math. I don't think we can change to American miles, but I suppose you can ask the ambassador."

I groaned inwardly. A car in a foreign country meant another set of problems—were there gas stations here? Do I just pull in? And if miles were in kilometers, what were gallons in? Do the attendants speak English? I took a deep breath. One step at a time, and kilometers first. Before Bangkok, I could barely figure out my change at the grocery store, but here, every day was a math lesson. I quickly figured that two-thirds times two was four thirds making my turn in a mile and third. One small victory.

"And you can check your mileage here." She pointed to the gauge. "That's in kilometers. You can use that to measure your distance."

I looked at the little odometer under my steering wheel. Mae was right. I pulled into the street, and at the GPS's prompting, I made all the turns I needed and when I turned onto the bustling Sukhumvit, I breathed a sigh of relief.

Mae directed me to a small parking lot on Suk 3, and when I eased the car into a spot, and turned off the ignition, I wanted to jump with joy. But I didn't. I followed Mae to the stalls and shops on the main street, and I picked through balls and crayons and coloring books until I found just the ones I wanted.

I watched in awe as Mae haggled over prices and walked

away from more than one shopkeeper before finally nodding to me. "This is the best deal," she said.

I paid only fifty-nine dollars for six balls, fifteen coloring books, fifteen boxes of crayons and one teeny pair of little girl sandals. At another shop, I got some cargo shorts, tee-shirts, sturdy trail shoes, socks and a sweatshirt, though I wasn't sure I'd ever need a sweatshirt in this heat. I treated Mae to a late lunch at one of the tea shops, and just as I was about to ask her about Emily, she spoke up.

"I completely forgot to tell you, but I've cut back Chai's hours." She stirred a packet of sugar into her tea.

I dropped my own spoon, the clatter against the table a sudden commotion in our quiet corner. I hadn't seen Chai that morning, and it had barely registered. Damn, I should have paid attention. Maybe one of those older, weary ladies on that street of misery was Chai after all. Mae was definitely trying to take back the responsibility she thought should be hers. "Excuse me?" I asked, my lips tight with anger.

"I spoke with Jim. You know I'm the admin assistant, correct? Well, that's a part of my job—overseeing the house, and he agreed with me."

I took a deep breath, but it did nothing to stall my pent-up rage. "I disagree, Mae," I said through gritted teeth. "And I want her back at the house tomorrow. I thought we'd settled this."

Her gaze narrowed, and she set her cup back down, and I immediately regretted the fury in my words. I reached out and patted her hand. "Sorry to sound so prickly, but it's hard trying to find where I fit in here, and what my responsibilities are. I like Chai. And I think she needs this job. But I like you too, and I just think I need you both. Okay?" I nodded and squeezed her hand.

She forced a smile so brittle I thought her lips might crack. We ate in awkward silence. All of my plans to ask about Emily had gone up in smoke, but I couldn't afford to alienate Mae any more than I already had. "So, we're still friends?" I asked when lunch was over.

Mae nodded and kissed my cheeks. "I'll call you soon," she said, rushing off.

I picked up a local newspaper, found my way back to the car, and headed home, my first time navigating through the streets entirely on my own.

By the time the guards waved me into my driveway, I was feeling pretty sure of myself. I crossed my fingers and prayed that John would be home. I had so much to tell him. But he wasn't, and with the knowledge that Chai hadn't been there, the house felt even emptier than when I'd left. I opened the newspaper to have a read, and almost fell off my chair. There on the front page, was a photo of me and the other ambassadors' wives lunching at the British embassy. *Diplomacy Starts At Home*, the headline read. Shit, shit, shit. This was exactly what John had told me to avoid. I peered closer and read.

> Nora Fielding, the wife of the U.S. ambassador joined the other wives in a special—

John would be livid if he ever saw it. For once, I was glad he was away. I tore the story and photo from the paper and slipped it into my pocket. I'd send it to my mom. She'd be impressed. I crumpled the rest of the newspaper and tossed it into the trash praying that wherever he was, there were no Thai newspapers.

The next day, I was still alone—no John, and only one message —and that was from Jim. He wanted me to have John call him. I didn't know why he hadn't just called John. He must be in touch with him, right? I called him back.

"Hey there," he answered. "Thanks for calling me back. I'm trying to reach John."

"I thought—" The wires in my brain felt suddenly disconnected, and I hesitated.

Jim sensed my confusion and rushed to fill the silence. "Not there?" he said. "That's okay. He probably told me where he was, but you know how it is—the right hand never knows what the left is doing, and God knows, that's never truer than in government work. I'll catch him later, Nora. Sorry to bother you."

"Speaking of the right hand—Mae said you both had decided to cut Chai's hours?"

There was a long silence. "Chai?" he finally said.

"Our cook, Chai, you remember her?"

"I don't think I do, but however many hours you need her, that's what she works. Okay? Does that clear up any confusion?"

It did. Mae was a smoother operator than I'd given her credit for.

Once he hung up, I plopped down on the bed to think. This house, as ordinary and elegant as it had first appeared, harbored a multitude of secrets of the people who'd passed through before me. My curiosity piqued by Mae and Chai and the embassy wives, I walked into the spare room that held Mae's crate and bent to it. It was sturdy and impenetrable—a little over the top for clothes and shoes, I thought. I tried to move it, to see if jostling it might not create a noise that would tell me what else was in there. But it wouldn't budge. It was too heavy. I ran my hand along the top edge and noticed that Mae hadn't even placed her name anywhere on the crate. If it were mine, and held my own private treasures, I'd have plastered my name all over it. I rose. Maybe we were just different, that's all.

I walked to the locked room, and jiggled the knob again, but this time, with weeks of frustration behind me, I leaned my shoulder into it and pushed hard. It didn't budge. I tried again—this time slamming my foot into the door with all of my might.

"Everything okay?" a vaguely familiar voice shouted from downstairs.

Damn, damn, damn! The door hadn't budged, and I'd left a nice black footprint smack in the middle of the perfectly white door. "All okay," I yelled back down, wondering who the hell was there. "I just dropped something. Be right down."

I pulled off my shoes and padded quietly to my own bathroom grabbing a white towel and soaking it through with water. I went back and began to scrub, but the footprint remained.

I gave up, wiped the trickle of sweat from my brow and headed downstairs. "Hello?" I said, poking my head around the corner.

Elizabeth Miller appeared from the kitchen. "The guard let me in. He rang and when you didn't answer, he thought it would be all right." She bobbed her head as if she was explaining it to herself. "He remembered me from the last ambassador."

I nodded. "It's fine," I lied, hoping I didn't look quite as disheveled as I felt.

"I just wanted to be sure we were all right, you know—with the gossip and all at the luncheon. I hope it didn't bother you too much."

"No problem. Would you like a glass of wine?" I asked, thinking that alone, maybe I could get more information out of her. "Have a seat," I said, leading her into the dining room. "Just give me a minute." In the kitchen, I pulled out a bottle of wine, scrounged together some leftover cheese and crackers, grabbed two glasses and headed back.

Elizabeth tapped her glass against mine. "To new friends," she said.

"To new friends," I echoed her toast and took a sip of wine. "I'm so glad you came," I gushed. "I have so many questions, and I know you couldn't really open up at the luncheon, but I feel as though I'm missing something that's right in front of me. You said the guard knew you today; that's why he let you in. So, I assume then you knew Emily Somerfield pretty well?"

She paused and looked over her shoulder as if looking for eavesdroppers, though she must have known that I was alone in the house when the guard let her in. Finally, seeming satisfied that we were indeed alone, she sat forward.

"Well, I guess I knew her as well as anyone could know Emily. She kept to herself, but not for the reasons the other wives mentioned. At least, I didn't think so. She was beautiful, mind you, but she was shy and so unsure of herself, she had trouble speaking when everyone was together. You can imagine how that group of ladies—as nice as they are—could chew someone up if they didn't like them and they didn't like her. And she knew it."

"Why didn't they like her?"

"She wasn't just beautiful, she was tall and slim and elegant, and when she did speak, she was articulate and charming. She was almost too good to be true, so they decided that nothing about her was real. They made up stories that she'd had plastic surgery, a multitude of lovers and that she'd married Tim for his money and influence. But the truth was that she loved him— more than anything—and that's why, for me, it's so hard to believe she just left. The other wives are convinced that her leaving proves them right." She sighed. "Maybe, it does. Maybe, I didn't know her at all."

I had unknowingly moved forward, my elbows on the table, my chin resting in my hands. I stayed like that—perfectly still and holding my breath—expecting more. But she'd reached for a cracker, and the plate was empty. I stood and quickly refilled it, anxious not to disrupt her train of thought. And it was then, I remembered, someone had said Emily had gone to Bân. I slipped the plate in front of her and sank into my seat. "What about Bân?" I asked. "Didn't someone say she'd gone there? Did she volunteer there?"

A light seemed to go on in Elizabeth's eyes. "That's right. I'd forgotten about that, though I admit she never spoke of it, so I'm not even sure she really went. It may have been one of those rumors started to stir up trouble." She reached for a cracker and swiped a bit of Brie across its surface before popping it into her mouth.

"Why would volunteering at Bân stir up trouble?"

"Oh, that's right," she said, sipping her wine. "You're working there, yes?"

I nodded; my fists balled up in my lap.

"What is it you do, exactly?"

And suddenly, I forgot about Emily. I was lost in my own stories of Bân—the hunger, the sadness and the children, and finally, of Suu. And Elizabeth seemed as mesmerized by my words as I was by the place.

"Oh, my, it does sound quite the adventure," she said, her eyes gleaming. "Perhaps, I'll come along sometime."

But she never mentioned Bân again. And, when I really thought about it, it seemed that showing interest had been her way of steering our conversation away from Emily.

CHAPTER FOURTEEN

The following morning, there was still no word from John, but Chai had reappeared. When she spied me coming around the corner, she bowed her head and placed her hands together in the traditional greeting.

"Thank you, Miss. Thank you."

She smiled, and I almost asked about Emily, but I didn't want to risk our unspoken bonding with one question. When she turned to check the coffee, I saw that her hair—pulled back into a tight bun—was without its usual net, and that allowed me to see the cluster of hairpins that kept her bun in perfect place. Hairpins! I wouldn't have to shove my way into the room; I could just pick the lock. Kelly and I had learned the art of lockpicking when she was a latchkey kid who had a penchant for losing her key. We'd become pretty good at picking locks, and I kicked myself for not thinking of it sooner.

"Chai, could I have one of your hairpins?" I asked, pointing to my own haphazard ponytail poking every which way out of my elastic band. "I was thinking of trying a bun or something different."

She smiled and plucked a long pin from her hair, pressing it into the palm of my hand. My fingers curled over it. "Thank you," I said. "I wish I'd thought of using a hairpin sooner." Feeling very Nancy Drew-ish, I smoothed my hair, tucking a few stray strands behind my ear to emphasize my need for a hairpin. My mother had read those old Nancy Drew stories to me when I was little, and here I was—living my own mystery of a locked room.

I spent much of the day in the garden, a pile of newspapers and books at my elbow, but it was the old gardener who had my attention. Intent on his work, he didn't seem to notice that I was there as he clipped and trimmed and arranged the flower bushes and beds. I cleared my throat and called out once, but he never turned, and finally I left him to his work and headed back inside. When I was certain Chai had left for the day, I tried the hairpin on the door again and again, but the pin was too flimsy, or maybe I just wasn't as nimble as I once was, but the result was the same—the mechanism wouldn't budge. Not even a tiny fraction. My fingers cramping, I stepped back and might've kicked the door again, but a tiny shadow of my footprint still remained, and I thought better of it. I heaved a frustrated sigh and made my way along the hall to the spare room where Mae's crate still sat. I bent to the first nail and tried to pry the board loose with the hairpin. But a funny buzzing sound stopped me cold. Was someone in the house? Was it Mae? I pulled the pin back, pushed it into the knot of hair at my neck and tiptoed out of the room.

"Hello?" I called. But there was no answer. I called out again before heading downstairs. But the house was empty, and I was alone. I held my breath and listened, but the buzzing— wherever it had come from—was gone. I exhaled noisily and prayed that John would be home soon. I was no good on my own.

Later that week, I called Lisa and asked if I could drive her and Renée to Bân.

"So, you've had a lesson?" she asked.

"Several," I lied. "I'd like to learn the route to Bân, and the best way for me to learn is to do the driving."

Lisa agreed to my proposition. "But Renée won't be with us today. She's off tormenting another aid group, so we'll have some peace."

An hour later, we were on our way. Once I made a U-turn, the route seemed pretty straightforward. I stayed on Sathon Tai which turned into Krung Thonburi and then into something else. I knew I'd never remember the street names, but if I was familiar with the route, and programmed my GPS, I'd be okay. I was relieved when we finally left the main roads and pulled onto the paths leading to Bân. And then I was even more relieved that the Toyota had all-wheel drive, a necessity on these rugged roads.

Once we were on the long stretch of road that led to Bân, I turned to Lisa. "Did Emily Somerfield ever come out here with you?" I asked.

She was silent, and I finally turned my head slightly and asked again. "Emily—the last ambassador's wife?"

It might have been my imagination, but she seemed to tense, her shoulders shifting forward. "No," she said. "At least, I don't think so. I don't know the name."

Another dead-end. Maybe Elizabeth and the others had been wrong. I turned my attention back to the road and took a long, slow deep breath. I was making too much of this whole Emily thing. It was going to turn out she had some pathetic affair and just took off, and God knows I had enough already to worry about—my new life, my often-missing husband, and how I could make my own way in Bangkok. My list was endless.

At the camp, I pulled only two of the balls and three coloring books and packs of crayons from the back seat. I wanted to figure out how many kids could play in our small space, and if too much of what I'd brought was out, we'd just lose it. I slipped Suu's sandals into my bag. I didn't want Lisa to see I'd broken her first rule—no favoritism. I followed Lisa through the camp, along the now familiar route to the clinic, and beyond that, to the play area. The crowd followed Lisa, only a stray dog chose to stick with me.

There was no sign of Suu as I made my way along the path behind the clinic, and my solitary trek allowed me time to appreciate everything around me—the trees, slick with morning dew, the flowers begging to lean in and be smelled, the sky, always a perfect blue, the hum every day everywhere of people chattering, birds calling, life being lived. And I wondered why I never noticed these things at home—the sky, the trees. At home, I noticed only the seasons. Was it cold or hot, snowy or rainy? Did I need gloves? It was all so familiar at home, I never really looked beyond the cold or the hot. I promised myself that the next time I was home—I'd notice it all.

A torrent of tiny footsteps broke through the quiet, and Suu appeared, all smiles and giggles. She ran right into me, throwing her arms around my legs. I squatted to her side, gave her a quick hug, and fished the sandals from my bag. I held them flat in my hand and held them out to Suu. She reached out and touched the plastic shoes, her fingers lingering along the soles. She gave me a wistful look, and I realized she didn't understand they were for her. I nodded and looked down at her feet.

"For you," I whispered, and though I wasn't sure she heard or understood my words, her eyes grew wide with the realization that the shoes were for her. I placed them on the ground and watched as she tentatively slid her feet into the sandals. She squatted down and patted the shoes before jumping up, hugging me and running off, the sandals slapping against the soles of her feet as she went. At that moment, nothing mattered more than Suu's simple joy.

Word spread, and more kids waiting their turn to be seen in the clinic arrived to our little play space. I took the balls and books from my bag and began a game of kickball though I suppose the boys would have called it soccer. Once they were engrossed in their games, I turned to the others, mostly girls, and we colored. I was surrounded by giggles and laughter, and more than one little girl leaned in to pat my face or my hair. I patted them right back and smiled the whole time.

Out of the corner of my eye I saw Suu approach, tugging at a small woman to follow her. Though young, a teenager perhaps, the woman wore one of the traditional long skirts that skimmed the ground as she walked. Her shirt was stained, her hair unwashed and hanging loose. She was shaking her head and casting sidelong glances at me to see if I was watching. And then she just stopped, Suu pulling on her hand before finally giving up and holding her little hands up in surrender.

Before the woman could scurry away, I hurried over, placed my palms together, bowed my head and smiled. She looked up straight into my eyes and smiled. She was an older version of Suu and so many of the other children—large almond eyes, soft gentle slopes to her face, and something else—a kind of innocence.

"Hello," I said, bowing again and wishing an interpreter were around. She pulled Suu close and pointed to herself.

"You're her mother?" I pointed first to Suu and then to the woman I assumed was her mother, but she was so young. Maybe she was only a sister, or maybe a friend. "Mother?" I asked again.

The woman giggled, the sound as soft and light as Suu's giggle. "Mawtha," she said, mimicking my Boston accent.

I laughed out loud, and watched as she pointed to Suu's new sandals, and then to her own bare feet. She said something that I didn't understand. I crinkled my brow, and recognizing my confusion, she bowed slightly, and smiled broadly.

"Sandals?" I asked. "Of course, you need sandals too."

She nodded, her eyes saying thank you in a way that her words could not. My heart melted. I was exactly where I was meant to be.

When Lisa and I drove away from Bān that day, I knew that a part of me remained there. "I know you're busy with your other projects, and I don't want to pester you all the time, would it be all right if I go by myself when you and Renée can't go?"

I thought she'd answer right away. I mean, it's a yes or no question, right? But she seemed to mull it over. Finally, she sighed, and looked back at the camp. "I think it can be kind of risky to go alone. There's so much going on there."

"But that's why I can help." I could feel my prospects dwindling. This was where I belonged, not with a group of stuffy diplomatic wives. I wasn't above begging.

Lisa shook her head. "I don't know. It can be a pretty chaotic place. The problem is that new arrivals are registered only once a year, and to get any help—shelter, food, education—refugees have to be registered. Families and neighbors share, but there's less to share these days, and that means less food, less nourishment, more diseases and poorer health. And Thailand is cracking down—they don't want people leaving the camp to work, so there's crime. Same as anyplace—people turn to stealing or trickery. It's a vicious cycle, so I'm just not sure."

"But I have nothing to steal—only soccer balls and coloring books—nothing of value."

"You have a car."

"And I have a cellphone. I could call for help if I really needed it."

"Not out here, you can't. There's no cell coverage."

I didn't realize there was no cell coverage—I'd never tried to make a call. I'd have to try another tactic. "But you've come alone, right? And you still have your car." I couldn't quite believe my own persistence.

"You just won't quit, will you?"

I smiled. "And—?"

"You win. But you have to tell me when you're going, and no more than twice a week by yourself. Maybe I can have you bring some supplies out for me too. It just might work. Deal?"

"Deal." I slipped my left hand from the steering wheel and shook her hand. With my eyes back on the road, I asked when she'd be coming back.

"I have meetings to attend, so not for a week at least."

"Do you mind if I come tomorrow?"

Lisa grinned. "It's okay. Just be careful."

"I want to try it out on my own, drive here, get to the play area and set up, which reminds me—I noticed some tarps all folded and piled outside the clinic. Can I have a few?"

"Sure, but what for?"

"My play area. I thought I could cover the ground and maybe create a shelter from the rain that will be coming soon."

Lisa nodded, and already I was planning the next day's trip.

CHAPTER FIFTEEN

The following morning, I rose early, and made the drive to Ɓān on my own. The solitary drive was lonely. I lost my car's radio signal halfway out, and even with my windows open, the roads were quiet—too quiet—and I thought maybe Lisa was right. This was a long, lonely drive and if I broke down out here —I'd be screwed. I shook off my anxieties, and kept my eyes on the jungle road, so rutted and furrowed, I was amazed my little Toyota could make it. When I finally spied the familiar smoke spirals of Ɓān, I heaved a sigh of relief and turned into the camp. It was only eleven o'clock. The drive had taken me just under three hours.

As soon as I stepped from the car, Suu came running to greet me. She must have had some kind of child radar to know I was there. She slipped her hand into mine and led the way to our play area. We stopped briefly at the clinic to pick up the tarps, and the balls and coloring books I'd left there. At the play area, I set out one tarp on the ground, and placed the coloring books there. The soccer balls, I placed in an open space with enough room for running and kicking balls. And then the kids came, all smiles and laughter and ready to play. I sat with Suu and the others who wanted to color, and I watched them all, reveling in their joy. A little boy came up and patted my head and smiled. Another leaned in close to my face, and just smiled. When a shy little girl reached out to take my hand, Suu swatted her away, and the tiny girl burst into tears. I gently chided Suu and took the other girl's hand. Suu turned her back to me, her anger apparent in the rigid line of her back. When I ran my hand through the tangled mat of her hair, she turned back and patted my cheek, and I knew all was right with my little piece of joy in Bân.

At one o'clock, I packed up to go. I wanted to be back in Bangkok early in case John made it home, and I wanted to get used to driving this route alone when there was plenty of light to guide me. The children surrounded me on the walk to my car, and along the way, we were joined by a few adults. I liked this—feeling as though I belonged here. As we reached my car, a man appeared beside me and grabbed my arm, his grip rough, his fingernails scraping against my skin. Lisa's warning flashed through my brain.

"Wait, don't go," he whispered, though his whisper sounded more like a hiss.

Suu kicked at him and scowled angrily. The man forced a smile and released his grip. I rubbed my arm, watching him all the while. He didn't look like the other refugees here. The Rohingya refugees had a kind of humility in their faces—soft, gentle eyes, and round faces that were open and kind. There was something almost elegant about them—the way they carried themselves with such quiet grace, their long-tapered fingers brushing against the baskets they balanced on their heads or on the babies they carried on their backs. Their voices were soft and whispery, and their bodies too, seemed frail and somehow vulnerable.

But this man had none of that. Beyond the slight similarity

in the almond shape of his eyes, and the color of his hair, his face was all hard angles, and his hands and even his fingernails, were crusted over with dirt. He stood stiff and straight as a pencil as if on full alert. But it was his gaze, direct and bold and piercing, that gave me a fright to be so near him. I backed away.

"Mrs. Fielding, you must listen." His voice was cloying, as though he'd practiced too long what to say and how to say it.

"You know my name?" I felt a chill. He knew me, and he spoke English. Something wasn't right. I turned away and opened my car door. The newspaper photo. Of course, that was how he knew me. John had been right. Damn it.

"I do, that and more. You must listen." He placed his palms together and bowed slightly, but it was a pose and a politeness that seemed forced. "Please. I have information. Just one minute."

I sighed noisily. "What is it?" I snapped as I slid into my car.

He leaned in close, shrugged a backpack from his shoulders, and pulled out an envelope. "You must take this—information for your husband." He held it out. "I have no way to get it to him unless you help. Please?"

What had John said? *Be careful—people will ask you for things.* I shook my head. "Just tell me what you want."

A scowl curled his lips, and he pushed the envelope toward me. "You must take it!"

A thousand questions swirled in my mind. Who was this man? And what did he really want? None of this felt right. It was all too risky, too strange. And John had been clear—stay away from risky political stuff, and no favors. I shook my head and placed my hand on the door handle. "Sorry," I said. "I'm not allowed."

His scowl deepened. "Then please, just tell your husband to come out here."

I rolled my eyes. Like I was about to do that. Yeah, right. This guy was crazy. I pulled the door shut and put the car in reverse and backed up. As I drove away, my hands trembling, my heart pounding, I could see him in my rearview mirror, a frown draping his lips, his eyes following me as I drove away.

CHAPTER SIXTEEN

I stayed away from the camp the next day hoping to speak with Lisa about the man with the piercing eyes, but she was busy in meetings every time I called. And John was still away, though I never considered—even for one minute—telling him about the man. I knew it would only give him a good reason to ask me to stay away from Bân. No way I wanted to do that. I'd just lay low until I could talk to Lisa.

But with John away, and Bân off limits, I was bored and acutely aware of just how different my new life in Bangkok was. In Boston, there was never enough time, and I couldn't remember ever being bored, or alone. Between work and family and friends, and my search for the perfect man, my life had been pretty full, and I'd always been surrounded by people close to me. I'd somehow expected that here in exotic Thailand, my life as the ambassador's wife would be a whirlwind of activity, but nothing could have been further from the truth. Here, all I had was time. I couldn't even really go for a drive by myself. Though I had my license and I'd pretty much mastered the whole wrong way thing, I'd never been a very good driver, even in Boston, so to me the prudent thing was to just stay off Bangkok's roads unless I had a specific destination like Ɓān, or the shops on Sukhumvit. And though I had acquaintances in Lisa, Renée and Mae, I had no real friends here. And the ambassador's wives, as nice as they were, just weren't my cup of tea. So, there I was—no Kelly to call at the last minute. No one.

Desperate for coffee and company, I headed down to see if Chai was in, and as I rounded the last corner, the now familiar scents of curry, chilies, and coconut filled the air. "Chai," I said almost too effusively as I entered the kitchen.

She turned and smiled. "Hello to you, Mrs. Fielding. You looking for breakfast?"

I shook my head. "No, just some coffee and maybe, if you're not too busy, someone to talk to." I plopped down into one of the chairs.

"Talk to me? No. You should go out. Find something to do with yourself, make new friends."

I laughed. She sounded like my mother. "Won't you just sit with me while I have my coffee?"

She pulled out a chair and plopped down, a flurry of lines creasing her forehead as she took a sip of her tea. I'd never really looked closely at Chai—she was older, she was busy, and I was busy trying to be the ambassador's wife. It was always something. But today as I sat across from her, I realized that, despite the series of lines and wrinkles and folds that crisscrossed her face, she was probably just about my mother's age. Her life though, had likely been much harder, and with Mae's recent attempts to get rid of her, I wanted to reassure her that her job was safe.

"Is everything all right here?" I asked.

She pursed her lips, or maybe she was biting down to keep hidden tears at bay. I reached out and patted her hand. "You know that John and I think the world of you, don't you? We have no plans to make any changes. I want to be sure you know that."

A wisp of a smile played at her lips. "I am grateful for that. Without this job, I am all alone—no home, only a shack to return to. I lose everything. You understand?"

I nodded. "Are you from Bangkok?"

She shook her head. "My old home is far away. I have a small room now here in town."

"What about your family? Are they here?"

She shrugged, an odd noncommittal response, I thought.

"Do you at least get to see them?"

"Not so—" She stopped abruptly, her face crumpling. "I've said enough. It's not my place to speak as though you are my friend."

I wanted to run my hand along her cheek and smooth the worries that had settled there, in the same way I wanted someone to smooth my own, but of course I couldn't. I had no idea either what to say, so I patted her hand again. "But—"

She stood and placed her cup in the sink, the clatter like a school bell dismissing me. "I have work to do, Miss. You should go out."

"I went out yesterday, but today, I'm back to being alone. Besides, I don't really know Bangkok, and I don't really have anyone to go out with. And, when I do go out, I have to pass by all the guards. It just always feels like a big deal. See my problem?"

She rolled her eyes. "You are the ambassador's wife. Just go out. Do something. Get your hair fixed up."

I ran my fingers through my hair. I was definitely due for some highlights, and I must have been overdue if Chai had noticed. I shrugged. "I'd like to, but I don't know any places here."

"Last wife went to small place over on Soi Ruam Ruedi."

"Was that Emily?" I'd taken to referring to her as just Emily —as though we were old friends, though we'd never met, and I knew almost nothing about her.

She nodded. "But we are speaking about you, not her."

"I'd like to go." I tugged at an errant strand of hair. "But I'll never find it."

Chai shook her head and cast a stern glance my way. "It's almost behind us. Of course, you'll find it."

"Behind us?" I stood and peered through the back window to the gardens beyond. But all I could see through the thick shrubbery were peaks of white fencing.

"No, no," she said, taking my hand. "I'll show you."

We stepped outside into the lush gardens. I trailed Chai through rows of flowers and bushes inhaling the sweet scents. As the gardens ended and the high privacy hedges began, Chai bent low and walked through a slight gap in the greenery, a gap I never would have noticed if not for Chai. I bent and followed her along a narrow and well-worn path. I watched as she stopped in front of the security fence, too high to scramble over, too sturdy to break through. Chai ran her hands along the fence until they seemed to catch on something.

"Come," she said, turning back to me.

She took my hand and ran it along the fence, until I felt something—a latch maybe? "What is it?" I asked.

"Secret," she whispered, unlatching the bolt and pushing lightly on the fence. I watched as a small gap appeared in the fencing, allowing the sounds of traffic and people and life to seep in around us.

I drew closer and had a look for myself, my eyes growing wide as I gazed through a narrow alley to the busy street just behind us. "Is this the street? Soi Ruam?"

She nodded solemnly and pulled the hidden gate shut. "No

one knows about this—another wife had it done some twenty years ago. The old gardener showed it to me, and I've told only you. And now you must promise to keep it a secret."

"Yes," I whispered, my hand over my heart. "Is the gardener the same one who works here now?"

"Yes," she said as she stepped back onto the hidden path.

"I've tried to speak with him, but he seems not to hear me or—"

"He cannot hear you, and he cannot speak. It is only with the flowers that he can communicate. Understand?"

I nodded and wondered if that was Suu's problem—if her garbled speech was a sign of a hearing problem. I followed Chai back toward the house, the hedges scratching at my arms. When we stepped back into the garden, I turned to check the path we'd just taken, but it was gone, swallowed up by the hedges and shrubbery once again. "Where—?"

She turned my head and directed my gaze upward to the swaying palms of a sturdy old tree. "I don't understand," I said, watching as her eyes tracked down to the tree's great trunk, and then I saw it. The great roots of the tree had pushed thought the earth creating a ropey mound right by the path. I stepped over the roots and back onto the hidden passageway, and from there to the secret gate. When I emerged back into the garden, I was alone. I checked the roots again and just as before, I found the path. I felt a bit like Mary Lennox in *The Secret Garden*.

I retraced my route back to the kitchen where Chai stopped her chopping long enough to nod her head toward a slip of paper on the table. "That is the number of the fancy place for your hair over on Soi Ruam Ruedi. Take that. You can go by yourself, just walk through the secret gate, along that small alley, and when you come out onto the street, you'll see the shops."

"And I'll be able to get back in the same way?"

"Let the latch fall loose when you pull the gate shut behind you. You'll get back in."

"May I ask why you've never told anyone else about the gate? And why me, now?"

The slightest of smiles draped her lips. "Other wives, other families, were always busy, always running to one place or another. They were never home long enough to say hello. But you—you are different, often home, and always alone. You need an escape. The gate will give you that."

I wasn't sure what kind of response the diplomatic protocol would have dictated, but I didn't care. I leaned close and hugged her. "Thank you."

I went upstairs, called the number Chai had given me and made an appointment for that afternoon at Plaza Hair. When I slipped through the secret gate, the latch hanging loose, I felt my pulse quicken. The street was filled with soaring towers, restaurants, hotels, fancy shops and people. The chaos was as familiar as any I'd find on my old street in South Boston and recognizing that made maneuvering it alone somehow less daunting. This, after all, was the adventure I'd hoped for. At Plaza Hair, I had the works—highlights and a trim for my long-neglected hair, and a fresh manicure for my raggedy fingernails. By the time I slipped back through the hidden gate, I felt like Cinderella. Once inside, I double checked the latch to see it had closed tight and hurried back along the path to the house. I checked my reflection in the hall mirror and smiled. Not bad for my first solo adventure. I tucked a stray blonde strand into place, and stepped into the kitchen to see Chai, but she'd gone. A handwritten note told me that dinner was in the refrigerator.

So, there I was—all dolled up, dinner in the fridge—and all alone. I distractedly picked at my dinner—a coconut curried shrimp that I would have devoured on any other night, but just not tonight. I cleared my dishes, poured a glass of wine and went upstairs determined to break into the locked room. The hidden path had somehow renewed my resolve to uncover the rest of the secrets in this grand old house. And the locked room was a mystery that had taunted me from my first days here. I took a deep breath, crouched over the unyielding keyhole and inserted Chai's hairpin, wiggling it to and fro until, almost magically, I heard a click and felt the knob turn under my fingers.

I held my breath as I pushed the door open, a flash of icy air rushing toward me. The air-conditioning for this room had apparently never been turned off, and the now frosty air had collected everywhere in the sealed room making it feel colder still and creating a kind of funny, musty smell. The shutters were pulled tight, the room in full darkness. With fingers aching from the sudden burst of cold, I flipped the light switch and watched in horror as hundreds of beetles, or maybe cockroaches, scurried away. I hadn't seen any in the rest of the house. Even the insects knew this room was locked tight and off limits to people. I held my breath, watched my step, and slipped inside.

The room was larger than mine, but held the same furniture —an oversized bed, cushioned armchair, and nightstands, all placed exactly as mine were. It looked like any ordinary lived-in room, not the long abandoned one I'd expected. The bed was made, the nightstand held a table lamp, alarm clock and a book. It looked for all the world as if its inhabitants had just stepped out. I picked up the book—*Wuthering Heights*—a book I vaguely remembered reading in high school, and as I flipped through the pages, a small card fluttered to the floor. I retrieved it and drew in a sharp breath. The card was identical to the one Lisa Bates had given me—her name, her position and her contact numbers printed on the front. I flipped it over—a handwritten number was scrawled on the back.

I was pretty sure I'd asked Lisa if Emily had gone to Bān,

and she'd said no. Maybe she just hadn't remembered, or maybe Emily hadn't gone after all, but they must have met, I thought. I'd ask her again. She'd probably just forgotten. I stuffed the card into my pocket, replaced the book on the night table, and stepped through an arched doorway into a comfortable sitting room. The master that John I and shared definitely didn't have anything like this. A television, bookcase and large couch almost filled the room, but it was the large wooden trunk placed in front of the couch that caught my eye, and I bent to it, running my hand over the intricately carved Asian scenes that covered the top and sides. The trunk's latch was unlocked and I lifted the lid and peered inside. Again, a hoard of bugs scurried this way and that looking for a way out.

Books, DVDs, an iPad, and several smaller boxes filled the space. I squatted down and began to sift through Emily's things as the beetles tried to hide. The books were more of the classics—*Little Women, Anna Karenina, A Tale of Two Cities*. Much as I hated to read, I'd read—and enjoyed—all of these in school. On the first page of each book, Emily had printed her full name in tight block letters, and I smiled. Kelly did that too—marked everything she owned with the same stiffly drawn letters. Emily was feeling more like a friend with every new discovery.

The DVDs, like the books, were old classics—*Doctor Zhivago, West Side Story, Casablanca*. The iPad was dead, or maybe just needed charging. I set it aside and lifted a small box out. This held odds and ends—a pair of silver hoop earrings—tarnished now, a lipstick, a mirror and a handful of cards—embassy business cards—identical to the ones I'd received. But, beyond her appreciation of all things classic, there was nothing here to indicate who Emily Somerfield really was, or why she'd left. I pulled out the next box and found only a pile of Post-it notes and cocktail napkins—all covered with almost illegible scrawls and numbers—and all indecipherable to me. Maybe they were codes for her friends here, or maybe she really was having an affair or two, and this was the proof—hidden from her unsuspecting husband. I replaced them in the box and was about to put everything else away when another small box caught my eye. I lifted it out and opened the tightly closed lid.

And my heart stopped.

CHAPTER SEVENTEEN

Inside, collected in neat piles and bound with paper labels lay neat stacks of one-hundred-dollar bills. My jaw fell open. There must be thousands and thousands of dollars in there and no cockroaches. Why wouldn't she have put it in a bank? Or taken it when she left her husband? Or was it only recently placed here? You wouldn't just leave this much money behind. I picked up one of the bundles and fanned through the crisp bills, the scent clean as new linen. I could take all of this money, and—unless Emily came back—no one would ever know. But I would know, and that was reason enough to loosen my hold on the stack that I held. Despite the deep chill in the room, a trickle of sweat ran along my brow, and I hurriedly replaced the packet of money and slipped the box back into the trunk. I sat back on my heels and packed everything else in just the way I'd found it.

I stood then at the entrance to the walk-in closet, Emily's clothes filling the space, dresses and shoes and blouses—all as elegant as I'd imagined—and likely just as she'd left them. I reached out to touch a sparkly silk dress, and just as quickly, drew my hand back. Why would a woman leave a pile of money and all these clothes behind? I wouldn't. I knew Kelly wouldn't either. It made it seem less likely that Emily had just left. I backed away, a sudden foreboding filling me with dread. As desperately as I'd wanted to get into this room, I was suddenly desperate to get out. It wasn't just the scurrying bugs. Something was very wrong but what could I do? I had to give this some thought.

At the doorway, I turned for one last look. Everything looked just as it had when I'd entered. I was about to pull the door shut when I spied her book. I'd read it, and maybe learn a little more about Emily Somerfield from what she was reading when she disappeared. I reached for it, did a quick check to make sure no insects had hidden between the pages, tucked it under my arm, turned the light off, and pulled the door shut. When I heard the lock click automatically back into place, I felt a sudden rush of panic. Did I leave the hairpin in there? I reached into my pocket and felt the small sliver of metal safely tucked away and breathed a sigh of relief. This hadn't been like Nancy Drew at all. The mystery of the damn locked room was a bigger mystery than before. I went downstairs, got a bottle of wine and curled up on my bed, the wine in one hand, *Wuthering Heights* in the other, and I began to read:

I have just returned from a visit to my landlord—the solitary neighbor that I shall be troubled with...

Two hours later, I raised my head, rubbed my eyes, took a final sip of wine and closed my eyes, my mind still spinning with thoughts of Heathcliff and Catherine and hidden money and secrets. I lay awake and sorted through the short list of people I might share the news of Emily's room with. I quickly eliminated Mae—she was waiting for the federal bids for a locksmith, and I'd likely broken some federal law by using a hairpin to get in. That left only Chai, or Lisa or maybe Elizabeth Miller, but none of them seemed right. I could call Kelly, but she wouldn't understand either. With all of those possibilities swirling though my brain, and my clock ticking out the passing minutes, I managed the impossible, and fell asleep.

It wasn't until late the next evening when John finally returned from Kuala Lumpur. I had just clicked *send* on an email to Kelly, hoping to arrange a time when we could actually talk instead of communicating by email, when I heard the front door bang open. I was in the house alone and, with the memory of the creepy man at Bān and the piles of hidden money in Emily's room, a tiny bubble of worry tugged at my brain. I hurried to the top of the stairs and peered down at the sweetest sight imaginable. It was John—sporting the stubble and sweat of his former life. Even his clothes—jeans and tee-shirts—were covered with a layer of dust as though he'd been tramping in jungles instead of foreign embassies. His shoulders slumped as he walked through the door and dropped his duffel bag on the floor. A tiny puff of dust rose from the bag as it landed with a thud.

It had been days or maybe even weeks—I'd lost count—since he'd left, and I felt weightless as I bounced down the stairs and into his arms. "I missed you," I said, conscious of the grime that now covered us both. He encircled me with his arms and kissed me, his fingers tracing the line of my jaw. The pungent scent of cigarette smoke and vodka surrounded me, and I stepped back. I'd never seen John smoke, not once, but maybe—

"I missed you, Nora. God, I missed you." And suddenly, I forgot what I was about to ask. His lips found mine, and we stood wrapped around one another, making up for days and days of lost kisses. He tilted my chin up and looked into my eyes, his dimples flashing through the bit of beard that covered his face. I rested my head in the crook of his shoulder and sighed as he ran his fingers through my hair. "You're beautiful," he whispered. "I could make love to you right here on the floor, but I won't." He lifted me into his arms, and carried me up the stairs, through our bedroom and into our bathroom. He reached in, turned on the shower, and began to peel off his clothes. "You too," he said, tugging at my clothes.

I laughed, pulled off my shorts and shirt, and stepped into the shower with John, where the cascade of water turned gray as it circled the drain. I scrubbed the layer of dirt from his back, and drizzled shampoo into his tangled mat of hair. I leaned into him, brushing my breasts against him as I ran my hands along his thighs, feeling him grow hard against me. And then it was his turn. He lathered me up, his mouth on my nipples, his fingers exploring the moist place between my legs. When I could bear it no more, he leaned me against the shower wall, moaning into my ear as he entered me. We groaned in unison and slipped to the shower's floor, where we made love again. And then again after that. Finally, John pulled me up, wrapped me in a thick towel, and carried me to bed. He grabbed another towel, dried off and slipped in beside me, wrapping his arms tight around me.

"I love you," he whispered into my ear.

I sighed and leaned into him, my heart still fluttering in my chest. "I love you, too." And I felt myself slipping into the happy oblivion of sleep.

It was hours—or maybe it was only minutes—later when I felt John slip out of bed, his footsteps padding softly down the stairs, and then pausing. And then, scratching, scuffing noises from the front hall broke through the deep quiet of the house. I pulled the sheet over my head to blunt the sound. Why was he unpacking now? I groaned and turned on my side. It wasn't long before I heard his footfalls plodding up the stairs, slower and heavier this time as though he was dragging something with him. The stupid bag, I thought. My eyes flickered open as he dragged the bag and turned for the closet.

"John?" I whispered drowsily. "Come back to bed."

His back stiffened at the sound of my voice, and he stopped dead, pushing the bag with his foot.

I reached out my hand. "John."

He leaned in and kissed my forehead. "Go back to sleep. I'll be back in a minute." He tucked the sheet around my shoulders and gently padded back to the closet, the sound of the bag's zipper opening almost lulling me back to sleep.

I nestled deeper into my pillow, the noises receding, the quiet descending on the house once again. I drifted back into sleep. And then a loud bang broke through the quiet, and my eyes snapped open. The closet door was pulled tight, allowing only a faint light to seep out around the edges. Shadows moved in the light. A rustling of paper was followed by a strange clicking sound and I wondered what on earth couldn't wait till morning. The sounds from the closet grew muffled and somehow distant. My eyelids grew heavy, and I felt myself sinking back into sleep.

It was the stream of sunlight that woke me. John stood by the mirror draping a tie around his collar when he noticed me watching him. "Good morning, beautiful." He leaned down and kissed me, and then tugged at his tie. "As long as you're awake, will you do this for me?"

I rubbed the sleep from my eyes and sat up, taking the ends of the tie and winding them over and around until they were perfectly knotted. I ran my hand along the smooth, stubble-free angle of his chin. "You look nice, all cleaned up and ready to go to work."

He winked and slipped his arms into a suit jacket. His polished appearance stood in stark contrast to his scruffy look last night, and my curiosity got the better of me. "You never said exactly what it was you did in Kuala Lumpur. Until I saw you last night, I didn't realize diplomacy was such dirty work." I raised a questioning brow.

He chuckled and brushed his lips against mine. "That's pretty good. I'll have to use that one." He retrieved his keys from the nightstand and turned for the door. "I'll try to get home early tonight."

I sat on the edge of the bed and let the sheet fall away, exposing my breasts. "I can't entice you to stay?"

He groaned in reply. "You're killing me, but I'm late already, and if I leave now, I can make it home in time for dinner." He blew me a kiss and disappeared out the door, his shoes pounding the stairs as he went.

I pulled on my robe, and headed for the shower, then stopped cold. His duffel bag, collapsed and likely empty now, was shoved up tight in the corner almost hidden behind a line of his suits. I leaned down and squinted into the bag. It smelled of dirt and sweat, a jungle smell not so different from Bān, but it was almost empty, save for his good luck piece, a smooth piece of lapis that he carried everywhere and that matched perfectly the piece he'd given me. He'd brought them both back from Afghanistan when we were dating and handed me mine with a flourish. "So, you'll always know that wherever I am, you're with me."

A few crumpled cocktail napkins sat at the bottom of his bag, and with Emily's stash of cocktail napkins fresh in my mind, I pulled them out to have a closer look. The name of the bar was obscured by the handwritten scrawls that covered the whole of it—numbers and names and symbols—not so different from the ones on Emily's napkins, but meaningless to me. Strange—two people who'd never met, with similar scrawls on cocktail napkins. But I was reading too much into everything, looking for conspiracy where there was none, and I knew I should just follow my mother's old advice—believe none of what you hear and half of what you see. It seemed especially apropos this week. I opened the bag wider to deposit the napkins back inside when a glint of metal caught my eye. I angled the bag to the light to get a better look and there it was— a gun.

In an instant, all my fears came rushing back. Why did an ambassador need a damn gun? He'd said not so long ago that he was just used to carrying one, but it didn't make sense. And then it occurred to me that he hadn't answered my questions about his latest trip. Just what was he doing in Kuala Lumpur? And now I had more questions—a gun? Cocktail napkins with messages? I shook my head. Tonight, I'd put my foot down and I'd just ask. I was his wife. I had a right to know.

CHAPTER EIGHTEEN

But that night, like so many others, there was no sign of John. He'd called around five to say he'd be late, and I should just go to bed. "I'm sorry, baby. I'll wake you when I get in if that's okay." I mumbled a noncommittal reply to hide the knot of misery that churned in my stomach and hung up. At three a.m., I woke to a shifting in the mattress. John had slipped in, and almost immediately, his breathing slowed, and he was asleep. He hadn't woken me. He hadn't even acknowledged that I was in the bed, right next to him. I slept fitfully and woke early ready to argue. But John, snuggled against me, opened his eyes when I threw back the covers.

"Where are you going?" he said, pulling me down and shifting onto his elbows to hover over me.

"I—I thought I'd take a shower." I wasn't ready to start an argument just yet. I'd argue over coffee, not in bed. Never in bed. I'd read somewhere that bickering in bed was the kiss of death for a marriage, never mind the secrets and lies between us. "I just—"

He covered my mouth with his own, smothering my words and even my thoughts, his hands exploring the parts of me he knew so well, and the remnants of my anger slipped from my thoughts. I was no Emily Somerfield and he was no Tim. All that mattered was this—he loved me. And I loved him back.

When we finally lay back, my skin slick with sweat, my heart still pounding, I waited for John to say he'd be home late, or away, or something that would crush my spirit. But he didn't.

"I took the day off," he whispered. "What would you like to do? Well—aside from this." He ran his fingers lightly along my lips and over my breasts and along my belly before resting his hand between my legs.

I sighed with pleasure and managed to push his hand away. "First, tell me, are you really spending the day with me?"

He kissed my neck. "I am. I'm sorry we haven't had more time together. I really didn't think things would be so busy here. You know that, right?"

A rush of tears pricked at my eyes, and I threw my arms around his neck so he wouldn't see. "I love you, John." And then I asked about the gun.

"Oh shit. I'm sorry, Nora. I always traveled with one before —Afghanistan, Iraq—you name it, they're places that demand protection."

"But—"

He drew his finger across my lips. "I'll get rid of it."

And that was that, or so it seemed.

We showered, gulped down coffee, left a note for Chai, and set off to explore Bangkok. We left the cars at home, walked the three blocks to Bangkok's sky-train—a cleaner, sleeker version of Boston's Red line—and hopped off after only two stops. I tucked my hand into John's and followed as he led me along luxurious boulevards lined with lush flowers and high-end shops, and then we ducked into side alleys where outdoor food stalls crowded the narrow paths, the scents of exotic spices and mysterious seasonings lingering in the air and reminding us that we hadn't stopped for breakfast. We nibbled on recognizable food—rice, noodles, ears of roasted corn, chicken satay, and little beef dumplings. I was stuffing another piece of beef into my mouth when a sudden shriek stopped me cold. I turned and saw John, a sly smile on his lips, holding a live chicken by the neck.

"For dinner?" he asked.

I shook my head, and he placed the poor, squawking chicken back into its cage. But he wasn't done. He took my hand and led me through another alleyway where the stalls were jammed so tight, there was barely enough room to squeeze among them. This lane held more live things—raw fish, more live chickens, and raw meat that could've been anything. But it was the live bugs and small turtles that made my stomach seize up. At one stall, giant grasshoppers, or maybe they were cockroaches, lay twitching in a long plastic tub.

"Does anyone really eat this?" I whispered.

John nodded to the smiling seller who plucked what had to be the largest insect from his bin and placed it in John's open hand. "Dare me?" he asked, his eyes locked on mine.

I shivered at the sight of the squirming insect. "Okay. I dare you."

And with that, he popped the bug into his mouth and chewed, the crunch making my skin crawl. He swallowed hard, and licked his lips, and then leaned in and quickly kissed mine.

"Yuck." I curled my lips and pretended to spit.

"I can't interest you?" He held up another bug.

I shook my head. "The only delicacy that will get me excited is a bag of Twizzlers."

He laughed. "So, red licorice twists are the key to your heart, huh? You're easy."

I swatted his arm playfully, and he pulled me close, locking my lips with his for one brief moment. "I forgot." He said, pulling away. "No close touching in public. The Thais are very proper. We'll have to save our kisses for private."

From the food stalls, we headed to the docks and boarded a river cruise along the Chao-Phraya River. The river, as muddy as Boston's Charles River had once been, flowed like a long meandering road through the city. Elegant temples, and soaring towers along the banks gave way to river shacks—fragile-looking cabins on stilts poking through the waves, their rickety supports looking as though a gust of wind or a boat's errant waves would wipe them out. But they were sturdy enough that barefoot children stood on the tiny front porches waving furiously. I waved right back thinking of little Suu, and how there was misery everywhere—not just in my beloved Bān.

We stood on the deck, the churning river beneath us, the exotic scenery of Bangkok life on either side, and held our faces to the breeze catching the water's spray. This was the way I'd envisioned my life with John, and I wanted this moment, this day, to last forever.

John was gone when I woke the next morning, but I could still taste his lips, and imagine the touch of his skin against mine. He'd left a note on the nightstand:

Love you, babe. I meant to tell you last night—I'll be away for a day or two. I miss you already. xoxo.

I read the note again, but, for once—with yesterday's memories still fresh—I didn't mind his leaving at all. I was clutching the slip of paper to my chest and floating on air when I stubbed my toe on the goddamn duffel bag that was now smack in the middle of our closet. I leaned down and tugged on the handle to push it back and noticed how light and empty it felt. I looked inside and saw—almost nothing. His lapis stone was gone—probably slipped into his pocket, and just as he'd promised—no gun, although he'd probably taken that with him, too. Only the cocktail napkins remained.

I sighed, relieved to know that John and I didn't have any real secrets—though I had secrets of my own now—I'd broken into Emily's room and found, not the answers I'd hoped for, but a pile of cash instead. But who could I tell? Not John. I should have trusted him enough to tell him, but I didn't want to admit to anyone, let alone John, that I'd broken into that room, although maybe I could say the knob just gave way. I heaved a long sigh. I supposed the real problem was that John and I had no history to draw on—no special song, no pet names, no private signals, no shared long-ago memories—we were still too new. There was no time I could look back on and remember when something similar had happened. We were only just now building that foundation and someday, I imagined I'd look back on this and smile. But right now, that someday seemed a million years away. I loved him but I simply didn't really know him. I didn't even know what his favorite color was. I rubbed my toe and stepped into the shower.

Later that morning, another invitation arrived—this one for *Ambassador and Mrs. Fielding*. I thrilled at the sight of our married title. I knew I should have been thrilled at the sight of my own name instead, but I was still new to this, and *Ambassador and Mrs. Fielding* looked pretty damn good to me. I slid out the silky invitation and read. We were invited to dinner at the residence of the Australian ambassador. I checked the date—one week away. Maybe we could go. If John knew ahead of time, maybe he'd be able to make arrangements to be here. I tucked the envelope into my pocket. I'd ask him later.

I spent the morning poking around the house, pestering Chai to teach me how to use the stove when Lisa called and invited me to a UN meeting on Myanmar's refugees.

"I'll pick you up at three."

Punctual to a fault, she arrived at exactly three o'clock. "We're headed to the UN conference over on Krungkasem. I think you'll enjoy this. The UNHCR wants to discuss how to move the refugees back to Myanmar, and we—the aid groups— are dead set against that. Renée will be there, so it should be a lively meeting."

I nodded and told her about the man at the camp, how he'd approached me and given me the creeps.

"Crazy, probably. What did he look like?"

And I described his piercing eyes and thinning hair and cloying voice, and I could have sworn that I saw a flicker of recognition in Lisa's eyes. "Do you know him?" I asked.

"No," she said. "But that description could match so many. If you see him again, let me know. He's probably harmless, but I'll make sure he doesn't bother you again."

She said that last part with such conviction, I was certain she would take care of him.

"Have you told your husband about him?" she asked.

"No. John isn't all that crazy about my going out there. I don't want to give him any reason to stop my work with the kids."

She smiled, and I sat back and twirled a strand of hair around my finger wondering how to ask about Emily. "Hey, did I ever ask—?" I began just as we pulled up to a large building with scrolled iron gates in front, and a flood of foreign flags waving overhead. Lisa rolled down her window, showed her ID, and we were waved through. My moment to ask had passed. It would just have to wait.

"So, this is it?" I asked. "The UN?"

"It's just an office—nothing fancy. For that, you have to go to New York or Geneva."

And it occurred to me that with John's job either of those was a distinct possibility for me. I stood a little taller as we entered the building and made our way through the long corridors to the meeting room. We were just finding seats when Renée hurried in, her clothes still steeped in the acrid smell of her last cigarette. *"Bonjour,"* she said, the thin red line of her lips stretching against her teeth as she smiled. She sank into a seat, her fingers nervously drumming the table as her eyes darted about to see if anyone of interest was in the room.

I settled into my seat and watched as the seats filled. The group sat around a long oval table. I was seated behind Lisa, in a chair against the wall. Lisa was there to represent her aid group whose name I always forgot—United for Health, or something like that. Renée was there to represent the UN. I sat forward as the introductions began. There was a handsome Frenchman from another aid group, his mop of uncombed hair almost hiding his piercing blue eyes, a Thai Ministry of Health representative—a small man with almond eyes and scant sprouts of hair on his chin as though he was hoping for a beard. It seemed an unlikely prospect from where I sat. There were other Thais—all women—one from the Ministry of Social Development, another from the Ministry of Education, and there were Europeans as well—from the UNHCR, WHO, UNICEF. I couldn't keep track.

The meeting, which I'd thought would be exciting, turned out to be dull as dirt. They talked about what the refugees needed, but in a way that seemed designed to complicate the issue, and then they veered off into funding and grants, and logistics, and blah, blah, blah. I didn't understand most of what they said. They'd lost me. For a time, I watched Renée watching the men, and wondered if she liked any of them. The

UNHCR guy was cute—German I thought from the sound of his accent. The WHO rep—an Australian man with a soft as butter accent, might have been a good choice for Renée, but her eyes skipped right over him, and I wondered if there was a story there.

After a while Renée's dating game bored me and I focused instead on the loops in the carpet, the reds and blues and silvers all woven together. I wondered if I should buy a rug for my mother. Was this rug an Oriental? Were Oriental rugs from Thailand? Maybe not, but I was here, so this would have to do. I'd have to remember to ask Mae about rugs.

The sound of chairs being pushed back, and the hum of chatter snapped me out of my reverie.

"Did you enjoy that?" Lisa asked.

I smiled. "Very much. Thank you for bringing me."

"Forget this place. Let's get a drink," Renée said, elbowing her way to the door.

"Cheap Charlie's?" Lisa asked, hurrying to catch up.

Renée shook her head. "No, let's try the Madrid. The rumor is it's owned by an American spy. Maybe you know him?" she asked, turning to me.

God, why did everyone think that every American knew every other American? I didn't even answer.

Lisa groaned. "Isn't that in Patpong?"

Renée smiled. "It is, and before you say it—not every place there is filled with *prostituées*. If it is, we leave. At least, let's see it."

I shrugged. "Okay with me, I guess." John wouldn't be home anyway. I was glad for the company.

The Madrid was in an area not quite as upscale as Sukhumvit Road. And though it wasn't quite six p.m., the dimly lit bar was crowded with expats—mostly men and several of them surrounded by small, pretty Thai women—girls really, who hung on their arms or sat on their laps. They seemed more like underage girlfriends than prostitutes, but who knew?

Renée knew, that's who. "So, perhaps the stories are true." She wrinkled her nose and peered up at the ceiling. "Ahh, but there are far more intriguing stories about the Madrid."

"What are you talking about?" Lisa asked as we claimed a table near the bar.

"Up there." Renée tilted her head back and looked up.

We followed her gaze.

"What? The ceiling, the wooden beams? Didn't know you were into decorating." Lisa smirked.

"No." A pout draped Renée's mouth. No matter the situation—she had an expression to match. "The area above the bar is said to have been a *clandestin* second floor, a safe place for the CIA and MI6 spies. It was in the old days, the seventies, the days of James Bond and the Cold War. They say the French were involved. You know, of course, we have a famous underground."

"Had," Lisa reminded her. "And James Bond exists only in the movies."

Renée raised a perfectly sculpted brow. "There is history here and, I think, a few unattached men." She sipped her drink, her eyes scanning the room.

"So, if not a diplomat, then you want to meet a spy?" Lisa asked.

"I just want to meet a real man, that's all. I am tired of men who are lazy. I'm looking for a man with—how do you say —*balls*. That's it—a man with balls." She exhaled a long plume of smoke before grinding the cigarette out in the ashtray on the table.

Lisa laughed. "What happened to your search for an artist? A man who's more interested in feeding his art and his soul, than his belly? Isn't that what you always said?"

A line formed between her eyes. "I am finished with all that. I want a man who'll drink with me, who'll have a smoke, a man who isn't afraid of anything. That's what I want these days. And, perhaps you, Nora, can help me find such a man." She clinked her glass against mine and turned her gaze back to the crowd.

"I thought she didn't like American men," I half whispered, half mimed to Lisa.

"Depends on the day," she whispered back.

And then I remembered the card I'd found in Emily's room, and I fished in my bag, my fingers fumbling. Lisa noticed my frantic search.

"What are you looking for?" she asked.

"I found your card in a book of Emily Somerfield's, the last ambassador's wife," I said, careful not to mention I'd been in the locked room just in case she knew about that too. "I thought I'd put it in my bag, but I guess not."

The color seemed to drain from her face, or maybe it was just the lighting in the bar that changed. "My card?"

"A business card, like the one you gave me the night we met. Do you remember her?"

She paused. "I-I suppose I might have met her," she stammered. "Though I can't remember for sure."

"What nonsense," Renée interrupted. "You knew her or not? *Mon Dieu!* One does not forget meeting an ambassador's wife." She shook her head in disgust.

A swath of red appeared on Lisa's neck, and she draped her hand there as if to cover it. "I probably met her, but I'm not sure. I'm an aid worker—it's refugees I remember. I'm not so impressed by titles."

Renée scowled, her red lips tight. "Oh. Please. We are all impressed by titles." She turned then to me. "Don't let that go to your head."

And I burst out laughing at the thought that Renée was impressed by me, or anyone for that matter. And that sudden bit of levity changed the mood. Renée laughed too, and after a minute or so, Lisa relaxed and laughed. But I never did get the answer I was looking for. I'd never met so many evasive people in my life. This whole crew in Bangkok could give the attorneys at Bain and Worth a run for their money.

"We should buy a round of drinks to impress Nora. *Oui?*" Renée asked Lisa who summoned a bartender.

I smiled and sipped my wine, my eyes surveying the room for Renée's potential mate, glazing over those men with pretty young Thai women on their arms. And then I saw him, and I froze. At the far end of the bar, his full attention on a pretty woman stood John. But it couldn't be. It was a trick of my eyes and the smoke. I squinted, the crowd shifted, and the man was swallowed up. It wasn't John anyway. *Working late*, his note had said. I sat up straight, craned my neck and the man bobbed into view once again.

There was no mistake.

It was John.

And he was with a woman.

CHAPTER NINETEEN

My breath caught in my throat. The questions, the doubts—little flickering warning lights—always pulsing through my bloodstream, suddenly exploded into my brain. My eyes were playing tricks. That's what it was. I blinked and looked again.

The woman—a beautiful Asian woman with shiny black hair falling past her shoulders, touched his arm. John whispered into her ear. She scribbled something on a cocktail napkin and handed it to John. He nodded and said something before folding the napkin and placing it into his pocket. She leaned in closer and said something, and he threw back his head and laughed.

Everyone else receded into the background, and all I could see was John and this woman. My heart stopped, and I felt the color drain from my face. My head was spinning, my mouth dry as cotton, and I knew I had to get out of there. I didn't want him to see me. I didn't want to make a scene. I gripped the table and set my glass down, my fingers trembling.

"I don't feel well," I said, pushing my glass away. "I think I'm going to grab a cab and just go home. I'll see you tomorrow?"

Lisa turned and looked at me. "You do suddenly look lousy."

She put her hand to my forehead, the way my mother did when I was little. "Fever?" she asked, almost to herself. She shook her head. "Maybe it's something you ate. Do you want me to take you home?"

I shook my head. "I'll just get a taxi. I'll see you later."

"Go home then, and rest. I'll call you tomorrow. Okay?"

I nodded, and then stood so quickly, my chair teetered ready to crash to the floor. I reached out and steadied it, and then—with one last glance at John and the woman—I pushed my way through the crowd, desperate to get away. Outside I gulped in the sticky evening air and hailed the first taxi I saw. I slid into the back seat as my first tears fell. "Forty-four Wireless Road," I directed the driver, a tiny gray-haired man with kind eyes, to an address that was up the street from the embassy and our house. The last thing I needed was a story about the ambassador's wife leaving a bar crying. Ambassador's wife? My ass, I thought as I sniffled away my tears.

When the driver let me off, I took a deep breath, kept my head down, and made my way past the high walls and ornate shrubbery that concealed the embassies and other homes on this street, to my house, suddenly aware that it wasn't just my husband who wasn't really mine, but the house as well. Aside from my moments with Suu at Bān, I had nothing in Bangkok, and I just wanted to go home.

It was almost seven when I nodded slightly to the guard out front and opened my front door. Once inside, I ran to our room, crumpled the dinner invitation we'd received that morning, and knocked our wedding photo to the floor, the sound of glass as it splintered into a thousand tiny pieces somehow comforting me. I slid to the floor and sat among the shimmering shards of glass and cried. I wore my growing distrust of John like a veil, seeing everything through suspicious eyes. I refused to be blinded by his seemingly endless good qualities. The images that stuck with me—him shouting into the phone in DC, the guns, the secret trips, the woman tonight—all of it flickered through my mind like pages in a book. Why hadn't I asked more questions? But I knew why. I loved him and I loved that he loved me back. I wasn't about to ruin that. I should have had more faith in myself.

"If it seems too good to be true, it probably is," my mother used to say, and here was the proof. I mean—John could have had anyone—so why me? And tonight just reminded me of my old insecurities. I wiped my tears away, and as soon as I did, a fresh stream ran from my eyes. My head ached with the pain of crying, and by seven thirty, I knew I had to get a grip—talk to someone—make some plans. I poured a long drink of bourbon, reached for my phone, and called Kelly, praying that she'd still be at home. She answered on the third ring, and it took all of my mettle to hold back my tears.

"Oh, Nora," she said, sounding as though she were sitting right next to me. "I miss you. Tell me everything."

And I did, and the floodgates opened. When I was finished, there was silence, as though the connection was lost. "Kelly? Are you there?" I asked, sniveling once again.

"Oh, Nora, I know you don't want to hear this, but he's got a big job. It sounds to me as though he was only laughing with a woman. And while he definitely owes you an explanation—you have to give him a chance to explain. I don't know much about your new life, but I know he loves you. And I know that you know that."

I took a long swallow of the bourbon, the burn of it in my throat stinging my eyes with fresh tears. "What should I do?" I stammered.

"Just ask him who the woman was. He loves you, Nora—just ask. I bet there's a damn good explanation.'

"It's more than that—it's not just that I'm lonely, Kelly. I hardly know John. We never really talk. I don't even know what his favorite color is or his favorite book." I took a good swig of bourbon, the numbness settling in my brain. "It all started too fast, and I was too eager to just jump in. And now, I'm halfway around the world and nothing is the way I thought it would be." I was slurring my words. "I..."

"Just give it some time. Give yourself some time. And remember, you married an ambassador, not the Hyundai salesman."

And with that image fresh in my mind, I finally laughed.

"And isn't that how life is?" Kelly asked. "It never turns out the way we think it will."

I knew she was right. At thirty-five, I'd already learned that not everything was possible, and that maybe all of my dreams wouldn't come true after all. But then I'd met John, and my dreams had shimmered with possibility once again. They still did. No matter what happened, I had to remember that.

But I lay awake long into the night replaying the scene of John laughing, the woman leaning into him, and I wondered if maybe it was my fault. I'd been nagging him—the locked room, the last wife, his frequent trips. Was he tired of me already? Was he having an affair? By the time the sun was seeping through the shutters, I'd changed my mind. If he was cheating, it was his fault, not mine.

Lisa called the following morning. "How are you feeling today?" There was genuine concern in her voice. "Any fevers? Do you need anything?"

A wave of guilt washed over me, but I couldn't tell her the truth. This thing with John was private. "I'm okay. Maybe it was the heat or the crowd. Thanks for asking."

"I'm going out to Bān this morning—"

I didn't even let her finish her sentence. "Could I come along?" I was desperate to go back, to get my mind off of things.

"Any other day, I'd invite you, but I think you need to just take it easy today. I'll call tomorrow."

I sighed. I just wanted to get out—out of the house, out of my own way. "Tomorrow? All right, I guess. And you won't forget? You'll call?"

"I can manage that. Go back to bed. I'll call you in a day or two."

Reluctantly, I hung up. I looked at my watch—too late to call Kelly. She'd be at work by now. I'd call my mother, but she'd forbidden calls. "I don't care what they tell you, Nora. A long-distance call like that is not free. We'll both be charged exorbitant rates, and your father and I will be in the poor house. Just write or send an email." It was the twenty-first century, technology had changed the world, but for my mother, it would always be nineteen-eighty, the year she'd left the workforce and married my father. The last of a dying breed— she still read paper newspapers, real books, and used her landline to make calls. When my father brought a bulky desktop computer home, she avoided it. "Another dust-catcher," she'd sniffed. In the end, she'd conceded and opened an email account.

But that didn't help me today—it was her voice I wanted to hear. I threw caution to the wind, and dialed her number, and the phone rang and rang. I couldn't even leave a message—they didn't have an answering machine. I sent off a quick email —*Miss you, Mom, Love, Nora*—and went back to my bedroom to sweep up last night's debris and retrieve the invitation from the Australian embassy. I smoothed the wrinkles from the invitation and slipped it into my pocket. I'd be optimistic and expect the best, and every time I moved, the crinkling sound would remind me to ask him when he did get home.

My cellphone rang at one and certain that it was John, I answered without looking at the caller ID.

"Hello there," Mae's sing-songy voice cooed. "How are you?"

If I didn't know better, I might think she knew about John, and was calling to needle me. "I'm fine," I said flatly.

"Oh? I spoke with Lisa today and she said you were under the weather last evening. I'm just calling to see if there's anything I can do."

"Oh that?" I said, feeling suddenly guilty for jumping to conclusions. "I think it was the heat or the wine, but I'm okay. Thanks for calling, Mae. I know you're busy, so I'll let you go. I'm sure you—" But Mae interrupted before I could finish.

"I have some good news for you."

I rolled my eyes safe in the knowledge that she couldn't see my reaction.

"The locksmith bid has been approved. We'll have you in that locked room in no time."

My stomach twisted into a knot.

"Nora? Did you hear me?"

"Yes. Sorry. I heard."

"Rest assured that I'll accompany the locksmith so we can get that room cleared. To tell you the truth, I'm anxious to see if there's anything of mine in there. But I won't keep you. We'll talk about it another time."

I clicked off and wondered what she meant. What could she possibly have left in there?

CHAPTER TWENTY

In the middle of the night, I heard John's footsteps bounding up the stairs. I curled onto my side and feigned sleep. I wasn't ready yet to see him, to ask where he'd been, or with whom. Morning would be soon enough. I clamped my eyes shut and slowed my breathing.

He leaned over me. "I love you," he whispered, his lips grazing my forehead.

My back stiffened, and I jerked away.

"Whoa, what's this?" He turned me toward him, my lip quivering. He switched on the light and pulled me close. "Jesus, what is it?"

I shook my head, almost afraid to share what I saw. This was bad. John could feel it too. I could see it in the set of his jaw and the way he drew his lips in, as though away from me. Tears stung at the back of my eyes. I bit down on my lips. I wouldn't cry. I wouldn't give in to the overwhelming urge I had to cry and scream and throw anything I could grab. That wasn't my style anyway. I was the quiet kill them with silence type. I turned away, but he cupped my chin and turned me back toward him.

"Please," he whispered. "Whatever it is, just tell me."

There was no use pretending or putting it off. I sat stiffly, pulling the sheet around me. "I saw you."

A tiny furrow creased his brow. "You saw me? Saw me where?"

I recapped everything I'd seen—the woman, his laughter, the stabbing pain in my heart at the sight of him with that woman.

He gripped my shoulders. "Hear this, Nora Fielding. I love you. That was nothing. It was work."

"You said you were going to be away, and instead you were right here—in a bar. What's an ambassador doing in a bar anyway?" I snapped. "A crummy bar at that. Aren't there rules against that?"

John smiled. "It's not really that crummy."

I scowled. "It's not funny. A bar? I'm supposed to believe that you were working? And, you said you'd be away. What about that?"

"Yes, I was in a bar or anywhere else I need to go to get things done. And I was working, though I admit I wasn't away. I said that only because I knew I wouldn't be home, and I didn't want you to worry. Last night, it was a bar. Next week, it might be something else. You just have to trust me. It really was work. I have other things I'm working on, and that's what this was. I just can't tell you everything. My anonymity is important to that part of my work, and that's why I've avoided publicity and more receptions. I'm not the typical ambassador." He held up his left hand and pointed to his ring finger, his wedding band still shiny and new. "I wear this all the time. It's no secret that I'm happily married."

He released his grip on my shoulders, and I heaved a long sigh. Were we happily married? And was this what really happened in marriage? Bit by bit, small wedges seeped in, tiny cracks appeared, and they just grew, and after a while you just learned to accept all the cracks and fissures, to turn a blind eye? I swallowed the hard lump in my throat. I didn't want to be that wife, that woman.

John could see the uncertainty in my face, and he continued on. "You've got to believe me."

And I nodded, not because I believed him, but because I so wanted to.

"That anonymity I've worked so hard at is precisely why we were able to go out by ourselves last week, and that's why I could go to a bar last night and have no one—except for you—notice me. Remember—this post is temporary. That can be easy to forget in this luxurious house, in this exotic city, but we won't be here for long. You understand that, right? We won't be here forever. And, when this assignment is over, it'll just be you and me—the way it's supposed to be."

He ran his finger under my eyes, collecting the last of my tears. "I love you, Nora. Nothing else matters. If you remember nothing else, remember that."

He kissed me then, a long, deep kiss that almost—but not quite—made me forget what I'd seen. I leaned into his caress, and slept curled in his arms, a tiny seed of doubt floating through my dreams.

John came home early that night and the night after that, and we had the kind of evenings I'd wished for every night since I'd met him. We made our own dinner—scrambled eggs, toast and wine—and ate while he regaled me with stories of the ambassador from Brunei or maybe it was Bhutan, showing up and asking for an invitation to the White House.

"When I told him I had no control over things like that, he offered to buy me a Mercedes. I almost spit out my coffee." He laughed and brushed my lips with his. "It was one of those days. It's so good to come home to you."

I'd pulled the dinner invitation from my pocket and read it aloud. "Please say we can go?" I asked.

He groaned. "I—" He paused, probably trying to think of an excuse I hadn't heard.

My smile collapsed in on itself, and I leaned hard against the back of my chair. "What is it this time?" I couldn't hide the irritation I felt, and my words crackled with anger.

"I'll be away, but even if I weren't, I couldn't go." He heaved a long sigh.

I felt a sudden heat creeping up my neck and onto my cheeks. "Really? What a surprise." Sarcasm dripped from my words, and I pulled my arms in close to my chest to prove I meant business.

"It's not what you think."

"How do you know what I think? You never ask, and you're never around—"

"Don't you think I want to be?" A crease formed between his eyes. "It's my job—and that means staying out of sight and remaining as anonymous as possible, and that means no events, especially ones like this. At least for me."

His eyes, the flecks of silver dancing in the light, locked onto mine and I felt my anger fade a little.

"You can go. You should go. Have some fun. But no photos, nothing like that. It's important that you remain anonymous too. Okay?"

"Too late." I told him about the photographer at the ladies' luncheon and the picture in the newspaper. This might have been the perfect opportunity to tell him too about the man at Bān, but I didn't want to. This little discussion was about us, no outsiders. I forced a smile to hide my little secret.

"Do you have the article?"

I shook my head. "I mailed it to my mother, so she'll have something to show her friends."

He chuckled and brushed his lips against mine. "If you see a camera, duck, okay?"

That nagging doubt I'd had since the night I saw him at the bar, surfaced again. "If I didn't know better, I'd think you have another life—maybe you're married and hiding from your wife. I mean, why can't you be seen? There's anonymous and then there's *anonymous*."

"I only have one wife. You—only you. Just trust me."

Trust me—a phrase that most women over the age of twenty-one have heard more than once—a prelude to a lie, or even the lie itself. *Trust me.* But he wasn't going to budge, not tonight at least. It was time to call a truce. We curled up in bed, sipped wine, watched TV and cuddled. I fell asleep in his arms, the hum and flickering light of the television lulling me to sleep.

He woke me the next morning with a kiss. "I'm off," he said.

I straightened his tie and kissed him back.

"Hey, about this—" He held out the embassy dinner invitation. "RSVP for two. I'll figure out a way to go. They probably won't even notice me with you on my arm."

"And you won't back out at the last minute?"

"No. I'll be there. I swear."

And my lingering doubts faded once more.

Lisa called the next morning. "I have supplies to deliver to Bân today, and Renée suggested I call—see if you're up for coming along."

I was, and an hour later, we were on our way—without Renée.

"She was called to another UN meeting," Lisa had explained. "But she wanted me to make sure you were okay, and to let you know she's thinking of you."

I nodded, a little surprised at Renée's gesture. Maybe she wasn't so hard after all. I settled in for the long ride, my pulse quickening as we rounded the last loop of the road before Bān. I was eager to see Suu. She had no way of knowing why I hadn't been back in almost a week. It had been our longest separation since we'd first met.

As soon as Lisa pulled in and parked, three men appeared, unloaded three more UNHCR crates and disappeared. Once they were gone, a group surrounded the car, children squealing their delight, adults just watching. I scanned the crowd, searching for the strange man, but there was no sign of him. Neither was there any trace of Suu, and I stood on my toes to peer over the crowd, but still there was no sign of my little friend. We headed to the clinic, Lisa to check the inventory and the vaccine supply, and me to pick up the play area tarps and toys. I bent to retrieve the coloring books and supplies, and suddenly, there she was—poking her tiny face into view, her hand reaching for mine.

I dropped what I was holding and swept her into my arms. She placed her perfectly beautiful and thoroughly grimy hands on either side of my face and peered into my face. She stared into my eyes, her nose against mine, her gaze steady.

"Missed me?" I winked. "I missed you."

Though she surely had no idea what I'd just said, she laughed, and buried her head into the crook of my shoulder. I hugged her tight, placed her down and she helped me carry the supplies to our play area. I bent down to spread out the tarp, and caught sight of Suu's bare feet—smudged with grime and dirt and who knew what else? I pointed to them and raised my brow to Suu as an unspoken way of asking where her sandals were.

She looked down, and as if remembering she'd had new sandals not so long ago, her bottom lip quivered, and she began to cry. I squatted and tried to pull her close. She hesitated for a minute, as if deciding whether to stay or to run, and then, before I could react, she shook me off and ran into the nearby woods. As I watched her go, I noticed how thin she'd become just in the last week. And more than that, her hair seemed more matted, her dress more threadbare and the skin of her arms and legs even grimier. Or maybe I was just seeing the stark reality that had always been right in front of me. My heart broke, and I started after her, but she'd moved too swiftly, and already she'd been swallowed up by the jungle. I pushed my way through the first layer of overgrown weeds and shrubs, my arms scraped and clawed by the thorny brush. And then I just gave up. My shoulders sagging, my arms raw, I stopped. I'd never find my way back. I'd just have to trust that Suu would come back to find me. She must have lost the sandals. Poor kid. She must have thought I'd be angry or disappointed or something.

I turned back to the tarp and the toys and before long, the play area was alive once again with the sound of children's laughter and friendly shouts of protest during a makeshift soccer game. I sat against the trunk of a tree and just watched. And I waited for Suu to come back, but an hour later, there was still no sign of her. I grew nervous that she might never return if she thought the sandals were a bigger deal than they were.

I stood and stretched. I'd have to find Suu if she wasn't coming back. I'd just ask Lisa to check to see where Suu and her family lived. Once I knew which section of the camp she called home, I could go and find her and let her know that one lost pair of plastic sandals didn't matter even one tiny bit. I made my way to the clinic, and found Lisa sitting with the staff, including—I was happy to see—Nath, the interpreter I'd met on my very first visit to the camp.

He stood when he saw me. "Allo, Miss, nice to see you." And then he saw the scratches on my arms. "What has happened?" he asked.

I shared with Nath and Lisa the story of Suu and her lost sandals. "I hope that you can check the camp register and see where she lives so I can let her know I don't care about the shoes."

He nodded. "It is not really such a surprise," he said, turning to Lisa. "I told you there would be problems letting them roam free here."

Lisa heaved a long sigh. "You did. She should never have been in here."

"What are you talking about? Who's roaming free? What's going on?"

"Suu and her family probably aren't registered, maybe don't even live here. She's avoided the clinic, and the un-registereds do that to avoid being discovered. There are hundreds, maybe more, who live beyond the camp's perimeter. But I can't be sure. She might be one of the orphans who scrounges dumps and trash bins to survive."

Nath waved his hand in the air. "We turn a blind eye. Allowing them in gives them a connection to their own community, and sometimes they can get food here, but they're still desperate and if someone from outside saw her brand-new sandals, they likely took them from her. Something like that, small as it seems, is precious out there. They're easily traded for food."

My heart sank. "Poor kid. But where out there does she live, and how can I find her?"

Nath shook his head. "She probably lives somewhere deep in the bush, in the rainforest, or in one of the dumps that border the camp. You'll never find her. That area is dangerous even for little Suu, where people will do anything to get through another day. They'll steal anything they can, and they don't care if someone gets hurt in the process. For you, a step into that world could be very dangerous. Just stay away and remember, bad luck never comes alone."

I wanted to roll my eyes. Bad luck? Luck had nothing to do with Suu's life. Nothing at all. I'd figure something out. I couldn't just desert Suu, especially now. If she was in trouble, I'd just have to find her on my own.

CHAPTER TWENTY-ONE

On the ride back to Bangkok, I peered through the windshield, paying careful attention to the jungle—or tropical forest or whatever they called it—that flanked either side of the road. How could people live in there? Lisa was talking about her day—the lack of supplies and dwindling money to pay for it all. With Suu still on my mind, I hardly listened, but every now and then, I muttered, "Hmm," and nodded. But Lisa was nobody's fool, least of all mine, and finally she cleared her throat to get my attention.

"You haven't heard a word I've said, have you?"

I cast a sheepish glance her way. "I guess not," I said. "I was thinking about Suu, about how tough her life must be in there." I turned my gaze back toward the jungle. "I had no idea she lived there. I thought living in a refugee camp your whole life would be bad enough, but this—" I swallowed the heaviness in my throat. "It's just mind-boggling."

Lisa nodded in sympathy. "It's absolute misery, but right now, there's no help for her and so many like her. If they're not registered, and they have no papers, it's as though they don't exist—they're invisible people just trying to survive in the harshest landscape imaginable." She patted my hand. "I know how you feel. When I first got into this work, I wanted to save everyone. It took me a long time to realize I couldn't. I had to make my peace with that. There are still those days I want to rescue everyone I see. And realizing that you can't help everyone never gets easy. You just learn to live with it."

"But there has to be a way," I pleaded, determined not to give up so easily. "What about doing something in Bangkok? Arranging—I don't know—a fundraiser, a conference maybe, to brainstorm? There's got to be something I can do for Suu, and the others."

"I don't know. It's all been tried. The people in the forest live the most hardscrabble of lives—nothing comes easy for them. And people feel less sympathy for them. It's not fair, but it's the way it is."

"But the orphans—"

She shrugged and turned her attention back to the road.

There was no use arguing. I drew in a slow, steadying breath and bobbed my head in pretend agreement. "Okay. I know you're right." But I didn't think she was right. I'd talk to John. There had to be some benefit to being the ambassador's wife.

By the time, Lisa dropped me off, we were friends again. "I'm going to talk to John. Maybe he can figure out a way to help."

Two days later, I slipped out through the back fence and had my hair done for the embassy dinner. I had a trim, a blow-dry, and had my highlights highlighted. And then I had my makeup done. At home, I slipped into my now well-worn little black cocktail dress and took a spin in front of the mirror.

John whistled and pulled me close. "Damn, you look too good for a bunch of embassy stiffs. Let's just stay in."

I rolled my eyes and playfully pushed him away. "Not on your life, buddy. We're going."

I helped him adjust his tie and watched as he slipped into the suit he'd worn at our wedding. This time, I whistled. "On second thought—"

"Say the word." He began to wriggle out of his jacket.

"The word is—we're going."

He sighed and looked at his watch. "The driver will be here in about five minutes."

"Driver?"

"Thought as long as we were going, we should arrive in style." He winked.

The drive was short—probably five minutes—and when we were waved through the main gate of another well-guarded, fenced-in metal and mortar structure, my gaze caught the sign at the entrance. Australian Embassy, it said. "I thought dinner was at the residence, not the embassy," I whispered to John.

He nodded. "One and the same for the Australians."

The car continued along a winding drive before stopping in front of a smaller building in the back. The main building had been an imposing piece of construction—an impenetrable towering fortress not unlike the other embassies I'd seen. In the movies, they were all so different, warm and inviting, but here in Bangkok, they all—or at least the ones I'd seen—seemed more like prisons. The house in the back, however, was a whole different story. It was a colonial style home, all shutters and flowers and quiet grace. The car deposited us at the entrance. "I'll text you when we're ready," John announced to the driver who disappeared into the car.

I patted my hair, smoothed my dress, and slipped my hand into John's as we entered the foyer. A butler offered us glasses of wine and directed us into a large room off to the right where a small group had gathered. A balding man approached us, his arm outstretched.

"John," he said, "so good of you to come." He took John's hand and shook it before turning to me. "And, of course, you're Nora. What a pleasure to finally meet you. You're every bit as beautiful as I heard."

Okay, so maybe it was a load of malarkey, but I couldn't hold back the smile that draped my lips. He gripped my hand with both of his and kissed first one cheek and then the other. I loved this European tradition. "So nice to meet you—" I paused. I didn't even know his name. I stood there, my mouth hanging open, waiting for someone to actually introduce us.

"I'm Harry, the Australian ambassador," he finally said, smiling. "I'll introduce you both to everyone."

He led us through the clusters of people talking and laughing, and each time he announced me as the American ambassador's wife, I felt a tiny thrill. Ambassadors and wives—and in one case, a husband—from England, Canada, France, Japan, and Sweden, Belgium, Greece and Argentina filled the room. I was dizzy with people's names and countries and by the time dinner was announced, I could barely remember my own name. We were ushered into a large dining room, an enormous and ornately set table in the center, elegant place cards at each table setting. While everyone murmured their appreciation, I looked anxiously for our names, and then frowned as I realized that husbands and wives were seated opposite one another. I knew it was designed to help us meet new people, but I wanted to be close to John. It wasn't like we had dinner together that often. I settled in and smiled through the centerpiece—a tall vase of flowers—that almost blocked my view of John. He was seated between two older ladies, who were both vying for his attention.

"You're Mrs. Fielding," a thickly accented voice to my right said.

I turned toward the sound. "I am." I recognized Anders, the Swedish ambassador. His accent was heavy, almost Germanic, and I was embarrassed to think I didn't know what language people spoke in Sweden. But at least I didn't have to worry about that tonight. Everyone seemed to speak English.

"You're enjoying Thailand?" he asked.

"Very much," I answered. "Though I haven't seen a lot of it, just Bangkok and the refugee camp at Bān."

"Ahh, so you're the wife working with refugees."

I groaned silently and fretted that he probably disapproved. I didn't really want to spend the evening explaining myself and my motives. I forced a weak smile.

He immediately sensed my discomfort and placed his hand gently over mine. "I meant that my wife and apparently several others admire your work, and your courage, I might add."

The man on my left leaned in, and I recognized Simon Miller, the Canadian ambassador and Elizabeth's husband. "I quite agree, Mrs. Fielding. My wife was quite taken with your energy and purpose."

I heaved a silent sigh of relief. I was sandwiched between two kind men who also spoke English. A hovering waiter refilled our wine glasses at the slightest hint of an almost drained glass, and that kept the conversation flowing. The sound of hushed conversations, a dash of polite laughter and frequently clinking glasses, meant the evening was going well. And then, the meal began. Attentive waiters delivered six courses in all—spring rolls, coconut soup, a salad, fruit and then chicken and prawns served over a bed of fluffy rice and a side of spicy green beans. When I thought I'd burst, they cleared our plates and served dessert—a mango sorbet drizzled with coconut.

My dinner companions made careful small talk—no politics,

no religion, no mention of Emily Somerfield, nothing to offend—during dinner. We talked about the weather, the food, movies and books. And I held my own at this international dinner of bigwigs. Every now and then, I caught a glimpse of John through the flowers. The women on either side of him were still busy competing for his attention, and John was nodding politely while running his hand through his hair, a gesture that I recognized as his only nervous habit. I stifled a laugh all the while realizing that this might just be our last embassy dinner.

Once dinner was over, we were ushered into a living room, where more drinks were served, and men were offered cigars. I watched as John took a cigar, his fingers running along the edges. When he finally exhaled, his eyes—sparkling in the fog of smoke that hovered above the group—caught mine. He nodded and cast a sideways glance toward the door.

Within minutes, we were in the back of the limousine laughing. "A conference call with Washington tonight? Really?" I raised a suspicious brow and whispered so the driver wouldn't hear.

John chuckled and brushed my lips with his. "I just had to get out of there. They were nice enough, but suits and ties and small talk make my eyes glaze over. Sorry if I pulled you away too soon. Did you have fun?"

I nodded and told him about my seatmates. "But I'm not very good at small talk either." I leaned closer and kissed him. "I'd rather be in bed with you."

And later that night, as I lay beside a sleeping John, his arm thrown over my chest, his breath hot on my skin, I curled into the curve of his body and ran my finger along the hard angle of his jaw. "I love you," I whispered. "I love everything about our new life." I brushed my lips against his and felt him stir against my skin.

"Hmm," he said softly. "I love you, Mrs. Fielding." In one

swift movement he was on top of me, his hips swaying above mine. "Shall I show you?"

And as leaned close and pressed himself into me, I closed my eyes and made a wish—that we would live and love like this for another fifty years.

CHAPTER TWENTY-TWO

Days later, as John and I sat on the balcony watching the sun set, I was ready to ask for help with Suu. I'd practiced what I'd say, and I'd decided to talk about Suu first. She needed help right now. I could bring up babies later, once the matter of Suu was settled. It all seemed pretty easy—at least in my mind. I took a deep breath and started.

"I want to tell you about a little girl I met in Bān," I said, fully expecting him to take my side in what was—in my mind at least—a moral dilemma with only one answer. We had to somehow support Suu and the others like her, and weren't we in the perfect position to do just that? And so I made my case. "What do you think?" I asked when I'd laid it all out.

"Christ, I had no idea things were that bad."

I sighed in relief. He did understand.

"I thought a refugee camp would be safe for you, but this puts a whole different spin on it. I almost wish you were doing something with the young prostitutes in Bangkok. What about the ambassadors' wives? Didn't you make any plans with them after that luncheon?"

I'd never mentioned getting together again with the other

wives. If I'd mentioned them at all, it would have been to say how sophisticated and different they were from me, and how out of place I felt in their company. I knew I had to try harder, but I also knew Bān was where I wanted to be. He was just trying to distract me, which only made me more determined. "I didn't make any plans with the wives, and as for the prostitutes, you said—"

"I know what I said. I was just trying to make light of it. I don't really want you working with the street girls either, but for different reasons. And I knew about the jungle people and the ones who scour dumpsters looking for scraps to eat. It's tragic, but Lisa's right. She's got a good head on her shoulders. Those refugees, those poor souls, who admittedly have nothing, also have nothing to lose, which makes them desperate, and makes being with them, or trying to help them, a dangerous proposition. You have to leave that to the government."

My jaw fell open, and I stood quickly, moving back into the house, knocking my full glass of wine onto the carpet, the perfectly pristine and perfectly white carpet that Chai or someone else had vacuumed and fussed over. Maybe it was those luxuries that made John forget who we both were. I reached down and dabbed at the stain with my napkin, my anger festering as I wiped.

"You're not mad, are you?"

And with that comment, I exploded. "Are you kidding me? We should all desert them because they have nothing, and the government's going to help. Yeah, right. That is friggin' convoluted logic. Count me out."

A sudden boom and a thousand shards of light suddenly filled the night sky. John jumped up, his hand on his hip, and pushed me down. "Stay down," he commanded, shielding me with his arm. He crouched low, his eyes searching for the source of the commotion, his body poised as if ready to strike.

But strike what? I didn't see anything. "Isn't it just thunder and lightning?" I asked just as the rain began, first a tiny spray and then a downpour. We hurried inside where we huddled by the window to watch.

"The start of the rainy season," he said with a chuckle. "Guess I overreacted—hazard of the profession." He pulled me into his arms.

"Hazards of being an ambassador?" I asked, remembering his gun.

He laughed. "Just an expression. So, where were we anyway?"

"Arguing," I said.

"Ahh, that's right, but you have to remember, I'm not the enemy. I feel the same way you do about the misery out there, but the truth is our hands are tied. I love you for wanting to help, for being ready to do whatever it takes, but some of those people aren't refugees. There's a criminal element out there too, probably a terrorist element hiding in the jungle as well. I know you want to believe that everyone's inherently good. But it's just not true. Most people are good, I'll grant you that. But the few evil ones are the ones we worry about. And I love you. I won't let anything happen to you even if it means you're pissed off at me. You have to—"

His words ran together, all blurred in my mind to one word —*no*. I'd have to think of something else. "I love you too, and I don't want this to come between us." And I didn't—since I'd seen him at the Madrid with that woman, he'd made more of an effort to be home in the evening. He still went away—there'd been two more quick trips—one to Jakarta in Indonesia and one to Afghanistan—that one he'd told me was *top secret*. But why was he even there? The Taliban were in charge, the place was a hotbed of intrigue and danger. I sighed. "Do other ambassadors travel this much?" I'd asked, and he'd smiled and kissed me and never answered my question. But tonight, all I wanted was help for Suu and the others.

"If you'd only seen her, this sweet little girl—"

He covered my mouth with his own, effectively ending the discussion. I wasn't angry. I knew he loved me. But I also knew there was a solution to every problem if you just paid attention to the details, and if there was one thing I'd learned at Bain and Worth it was how to pay attention to the details, though I often didn't.

Of course, if there was another thing I'd learned, it was not to let opportunities slip by. And I was still doing that too. With all of my attention focused on finding Suu, I'd almost forgotten Emily's room and the money. And though Mae had said a locksmith had been approved, the room was still locked tight.

Except to me.

CHAPTER TWENTY-THREE

The rainy season turned out to be every bit as bad as I'd been told it would be. Clouds—small smudges of white—appeared in an otherwise perfectly clear sky, and if you were new to Bangkok, as I was, you might be lulled into thinking how mild it all was. But those inconsequential clouds soon gave way to gray skies and then to rain, unrelenting and unforgiving and pouring down in never-ending sheets of wet that disappeared as quickly as they'd appeared. But, either way, the result was the same—the roads were too wet, John said, for travel to Bān.

And though in Bangkok the rain was a nuisance, just beyond the city, it greened up already lush plants and vegetation, and that included the thriving brush and greenery in the jungle along the road to Bān. Though the forest blossomed and grew more arid with the downpours, the road suffered. The ruts grew deeper as the water settled into channels that ran the length of the unpaved paths. Even the smooth bits of motorway were altered—the road buckling and cracking—making the drive longer and more treacherous. But I didn't care. I had a plan, and that involved driving slowly so that Suu, who I was sure was watching for me, would know that I was watching for her.

The first morning after the rain ended, I rose early enough to kiss John goodbye, and tell him I'd heard the roads were safe, though I didn't say just who'd told me that, and he never asked. I promised to heed all of his warnings, and to call if I needed him. I neglected to tell him there was no cell service out near Bân. That would only put a bee in his bonnet, as my mother would have said, and might have resulted in another argument. And, with our newfound solid footing, I wanted to avoid that.

The roads in Bangkok were bone-dry. If I hadn't seen the torrential night rains with my own eyes, I wouldn't have known we'd had them. But the dry streets ended an hour out of Bangkok. Potholes, crevices, cracks in the highway, and large sloping puddles kept my eyes glued to the street in front of me. By the time I reached the unpaved sections of road, I'd been driving for four long hours and still had another forty-five minutes to go. Damn—at this rate, I'd get there in time to just turn around and head home while there was still light to guide me.

I slowed to a crawl, peering into the overgrowth of greenery that lined the road, but there was nothing to see—not even birds disrupted the eerie quiet. I finally gave up, deciding that I needed to get to the camp. The kids deserved whatever bit of play time I could offer, and maybe Nath would have word of little Suu.

I pulled into the parking area almost five hours after I'd left Bangkok. That only gave me half an hour for play with the kids, and it still meant I'd be driving at least part of the way home in the dark. But, as long as I arrived home before John, I'd be okay. I made my way to the clinic, the roads here still muddy, the shelters now soaked through, some probably washed away. I wondered how Suu could survive without even a shelter. A crowd of children joined me, keeping pace, chattering the whole way. I searched their shining faces looking for Suu, but she wasn't among them. I couldn't hide my disappointment, my lips curling into a frown, but the kids didn't seem to notice. They giggled and laughed and helped me to collect and then set up the tarps and toys, and while they were playing, I went back to the clinic in hopes of finding Nath inside.

As I entered the clinic, I blinked away the sudden darkness. Had it always been so dark in here or was it yet another reminder that it was later in the day?

"Ahh, Miss Nora," a male voice said, and I turned to see Nath stepping into the clinic. "Can I help you?"

I smiled. "I hope so," I said. "I came to see you."

He pulled out one of the straight-backed wooden chairs and motioned me to sit, and as I did, he settled himself across from me. "What can I do for you?" He placed his hands politely on his lap.

"I'm here about Suu."

He nodded knowingly. "I expected as much."

"I'm worried, and I feel as though I can't give up on her. What if she's in trouble?" I crossed my legs and leaned forward. "She's just a little kid. I'd like to find her."

"You heard—"

I put up my hand. "I heard. I understand. I'm not going into the jungle, but someone here knows her, knows how to find her. She came every day I was here. I think she's close enough to see me driving in, to know when I'm here. I'm sure of it."

Nath nodded his understanding, and a wave of relief swept over me.

"I can ask the children, and some of the adults. You're probably right. Someone knows something, and she's probably living very near."

The way he'd said that—*someone knows something*—made me think of Emily again. I nodded. "That reminds me, did you ever see the last ambassador's wife—Emily Somerfield—out here?"

He smiled, his eyes sparkling with the memory. "Did you know her?" he asked. "She wanted so much to help out here. She carted supplies out here for Lisa. She was a great help. I was sorry to hear she just left."

I could almost hear the acid in my stomach churning. Why would Lisa lie? Maybe the money I found was involved, maybe it belonged to the refugees, or to Lisa's aid group. Shit—did Emily steal it? Maybe Lisa was just trying to protect Emily from Renée and her audit. I wanted to stay, to ask more questions, but though I'd been in the camp for less than an hour, I was in a race to get home before sunset. Even though it was July—the month of late day sunshine at home—here the sun set before seven p.m. It was almost three, so as long as I hit the outskirts of Bangkok before sunset, I'd be okay. Except of course if John made it home before me, in which case, well, in which case, I'd think of something.

The muck and mud of the roads around Bān were as tenacious as ever, but I focused, drove slowly and kept my eyes on the prize—arriving home before John. When I made the final turn onto Wireless Road, I crossed my fingers, and when the guards waved me in through the gate at home, I breathed a sigh of relief that John's car wasn't there yet. Tonight would likely be the only time I prayed for him to be late, and in the dark about how late I'd been.

John and I were finally settling into marriage, and more importantly—we were on the same page. At least, I hoped we were. I'd come to understand my role as the temporary ambassador's wife—head down, mouth shut, eyes on the future. Our future. The sight of him still made my heart flutter and my knees go weak. There were days I pinched myself, not quite believing how far I'd come from the invisible Nora Buckbee to the ambassador's wife. It wasn't just my head that was spinning, it was my heart, it was my world, it was everything.

And, even with my worries about little Suu, and Emily's room, and now her connection to Lisa, I'd have to say that my life had never been happier or more fulfilled.

But if I'd learned anything, and then just as quickly forgotten, it was that good things never last.

CHAPTER TWENTY-FOUR

John didn't come home that night, so instead of counting my blessings, I was busy reassuring myself that it was only his work, whatever that was, that kept him away. And though I tried to keep my questions at bay, I still hadn't quite reconciled myself to what an ambassador did that required so many secretive overnight trips. I was determined to stay positive, but he seemed to see Jim Leo, the liaison guy at the embassy, and that guy—Dave— more than he saw me. They were in almost constant communication—cellphone calls, text messages, emails. Sometimes, they seemed like teenage girls, but of course I never said that.

And then the rainy season really arrived—not the pleasant evening storms I'd come to love, instead we braced for flooding and downpours that kept me trapped in the house, the wind knocking the shutters wildly against the house, the rain seeping in, the dark descending like an all-enveloping fog. I'd never seen rain like this before. It flowed through the streets, and into gardens and stores and even homes, soaking everything in its path. It slowed traffic, shut down electricity, and twisted umbrellas this way and that rendering them useless. The rain kept up, some days with drenching sideways downpours, other days—just a steady trickle. Someone from the embassy would pick John up, and he'd invariably turn to me, his blue eyes shimmering, a trace of a sly smile at the corners of his lips, and he'd whisper, "No need to get dressed today, Nora. I'll be home for lunch." And so, even though I couldn't get to Bân, I cherished the extra time with my husband. My husband—how I loved that phrase.

We ventured out early one evening, in the midst of a downpour, to the Emporium Mall to see a movie. "The rain," John explained, "will keep most people away. We'll probably have the theater to ourselves."

He ran first his fingertips and then his lips along the curve of my throat, and just like always, a ripple of pleasure surged through my veins. At the mall, we slipped into the darkened theater, and slid into our seats. Suddenly, a picture of a silver-haired man, dressed in white military garb, a flurry of medals and a gold sash across his chest, appeared on the screen. There was a hushed rustle of movement as everyone rose. I stood beside John. "What is it?"

"The King's Anthem," John whispered as music began to play.

And I remembered that someone in DC, or maybe it had been here in Bangkok, had told me about the Thai's devotion to their beloved royal family who'd served for so long. I liked the respect inherent in a gesture like that, even if it was required. And it was a reminder that here, things were different.

We sat back down only after the final strains of the anthem had faded away, John's arm wrapped around my thigh, my head on his shoulder—an ordinary couple on an ordinary day. I couldn't even tell you what the movie was about. The only thing that mattered was that we saw it together.

But when I wasn't being wooed by my husband, I was at

home—alone. The house in Bangkok was designed to shield its inhabitants from terrorists and petty criminals, and those safeguards, though important, kept us locked up tight. Too tight, I thought. If I opened my windows in South Boston, I looked out onto life—bustling streets filled with people hurrying this way and that, traffic darting through lights and intersections, drivers beeping and shouting, police sirens blaring. It was real life. But here, I looked out onto quiet gardens, the street view blocked by swaying palm trees and high security fences. When I went out through the front gate, the guards silently watched, assessing how I presented myself as the ambassador's wife. If it weren't for the secret gate which allowed me an easy exit onto a main road, and an occasional solo outing to have my hair or nails done, a chance to be blissfully invisible once again, I'd have gone stir-crazy. So, when Kelly called out of the blue, just to say hello, it was as if she'd read my mind.

"I miss you," I shouted, not quite convinced that she could hear me so far away.

We chatted about everything and nothing, as if there weren't thousands of miles and a whole world between us. I told her about John and Bān and my dull life in Bangkok, and she told me about her new apartment and her new boyfriend. "You won't believe this, but—" she paused as if for effect. "He's a salesman at Hyundai. He knows George."

We both began to laugh. "Tell me everything," I sputtered.

"You should have seen George's face when I told him who you'd married. I thought he was gonna cry. He just kind of nodded and walked away. I felt sorry for him."

"Ahh, if you remember, *he* dumped me. And thank God, huh? Though if you marry this guy, we coulda been Hyundai wives."

"Oh, great," Kelly said. "That's an image I could live without."

It felt good to be the old Nora, if only through the phone lines, and when we finally said goodbye, I was feeling pretty good about the way my life was turning out.

"Think we can go home for Thanksgiving?" I asked, one rainy morning. It was only three months away, and I wanted to start planning our trip home.

John's dimples flashed. "I think we'll be home by Thanksgiving if things work out the way I expect they will."

"Really?" I asked, throwing myself at him.

"Really. I told you this post was temporary. A few more months and we should be outta here. No more *Mr. Ambassador*. First stop—Paris, and then home."

"DC?"

"Eventually, but first Boston and then Minneapolis to see our families, and then DC, where we'll need to find a larger apartment, or a house maybe."

My life was full, rain or not.

The next morning, Chai, who'd come faithfully during the heavy rains, greeted me with a deep frown. "I need to ask permission, Miss," she said, her voice raspy as if she'd been crying or shouting.

"What is it, Chai?"

"The old gardener—Patiwat—has a family problem. His granddaughter... Well, because he cannot speak, he has asked me to help. And for that, we will both need a few days off."

"Of course. Can I do anything to help?"

She swallowed hard, and the line of her jaw tightened. "Please, Miss, do not tell Mae. And if she asks, just say that Patiwat and I have some days off."

"I won't say anything, but can you tell me why?"

She shook her head and blinked as if heading off tears. "Thank you, Miss, from both of us."

CHAPTER TWENTY-FIVE

Two days later, with Chai and the gardener gone, the rain finally slowed, and Renée called. "Nora? Are you here in Bangkok?"

I held the phone tight to my ear—her French accent seemed deeper, harder to understand on the phone. Or maybe it was just that she spoke the way she seemed to live—everything rushing by in a blur. I hadn't had time to answer before she rushed on.

"I haven't been to the camp in weeks and with Lisa away, someone has to go. *De sorte qu'il est de ma responsabilité—*"

"Renée," I interrupted quickly before she could get another word out. "I don't understand French."

A throaty laugh snaked through the line. "Forgive me. I forget. So, you know Lisa has been called away by her aid group? And someone has to go to Bân. You understand?"

She was speaking slowly, enunciating each syllable so that I would understand her English. A laugh escaped my lips.

"You do not understand?" she asked.

"No, no, I do. I'm sorry. I didn't know that Lisa was away. So, are you going to Bân?"

"*Oui.* And with the roads so—you know—wet. I don't want to go alone. I have the big Range Rover. Are you busy? Will you come?"

And, just like that, I was finally on my way back to Bān. And with Renée, no less. Though I hadn't hosted or even planned my promised fundraisers for the forgotten refugees during the days I'd been rained out of Bān, I'd had enough money to do a little shopping on my own. I'd made my way back to the storefront shops on Sukhumvit, and I'd replenished my toy supply with dolls, trucks, books, pencils and notebooks, and a few pairs of sandals. I lugged them out to the car when Renée arrived.

"Ahh, for the children, very good," she said as she helped load my things in the back.

I nodded and climbed into the front. Renée, a cigarette dangling from her lips, one hand gripping the steering wheel, the other on the gearbox, barely opened her mouth except to inhale or occasionally, to cough. The smoke drifted toward me, the haze of it stinging my eyes. I cleared my throat, and Renée ground her cigarette into the ashtray before casting an exasperated look my way. I tried to start a conversation with no luck.

"It is best," she said, "if I focus on the road." She nodded toward the road. "You understand. *Oui?*"

It was just as well. With Renée at the wheel, I could concentrate on scouring the roads and the bush beyond for any sign of Suu. As we moved further from the city and closer to the camp, my eyes burned into the jungle looking for any sign of little Suu, but the heavy rains had made the trees fuller, denser and almost impossible to see what might lay beyond the lush greenery. As we neared the camp, I noticed soldiers, or maybe they were police, patrolling the roads. I turned to Renée. "Why are they here?"

She shrugged. "They are always here. Sometimes we see them, sometimes not. They provide security."

"That's good, isn't it?" I asked, remembering that man who'd approached me.

"Who knows? *C'est la vie.*"

When we pulled into the camp, I threw open the car door and jumped out searching the gathering group, and still there was no sign of Suu.

My shoulders slumped as I pulled out the new toys and handed Renée a pile to carry. "Does Lisa bring supplies when you come with her?" she asked.

I hesitated and wondered if I should mention what Nath had said about Emily helping with supplies. But that probably didn't matter unless the money in Emily's room was connected to Renée's audit, and then I'd be the one in trouble. I'd not only be the one who'd broken into the room, but I'd also discovered the money and hadn't said a word. I didn't want to cause any trouble—for any of us—but I didn't want to lie either. I nodded. "Some UNHCR crates." And an image of Mae's crate in the spare room flashed in my mind.

"And did you see what was in the crates or where those supplies went?"

I shook my head. "No, they were closed up tight, and once we arrived here, some men just came, as if they'd been waiting for us, and carted them away."

Renée's brow wrinkled. "And have you seen them again— those crates or new supplies—maybe in the clinic?"

And I realized I hadn't seen the crates once the men had taken them. "No, I guess not," I answered, hoping Lisa wouldn't be in trouble. "But I'm only in the play area by the clinic. I'm sure the supplies are here somewhere. She brings them for the refugees."

"Hmm," was Renée's only reply as she tucked her arms tight around the toys she held.

As we headed toward the clinic, a small boy, his toes peeking out from his tattered sneakers, and a wide smile bursting onto his lips, kept pace with me. His little face turned up to me, he reached for a truck. I held on tight, afraid they'd all fall away. But this little boy was determined. And finally, hands on his hips, he stopped and shouted at me. I turned and shrugged my shoulders in an *I don't understand* pose. He giggled and led me along the path to the front of the clinic where the tarps and the rest of the toys were kept. I emptied my pile onto a tarp and folded the corners up making a kind of pouch. While the small boy bent to gather the coloring books and crayons, I poked my head into the clinic just as Renée caught up.

She deposited her armful onto another tarp and exhaled noisily. "*Beaucoup jouets*," she exclaimed, wiping the tiniest trickle of sweat from her brow. She was dramatic, but I liked that about her—that ability to make everything bigger than it was.

"*Merci beaucoup*," I said.

"*Tres bien*! You will be speaking French in no time. *Peut être*, which means maybe. You see? One word at a time."

I laughed. "Lesson two on the way back then."

"*Peut être*. I will see you in an hour. Yes?" She turned to leave the clinic area.

"Wait. Do you know if Nath, the interpreter, is coming today?" I asked.

She shook her head. "No, he is in Bangkok with UNHCR this week. I saw him this morning. You need to see him?"

The corners of my lips instinctively turned down. "Damn it," I muttered.

"Problem?"

"He was going to ask around for Suu, the little girl. We learned she doesn't live here in the camp." I explained that she wasn't registered, and in addition, may have been an orphan.

She nodded. "That is a big problem. There are too many of them out there. But she's the little one who has made a special connection with you. Yes?"

I nodded.

Renée's face softened, and she patted my shoulder. "She will be back. The child needs this place—as bad as it is—and you, more than you need her. Understand? This place offers her hope, and you offer her love. She will not give that up so easily."

"You think so?" I asked, suddenly smiling. Renée was not the type to say something to make me feel better. If she said it, she surely believed it.

"I do. You must keep your eyes open. She will hide in the *buisson* just beyond the camp, and she will watch for you. When she feels that it is safe, she will return. There is too much to lose if she stays away. Yes?"

Renée's words both buoyed and dampened my spirits. I wanted to see Suu again, to know she was safe, but the thought that she had *too much to lose*—at such a tender age—broke my heart. I felt a tug at my shirt and looked down to see my mystery boy trying to add the soccer balls to his little arms already filled to overflowing with books and crayons. I smiled, gathered the corners of the now full tarp and carted it to the play site, all the while glancing through the trees and brush surrounding Bân.

With the help of the small boy and other children who had appeared, we gathered the rest of the toys, and set up the play area but, instead of sitting to color or giggle with the girls, I strolled around, and kept my eyes glued to the edges of the area searching for any sign of Suu. A tiny rustle of brush made my pulse quicken, and I spun around, my ears and eyes alert.

"Suu," I called, but there was nothing, no answer, no more rustling, and finally, it was time to go.

"Come on," Renée said an hour later, bending to help clear the toys. "Time to go. No sign of your *petite fille?*"

I shook my head, and reluctantly I turned away from the jungle. In that millisecond, a flash of movement caught my eyes, and I froze. It wasn't just a feeling, I could see *him*, I was certain of it. And though I'd almost forgotten his face or that moment when he'd approached me, it all came rushing back, a tiny knot of fear creeping into my brain. I steadied my gaze and looked through the trees, and there he was, clear as day—his knobby head, his cold eyes—and he was watching us. A shiver ran down my spine. I nudged Renée, tilting my head to the tree line. "Look over there," I whispered. "Do you see that man watching us?"

She peered around me. "Where? What man?"

CHAPTER TWENTY-SIX

Emboldened by Renée's presence, I turned to point him out, but he was gone. Oh shit, I knew he'd been there. My shoulders sagged. "It was a strange guy. I've seen him before." And despite how silly I knew it sounded, I told her how he'd approached me weeks before, frightening me into a kind of stupor.

Renée raised a brow. "And you told Lisa? What did she say?"

"She said to tell her if I see him again, that he was probably harmless, but I just don't believe that. There was something sinister about him. It's hard to explain. I know it sounds stupid, but—" But Renée seemed interested and so I did explain, even describing his beady little eyes. She helped me to gather and then store the toys before we headed to the car.

"And what did your husband say?"

I shook my head. "I didn't tell him. He worries enough with me here alone. And this guy, he just—"

"And you will recognize him if you see him again?" She slid into the driver's seat, and I scurried around so that we could continue our conversation.

"Yes, I'm sure of it." I rolled down my window.

"Ahh, that is good. So, you must promise—if you see him again—you must tell me right away. I'll let the authorities know, and they will take care of him. And you must not tell Lisa again. I will take care of it."

I let out a long breath, relieved that someone understood. At least I wasn't alone in that. But why didn't she want me to tell Lisa? Not that it mattered, but with my luck, he'd show up again when I really was alone.

"Want to stop at Cheap Charlie's for a drink?" I asked, eager to talk more.

"Any other day, I would say yes, but today—with Lisa away —I must write a damn report."

She lit a cigarette, the plume of smoke heading straight for my eyes. I blinked away the burn. Renée tapped her cigarette ash out the window, and I watched as the tiny cinders blew back and landed in my lap. Despite her incessant smoking, and her tendency to bitchiness, I liked her. There was nothing pretentious or phony about her. What you saw was what you got. Added to that—our shared uneasiness about the man with the beady eyes—and we were almost friends.

As though she could read my mind, she spoke up. "The report, I think, can wait," she said, her eyes still on the road, the cigarette dangling from her fingers. "A drink sounds far more appealing."

We drove toward Cheap Charlie's but the traffic on Sukhumvit was at a near standstill. "The Madrid?" she asked.

I felt a knot in my stomach. "How about one of the hotels? They all have bars, don't they?" I'd even passed one or two on Soi Ruam Ruedi. I mentioned the street.

She scowled and looked me up and down. "We are not dressed well enough, either of us, for places like that.

Understand? I think it is Cheap Charlie's or the Madrid or none? *Oui?*"

I nodded and tried to ignore the acid that churned in the pit of my stomach. John had explained what I'd seen that night, so why was I feeling so queasy?

At the Madrid, we slid into a booth near the back, Renée facing the rear wall. When she realized that her view would be the entrance to the bathrooms, she asked me to swap places. "You don't mind, do you? I want to see who comes in. You are married, so for you the view is not so important. *Oui?*"

I laughed. She did have a way. "No problem," I said, sliding out of the booth and into the narrow space between booths.

"*Merci.*" Renée stood quickly. "You, *mon cheri*, are a good friend." In her haste to move, she inadvertently knocked my bag to the floor. I reached to pick up the scattered contents.

"No, no," she said. "My fault. I will collect your things." She bent and began to retrieve the few items in my bag. I didn't carry much—my wallet with some Thai *bhats* and always twenty American dollars, my Thai driver's license, a few photos, my iPhone, a small makeup bag that held blush, lipstick, a comb and a few hair elastics, and that was it. It had never seemed like much until I saw it all strewn on the floor around us. Finally, Renée handed the bag to me. "My apologies. I am clumsy sometimes. Perhaps that is why I have trouble finding love." She winked and slid back into her seat. "Ahh, if only it were that easy."

We sat back, drank wine, and watched as the crowd grew just as it had the last time we'd been in here. Each time I heard the door open and saw the swath of light cut through the dim space, my stomach tightened a little more. Renée sensed my unease.

"What is it, *mon cheri?* You seem—I don't know —distracted."

I forced a smile. "I'm fine," I lied. "Not distracted, just tired, I guess. How about you?"

She shrugged in her now familiar way. "It is life, I think, to be tired. *Oui?* It means your life is full."

A woman passing our table bent to the floor and placed a photo on the table. "Yours?" she said, walking away before either of us could answer.

Renée picked it up before I could see it, her fingers tracing the lines of the image, a small line forming between her eyes. She held it out to me. "This is yours, perhaps?"

I reached for the photo, and instantly recognized a snapshot of John I'd taken in Boston after one of his mysterious trips. His uncombed hair was longer than usual, a small beard hid the angles of his jaw, but his eyes—his perfectly sparkling blue eyes—looked right into the camera. I'd taken it at the Four Seasons, and I loved it still—my rugged, beautiful man. I smiled realizing that Renée had never met John.

"You know this man?" Renée interrupted my thoughts, her voice excited.

I nodded. "He's—"

"A man I have seen," she said, making no attempt to hide her interest. "I know him. Well—maybe I don't know him—but I have seen him many times. He is handsome, yes?"

The tiny knot that had formed in my stomach expanded into my throat. I tried to swallow it away.

"So," she asked, reaching for the photo again. "Is this your husband?"

Her voice was a blur as my brain tried to process the possibilities. She'd seen someone who looked like him. He was recognizable in this photo, only to me. She was mistaking him for someone else. In the quickest recovery of my life, I shook my head. "No, I don't really know him. I think he might be a friend of John's. I'm not even sure how I wound up with this picture. How about you? How do you know him?"

"Ahh, I have seen him, you know, around." She smiled, lost in some memory.

I didn't know. Around Bangkok? At events, though that couldn't be—aside from that one dinner, we weren't doing events. *"We're keeping a low profile,"* he'd said. *"So we can move around easily. It's safer that way, too."*

"Here in Bangkok?" I asked, my voice cracking.

"Bangkok? No." Her voice was firm, but her eyes were dreamy like mine had been when I'd first met him. "Maybe it was Pakistan or maybe Iraq, and maybe it was last year, or maybe the year before that. I can't be sure, but I think he bought me a drink, or maybe more. But that was all. He was always with exotic foreign women, all whispers and kisses, you know." She kissed the air for emphasis and ordered another round. "You must promise—if you see your husband's friend—to ask if he remembers me."

My shoulders, which had been hunched up tight, relaxed, and I exhaled slowly. John was with the State Department, Renée with the UN. It wouldn't be so unusual that their paths had crossed, and I couldn't be jealous of that. Well, maybe I could, but at least I wouldn't show it. "Pakistan, Iraq, you've worked there?" I said, hoping to move the subject away from John.

She nodded, her finger circling the rim of her glass. "Yes. So many places, I forget sometimes who I've met and where. Was it Paris on break, or Geneva with the UN, or maybe a miserable bar in some miserable place? I think I should find my own ambassador and stop moving around the world. What do you think?"

I clinked my glass against hers. "I think that's exactly what you should do."

Renée ordered more wine. "A bottle," she said.

"I don't think I can—"

"It's less expensive," she replied to my questioning glance. "So, who do you think—?"

Oh, damn she was going to look at John's picture again. I opened my mouth to change the subject, but Renée continued on.

"—that man at the camp is? Could he be with the government, maybe? There are more soldiers around there these days."

I laughed. "I don't think so. If he were, why would he need to speak with me there? Why not in Bangkok? Why would he bother?"

"Ahh, you know what I really think—I think he is lonely and looking for love." She raised a brow and winked. "And that, I can understand." She raised her glass and took a long, slow sip before turning in her seat to get a better look around the bar.

I took a sip of my wine too, but I hadn't really eaten, and almost immediately, my head was spinning. I put my glass down, and when Renée tried to refill it, I put my hand up. "No more for me."

"More for me, then. You Americans don't know how to drink, do you?" She chuckled and filled her glass to the brim.

I smiled and watched as her eyes scanned the room, pausing to assess every potential suitor before moving on. I was glad I'd told her about the man at Bān. She did have a way of deconstructing my fears, and maybe they *were* unfounded. Maybe we'd both overreacted. There was nothing like a little wine and the dim lighting in a bar to allay your fears.

We lingered there in the bar, and I watched as Renée drank more wine than she should have and refilled my glass more than once. When she suggested it was time to go, I offered to drive. She scoffed at my suggestion. "Americans cannot drink wine the way the French can. I'm fine. I could drink another bottle, and maybe I will, later. But let's get you home before I am—you know—drunk."

I laughed and walked to the car, stumbling only once. And that was probably due to the rain which was pouring down as we left. Renée laughed out loud.

"You see," she said. "Americans can't even manage two or three drinks."

If I was intoxicated, and I'm not saying I was, it was on the knowledge that John loved me, and the little kernel of doubt that had lodged itself into my brain, began to dissolve. Maybe I'd even ask him if he remembered meeting Renée.

But he never came home that night, and I never got the chance. And when he did come home the next day, the little seed of doubt had blossomed again, and I was afraid to ask.

CHAPTER TWENTY-SEVEN

A few days later, the downpours seemed to let up altogether, and even though it was still rainy season, it wasn't quite so wet. The rains swept through and then out, and the sun shone, and dried the streets and the puddles, and all that was left of the rain were the rainbows—splashes of color that filled the sky and hung low over the city—and the promise of cooler days and clearer skies. And I realized that I was seeing the things I never even noticed at home—a night sky blanketed with stars, glistening raindrops on rose petals, the pleasure of a small breeze, the giggles of small children, the hush of the Bhuddist temples as I passed, so like and yet so different from my own church in Boston. The scents—the hint of jasmine and wet trees hanging in the air, and the tastes—the spices in chicken satay or sticky rice. Thai food had never tasted like this in Boston. Even the wine seemed better, at least at the Madrid, but I supposed that it was just that everything was so new—that was what made Thailand so exotic and so familiar all at once.

One morning, John and I watched as a rainbow—perfect bits of fairy dust—sprang into view, and then faded just as quickly from the sky. He drew me close and kissed me, a soft lingering kiss. He opened my robe and kissed the tips of my nipples. I felt the familiar tingle, and I arched my back to him, and I knew I had nothing to worry about. He loved me.

And suddenly, he closed my robe and stepped back. "I don't know what the hell I'm doing. I'm late already." He ran his fingers through my hair and kissed my forehead. I've got to run, babe," he said. "I'll see you tonight. We'll finish this then."

My shoulders sagged a little as I watched him dress, but I nodded and kissed him back. "Have a good day," I said with a quick adjustment to his tie.

He turned toward the door and stopped, as if he'd forgotten something. He pulled me close and then closer still, his body pressed to mine, as though he were trying to memorize the planes and curves of my body. He let out a long sigh. "I love you, Nora. I really love you. You know that, right?" He planted a quick peck on my cheek and ran his finger along the curve of my chin. "I just want to be sure that you know how much I love you. That's important to me."

"I love you, too," I whispered as I watched him go.

And I listened as his footsteps banged down the stairs, and then, at the bottom, he hesitated. "Nora," he called out, his voice trailing up the stairs and down the hall to our room losing any urgency he might have intended. "I forgot to mention Bân. There are some issues there, so I need you to stay away until I have more information. Okay?" And then, without waiting for an answer, he was gone, and I was left to wonder if Renée's audit was the issue, and I wondered why that meant I should stay away.

I drew in a deep breath and hugged myself. I loved being married. I loved waking up beside John, and knowing he'd be coming home to me at the end of the day, well, maybe *hoping* was a better word. But there were plenty of things I disliked— his secret trips and his long hours topped my list. But I supposed

I had secrets of my own these days—the wet, muddy roads that made travel to Bân risky, the lack of cell service out there, the creepy man who sent a chill through my veins and, of course, Emily's room and the money stashed there. I knew I had to tell him everything—and I'd start with Emily's room. But not yet and until then, I couldn't stay away from Bân. I wasn't used to anyone telling me what I could and couldn't do. I'd planned to go once the rain let up to see if there was any news of Suu. I wouldn't change those plans, not today at least.

I finished my coffee and decided to get an early start on the drive. Just as I stepped back into our bedroom, I saw John's phone there on the night table, probably forgotten in his morning rush. I knew he'd be frantic without it, and that I'd have to get it to him before I headed out of the city. I tried his office but got only the answering machine. I didn't want to just leave a message. What if no one ever checked the machine? I wanted to be sure he'd get it, so I called Mae, and she picked up on the first ring.

"Hello, Nora, how are you?" she said.

We chatted for a few minutes until I realized that every minute I spent on the phone, even with a friend like Mae, was a minute less at Bân. "I hate to cut this short, it's been so good to talk with you, but I'm actually looking for John. He left his phone here, and I know he'll need it."

"Of course," she answered. "I could come and get it. Perhaps we can have coffee."

I couldn't let her come to the house. Without the scents of food preparation and fresh flowers in the house, she'd realize that Chai and the gardener were gone, and I'd promised Chai to keep that bit of information from her. "I can't, not today," I answered quickly. "I'm heading out to Bân and I want to be sure I'm home before dark." Damn, damn, damn! Why had I told her that? I was so intent on keeping Chai's secret, I gave my own away. She'd probably tell John.

"Ahh, B̂ān. I was going to ask how that was going. Do you get out there much?"

I paused and tried to angle my phone with one hand and slip John's phone into my bag with the other. I was considering my response when Mae piped in.

"You know, with the rain and all, I assumed the roads were out, but perhaps you have been able to go?"

"The roads were terrible, but Renée and Lisa have a Range Rover, so I was able to go with them."

"Ahh, so will they take you today?" she asked.

Why was I telling her so much? "Uhh, no, I'm going to take the Toyota and pray for the best. Not even sure I'll get there." There, I'd recovered nicely, I thought. I paused, waiting for Mae to warn me about the issues that John had mentioned, but she didn't, and I wondered—if there were *issues* at B̂ān, wouldn't she know about them too? I considered asking again about the locksmith, but that would only delay me more. I'd ask another time.

"The locksmith can come this morning. You won't be home, then?"

"No, I..."

"Ahh, so you're in a hurry. No problem. I'll meet you in front of the embassy's main gate in five minutes. Is that okay? And perhaps we can have lunch one day soon?"

"I'd like that."

We said our goodbyes and I hung up. I hurriedly packed a snack and bottle of water for the road, and just as I opened the door, my phone rang again. This time, I was certain it was John, but instead, it was Renée.

"*Bonjour, mon cheri.* How are you?"

"I'm good, on my way to B̂ān. Any chance you can come with me?"

"No, no, I have work here in Bangkok, but perhaps we can meet tonight for a drink? You can tell me all about B̂ān."

"Any other time, I'd love to, but I'm planning a special dinner for John." I hadn't known I was until I said it, and then the idea kind of took hold in my brain. I'd come home and cook. That's what I'd do.

"So, have a good day. Perhaps tomorrow?"

"Sounds good, Renée. I'll speak with you then."

I headed out to the embassy. Good as her word, Mae was out front waving as I pulled up. I handed her John's phone, and waved goodbye as I pulled back into the traffic. I didn't want to give her any more opportunity to ask about B̂ān, and the earlier I got there, the better.

The roads were clear, the sky even more so as I drove out of Bangkok, my head filled with plans for John and me that evening. Maybe instead of cooking a mediocre meal, we could go out to dinner. We'd done that only once in the four months we'd been here, and before we packed up and left Thailand for good, we needed to experience more of the local culture and just do more. Maybe, I'd ask him about having a small dinner for the Australian and English ambassadors to reciprocate our invitations—just a small dinner, nothing elaborate. Maybe invite Elizabeth Miller and her husband, the Canadian ambassador, as well. I didn't want to get home with regrets about all the things I'd missed. John had been a traveler for a long time. He could afford to be cavalier—he'd lived a life of adventure. Even Renée, it seemed, could attest to that.

Three and a half hours later, as I made the final turn to B̂ān, I slowed and marveled at the lushness of the foliage and trees. There'd be no seeing little Suu through all of that, unless she decided to come to me. I crossed my fingers, and as I pulled into the parking lot, I saw a military vehicle and soldiers with guns. They seemed to be leaving. I knew they patrolled the area, but I'd never noticed them right in the camp. Maybe there really was something going on. I shook off my foreboding, and as I jumped from the car, a small group of children quickly gathered. They followed me, chattering the whole way. When we arrived at the clinic, Nath stuck his head out. "When you're finished setting up, come and see me."

There must be news of Suu, I thought, and a tiny kernel of hope lodged itself into my heart. I nudged the children who began the familiar collection of tarps and toys, and we trooped to the play area where I laid out the tarps, and set up the dolls and trucks and balls and coloring books faster than ever. Within minutes, the kids were shrieking, the balls bouncing off trees and anything within reach, the tiny trucks whizzing through the dirt. I headed back to the clinic, the screeches of happiness fresh in my ears, and found Nath.

"Hey," I said, poking my head inside. "You wanted to see me?"

"Come on in." He motioned me to one of the familiar straight-backed wooden seats.

I sat and crossed my arms, trying to gauge his mood. Was he smiling? Good news. Scowling? Not so good. But it was neither. Nath had a face devoid of almost all expression. So, caving in to my own anxiety, I frowned.

"Are you okay?" he asked, a tiny line appearing between his eyes.

I forced a quick smile. "I'm fine, just eager to hear if you've learned anything about Suu."

"Ahh." He bobbed his head up and down and took a seat across from me. "I have, but not very much, I'm afraid. I think she lives about four or five kilometers from the camp, just outside a large dump. It's not clear if she's actually a Thai citizen or refugee from Myanmar. And that's the problem. If she's Thai, I can't do anything for her, and if she's a refugee, I'd need proof."

"But, what about her mother? I met her. She can tell us if they're refugees."

He shook his head. "You probably met someone who hoped you'd give her new sandals, too. There's no word of her mother, so she might have been a prostitute, but either way, Suu's all alone from the little I learned. People are reluctant to share any information about these kids. They worry that it's really the Thai police or military asking. And there's so many kids just like her. It's a shame, but it's not an unfamiliar story."

I crossed my legs and remembered some distant warning about that being impolite. I quickly uncrossed them, my hands bracing either side of the chair. "There's got be something we can do."

For the first time, Nath's mouth bowed into a kind of half smile. "If she shows up, we can try to get her to an orphanage, but aside from that, there's not much we can do."

"An orphanage?"

"It's better than where she probably is right now. If you'd like, once the roads clear up, I'll take you to some of the dumps, see if we can find her. Until then, we wait, and see what happens." He sighed, and stood, a not-so-subtle hint that our conversation was finished.

"So, maybe I'll check back next week?" I guess I could check out the orphanages in Bangkok, ask John to help, and maybe I could get her a dress, some new sandals. I caught myself—I was getting ahead of things. Nath was right. I just had to wait.

An hour later, I slid into my car and turned for home. I knew the route—the ruts and curve of the road, the angle of the sun by heart, and I drove distractedly, preoccupied with my plans for Suu, and my dinner with John. Maybe, I could convince him to come to B̂ān with me. If he could help to get donors interested, there was no limit to what we could do there. And that, I thought, was exactly why Renée and Lisa had invited me in the first place.

I pulled onto the paved stretch of road and glanced quickly at my watch. If I got home early enough, maybe I could make something, and John and I could stay in, and—

Suddenly, a small child darted into the road. I tried to brake, to swerve, but there was no time. I veered wildly to the left, and then to the right. I put all of my weight onto the brake, but I couldn't seem to slow the car, which was hurtling into the brush and trees that lined the road. I held tight to the steering wheel and prayed. If I could just get control and turn away from—

And then, as quickly as the child had appeared in front of my car, she disappeared, as though she'd been swallowed up. My heart was in my mouth.

Was it Suu?

CHAPTER TWENTY-EIGHT

My car came to an abrupt stop in a patch of weeds and thistle on the side of the road. I released my white-knuckled fingers from their grip on the steering wheel. Overgrown brush and branches covered my windshield and the passenger windows, and all I could see was jungle. A trickle of sweat ran along my forehead and into my eyes, clouding my vision. Swiping my sleeve across my eyes, I pushed against the door, the shrill squeak of it startling me as it broke through the eerie quiet of the jungle.

"Suu," I shouted, my words hanging in the full, soupy air. I stepped from the car, my shoes sinking in the muddy earth. "Suu," I called again, and again there was no reply. A tiny crackling sound, footsteps maybe, pierced the quiet and I spun around looking for the source, but there was nothing there. It was as though she'd never been there at all. I turned back and pulled the brush from the front of my car to have a closer look, but there was nothing much to see—a splatter of mud along the sides, and a few scratches to the fender from the tree branches that had slowed me down.

I slipped back into the car. I should probably make sure I

wasn't stuck in the damn mud. Just as I turned the key in the ignition, a hideous thought came to me—was she trapped under the car? My heart in my mouth, I stepped from the car and squatted low, my eyes trying to focus underneath, but there was only blackness there. I crouched lower still. And I was there—suspended in time and fear—desperately praying for Suu, when I felt something touch my back. I scrambled to my feet, a tiny sliver of hope nipping at my heels. Was it Suu or merely a stray branch fluttering over me?

I turned and caught a glimpse of someone running. "Suu?" I called, but I couldn't be sure. I'd caught only the barest glimpse as she ran into the forest.

"Hey," I shouted, taking a few tentative steps after her. "Are you okay? Come back." But she was gone, vanished as surely and swiftly as if I'd only imagined her. I exhaled noisily and leaned back against my car. I couldn't just let her go. I pulled open my car door and stood on the rise. "Come back, Suu," I shouted one last time. This time, there was a rustle of movement, and the jungle seemed to open, the swaying branches parting as if by an unseen hand. And then a tiny hand appeared, and then the child behind it.

My heart stopped.

It was Suu. She was covered with mud and dust, her hair more matted than ever, her too-big dress sliding from her bony shoulders, and her little feet—bare and covered with healing cuts and scrapes, and on top of that, a layer of dirt. She ran the last few steps to me, and I bent to her, lifting her into my arms and holding her so tightly, she finally pulled back a little. She reached one grimy hand to my face, and as she'd done so often before, she traced the line of my jaw with her fingers.

"Hello, Suu," I finally said when I could speak.

She giggled in reply, the sing-songy lilt of her laugh playing in my mind like a longed-for melody. She pulled back a little more and pointed toward the thick brush through which she'd just emerged. Bobbing her head, she dropped to the ground and tugged at my hand, and I knew I was meant to follow. And I also knew that I shouldn't. But if I hesitated at all, it was only for a millisecond. Every warning I'd heard—from John and then Lisa—held no sway over me at that moment. I reached in, turned my car off, locked the doors, pocketed the key and nodded to Suu who smiled and pulled away the first low branches that were blocking our way exposing a small well-worn path that seemed to weave through the jungle. Confident that I'd find my way back, I followed.

We walked in silence and in darkness, the trees and shrubs allowing only the barest of daylight to poke through. But it didn't matter to Suu who seemed instinctively to know where to place her feet to avoid the prickly bushes and sticks that littered the ground. Occasionally she broke stride to glance back and pat my hand, as if sensing that with each step we took, my unease grew. I knew my following her into the jungle was crazy, but I was helpless in the presence of this little girl.

After what seemed like miles, but was likely not even one, the sweet scents of the jungle were replaced by a stench of rotting food and long forgotten garbage that moved toward us like a fog, and I knew we were nearing the dump, the place that Suu called home. She picked up her pace, her little feet gliding over the ground, her joy palpable, and suddenly we emerged into daylight, and I stopped dead.

In front of us, spread out over what might have been miles, was an enormous never-ending landscape of garbage. Suu began to run ahead, but I stayed where I was and just looked. Enormous flies seemed to swarm everywhere; their sound a constant grating drone, a kind of hideous symphony to the scene before me. Off in the distance two trucks unloaded tons of fresh trash, a crowd at the ready—arms outstretched—to catch it as it was hurled to the ground. A heavy-loader pushed the piles to the center of the landfill, so for the people who stood by the emptying trucks, it was a race of sorts to gather the best of the trash before it could be moved. Children were scattered about picking through the trash on the periphery where small fires burned. Although at first glance, it might have seemed a scene of sadness and desperation, there was a kind of hopefulness there. And I forced a small smile so that if Suu was watching, she'd see that I wasn't shocked at the sight.

As my eyes adjusted to the scene, I realized that some of the children were sifting through items in what had to be makeshift shelters, most made of branches and old plastic bags, a few with roofs made of grass. Old mattresses, long discarded and now stained, and with springs poking through worn fabric, served as the only furniture I could see. On one, a young woman laid on her side, a tiny baby suckling at her slack breast.

Although daylight leaked through, the blue of the sky was obscured by the thick layer of murky steam that rose from the garbage creating a kind of veil between the earth and the sky. Forgetting for a moment what lingered all around, I took a deep breath, and my lungs filled with the sour air that flowed everywhere—the whiff you'd catch if you were behind an open garbage truck, the smell that could cut your breath in an instant. My eyes watered, my hand fluttered to my mouth, and suddenly Suu was at my side.

I looked down and smiled. She slipped her hand into mine and pulled me forward. The closer we got to the center of the dump, the more I could see. Much of the garbage seemed to be in those plastic bags we get at the store at home. There were thousands and thousands in among the trash.

The garbage pickers, canvas bags slung over their bony shoulders and gripping long handled tools, worked swiftly. Their eyes moving over the fresh trash, they pierced the choicest bits—food and fabric and plastic bottles which might fetch cash —before someone else could grab it. Rats competed for the spoils as well, darting boldly through the piles of trash, while dogs gave chase amidst the debris, and birds swooped in for whatever was left. As heart-wrenching as the sight was, it was also eerily quiet, no fights breaking out, no anger, no shouts, just quiet nods. And in that politeness alone, it was like the refugee camp, which now seemed a luxurious place compared to this. I wondered how Suu and the others managed to survive at all. I was having a tough time just standing here. I had to do something. I'd bring John out here, that's what I'd do. It's one thing for him to hear about the garbage pickers and dump dwellers, but quite another to actually see it. And, once he saw it, I knew he'd want to help as much as I did. He'd described these people as *desperate*, but this was a polite, hopeful kind of desperate, so different from the *desperate* he'd described.

"Aay," Suu shouted, a garbled sound, and nudged me with her elbow to get my attention. When I looked down to see her at my side, she smiled and gripped my hand a little tighter. I let her lead me to a makeshift hut that I thought must have been her home—a small piece of plywood on the ground created a kind of floor, which had been covered with discarded plastic and one long piece of torn fabric. Her roof consisted of a long piece of plastic held up by wooden sticks. A cardboard box held her treasures and she held it up to me so that I could appreciate her prizes. She had an old book, its binding broken, a plastic doll with no legs and missing one eye, a handful of old buttons, and another tattered dress. She plopped down on an old baby mattress. Covered with mysterious stains and missing a large chunk off the end where something had chewed all the way through, it seemed a source of pride for her. She patted the place beside her, and I sat down, pulling my legs up under me. She took out the doll and played, bouncing it along her legs. She exuded such simple joy, such pleasure in that moment with her doll and nothing else. I bit back the tears that I could feel gathering in my eyes. Two more children approached, their eyes wary, their footsteps slow and tentative. They looked much like Suu—dressed in rags, covered in muck, one chewing on a bit of gristly meat. Suu smiled and beckoned them closer, and I wished that I could speak their language. Suu—the little hostess—was busy pointing first at me and then at herself and smiling, and the children's heads bobbed in understanding, and they turned and chatted with each other. Suu didn't speak to either of them, and I realized then that the sounds she made were just that—sounds—not words. Nath had mentioned the first time I'd met Suu that maybe she couldn't hear. My heart sank. I had to get her out of here. She'd rot away like all this garbage if she stayed here.

I looked back at the two newcomers, and wished I had something to give them, some piece of food or anything. I fished in my pockets praying for gum or peppermints but all I could find were my keys, the feel of them, along with the dwindling light, reminding me that it really was time to go. I pulled myself up and motioned with my hands to mimic driving, and then I pointed back to the area through which we'd come. Suu frowned but jumped up quickly and took my hand to lead me back.

"No, no," I said, taking my hand from hers. "I can find it. It's okay."

And for all our language differences and her likely deafness, she clearly understood my intent. With a long pout, and her hands on her hips, she shook her head angrily and pointed to me and then the other children. They seemed to come to some kind of agreement, Suu taking my hand and another girl taking hold of my other hand. They pulled me along until I gave up. "Okay," I said. "Let's go."

I followed them back to my car, the dark in the trail even deeper now. When we stepped out of the path and into what was left of the afternoon's sunlight, the children spied my car, all shiny and so exotic-looking after the stench and chaos of the dump, and shrieked with delight, running to touch it. When I unlocked the doors, they climbed inside and patted the seats, running their hands along the slick leather, and the shiny instruments. They smiled and laughed, and my heart broke that such a simple thing as a car could bring such joy to kids who had so little. When they finally clambered back out, little heads nodding approval, I bent low and gave each of them a hug and a quick kiss goodbye before Suu stepped in front of me.

"Aay," she said, the sound she made most often. She giggled at her own cleverness and threw her arms around my neck.

"Okay," I whispered, afraid I was about to cry. I pulled her close and buried my face in the bony curves of her tiny shoulder and wiped away a tear before she could see. "I'll see you soon little friend. *Soon*. Understand?"

"Aay," she said again.

"Soon, Suu," I said, and she giggled again, shaking her head at my inability to just leave.

I slid into my car and watched as the tiny trio slipped back into the jungle toward home. I inhaled the fresh air all around me, started my car, put it into reverse, and was turning the wheel to back up onto the road when something behind me caught my eye. I slammed on the brake and turned my head to get a better look, and I froze.

It was *him*—the man with the cold eyes.

CHAPTER TWENTY-NINE

H e was behind my car and hurrying toward me, his eyes locked firmly onto mine.

"Stop," he shouted. "My name is Yut. Wait! I have something to—"

I looked away and willed myself not to listen. This crazy bastard must have seen my car and been waiting for me to come back. Shuddering at the thought, I glanced back and saw he was getting closer still. I had only seconds to turn and get out of there. Pushing the gear into drive, I stepped hard on the gas, my car skidding and spitting mud into the air, and the car spun forward, my fender swiping a sturdy tree. I stepped hard on the gas, and as if by magic, the wheels glided forward and suddenly, I was back onto the road. I checked the rearview mirror to see the man receding from view, his arms waving, an angry scowl on his face.

For the first time since he'd appeared, I breathed. I mean really breathed—a slow deep breath to clear my head. Except that it didn't. I was shivering—despite the heat of the jungle around me—I felt cold, my legs and arms and hands trembling. And I knew I had to get home. The roads, still rutted and pockmarked as ever, kept my speed down. It was an hour before I hit the paved roads heading to Bangkok, and once there, I knew I'd be all right. I turned the radio on and turned the volume to high, hoping to block out all thought from my head. I couldn't let myself think—not yet, not until I was home. And tonight, I'd tell John everything—the dump dwellers and trash-pickers, that man, Emily's room, all of it. He'd know what to do. And I'd be rid of my secrets at last.

When I finally pulled onto Wireless Road, I quickly smoothed my hair, dabbed a tissue under my eyes to wipe off any mascara stains, and took a deep breath. I turned into my drive and waited as the guard opened the gate. He began to wave me through but stopped me when his eyes landed on the scratches and mud.

"Hold on, Mrs. Fielding," the young Marine said.

I rolled my window down. "Good evening," I said, trying to keep my voice steady. "Everything all right?"

"I was just about to ask you that. You know you have some front-end damage?"

I nodded. "I thought I was in reverse. Turns out I was in drive. I'll have some explaining to do tonight, I guess." I forced my voice to sound light, and I tried to bolster my veracity by smiling.

"Okay, ma'am, have a good night."

He stood back and I drove right in. When the gate clanged shut behind me, a wave of relief washed over me. And then I remembered—beyond not following John's advice to stay away from Bân, I hadn't done anything wrong. Why did I even lie to that Marine? I shouldn't be breathing a sigh of relief. I'd tell John what happened. He'd know what to do.

I gathered my things, slid from the car, and let myself into the house. "Chai," I called, but there was no answer. She was still away. "John," I shouted, praying that he was home, but there was only silence, my words echoing in the long hallway. A sudden buzzing sound made me jump, and I turned. There was nothing there, but the buzzing continued. It was then I realized it was coming from my pocket. My phone. I pulled it out, a smile on my face for the first time in hours. I held it up and looked at the screen. It was a message from John—at least he'd gotten his phone.

Problems at work—won't get home tonight.
Will try for tomorrow. Best, John.

Best? Huh? He never signed anything with *best*. Was he angry? Did he know I'd gone to B̂ān? Damn—my little white lies were catching up to me. I didn't want to be caught up in a tangled web of lies. I'd confess to everything when he came home. I'd let everything go too long as it was. I blew out a plume of air and looked closer at the message. The time stamp indicated he'd texted me hours and hours ago, but I'd probably been too far out of range. And there were five other calls too—all from the same number—a number I didn't know, but maybe they were from John. I tapped *call back* and listened as a funny, tinny ring sounded. And then it stopped, and there was nothing —no voicemail, no message, nothing. I tried again and got the same. Damn—it was probably a wrong number.

A note on the hall table caught my eye. I picked it up and read:

The locksmith changed the lock. New key in the door upstairs. I've kept a spare at the office, just in case.
Talk soon,
Mae

Too tired to care just then, I dragged myself upstairs, turned on the shower, checked my reflection in the bathroom mirror, and drew in a sharp breath. It was a good thing John wasn't home. I looked a sight—slick with sweat, my hair plastered to my head as though I'd been caught in a rain shower, and the pungent scent of garbage on my clothes and skin. I turned the water to hot, peeled away my clothes and stepped in, the water and the soap washing away the last traces of my visit to the dump. I toweled off, threw on a robe, and heated up some of Chai's frozen sticky rice and chicken satay.

I sat down to eat and had the fork halfway to my mouth when a fresh image of little Suu flashed in my mind. I paused. I'd just come home, turned on the lights, taken a shower, and was about to eat—all luxuries to little Suu and the people I'd met today. Suddenly, I had no appetite. I dropped my fork, pushed my plate away and took a sip of wine while I considered what to do. I could call Mae, thank her for getting the phone to John, and see if she wanted to go out, maybe to Cheap Charlie's. I put my plate in the refrigerator, picked up my phone, and got only her voicemail. I left a quick message and wondered who else I could call. I wanted to go out—talk about the day. Maybe Renée—she'd asked about just that this morning—maybe she'd go. I dialed her number but reached only her voicemail as well. Where was everybody? With Lisa away, that was the end of my *friends to call for a drink* list.

I went back upstairs, the lure of Emily's room not quite as urgent now that there was a key. Although it did mean I wouldn't have to say I'd broken in. I could just say I'd found the money when I was having a look around. I slipped into bed, clicked on the TV, crawled under the covers, and fell asleep to the dull glow and easy hum of the television. Tomorrow couldn't come soon enough.

I slept until a swath of sunlight leaked in through the shutters nudging my eyes open. I sat and stretched. Might as well get up, try to call John. My phone buzzed just as I reached for it. And this time I was certain—it was John.

But it wasn't. It was Jim Leo. "Hey, Nora, I need to see you. Are you home?"

"Just woke up. Is John with you?"

There was a long pause. "Uhh, no, he's not. Can I stop by?"

His voice was awfully serious for so early in the day, and I wanted to say no. I'd just woken up, and I was a mess. And John wasn't here. What did he need me for? I ran my fingers through my tangled hair and sighed. "Sure, give me ten minutes."

I splashed water onto my face, pulled my hair into a neat little topknot, and slipped into a pair of sweats. I ran downstairs, gulped a cup of instant coffee, and by the time Jim arrived, I was wide awake, and feeling pretty good.

Until I opened the door.

Jim stood there, the corners of his mouth drooping ominously. "So sorry, Nora, but there's just no easy way to say this. I have bad news." He wiped away a bead of sweat that lined his forehead.

"It's John."

I stepped away from the door afraid to acknowledge what he'd said. I couldn't have heard him right, unless—oh, damn —had they heard about my going to B̂ān? Was John in trouble because of me? Jim's face was drawn, concerned.

"Is it B̂ān?" I asked, a surge of remorse ringing in my voice. I shouldn't have gone. "John told me not to go, but I can explain."

Jim shook his head, a puzzled look on his face. He stepped inside and closed the door quietly behind him. "B̂ān? No, no. I'm here about John. And I'm afraid, it's not good."

He reached out and placed his hand on my shoulder. I shook him off. "What's not good? What are you talking about?" A thousand possibilities raced through my mind. Had there been an accident? No, I would have heard something. Wouldn't I? Or was that what this was? No, I couldn't think like that. It had to be something else, but what? Was John in trouble because of me? No, that didn't make sense either. But so far this morning, nothing was making sense.

"It's John. He's—"

Jim's voice was hollow, empty almost, and his face was crumpled, his lips almost hidden in the downward folds of his face. And I suddenly knew that whatever he wanted to tell me, I didn't want to hear. I wanted to cover my ears and run. Instead, I shook my head decisively. "Don't—" I turned and started along the hallway. I'd make breakfast, or dinner. That's what I'd do—start on a special dinner. Maybe John would be home tonight.

"Nora," he shouted. "Stop! Just stop and listen."

I turned back, tears pricking my eyes. "Please," I whispered. "Don't tell me anything bad."

Jim came to my side. "Come on, I'd like you to sit down and listen to me."

His eyes, I noticed then, were shot through with red, his brow furrowed. "Come on, honey," he said softly. "Please just sit."

I shook my head. "Not here," I sniffled and led him upstairs to our living room. I plopped onto the couch, hugged a pillow to my chest, and pulled my legs up under me. Jim sat across from me, his hands folded in his lap. He took a deep breath, and then let it out in one long sigh as though he was stalling, thinking what to say. After what seemed forever, he finally spoke.

"John was on assignment yesterday, and he's gone missing." For all of his delay, he spit out his words the way you might spit out a sour tasting lemon. He leaned forward. "We've had no communication with him, and—"

My brain was on fire, all synapses exploding but not connecting. I didn't understand, or maybe I just didn't want to. I threw off the pillow and leaned forward. "You're not making any sense. It's like you're speaking a foreign language, but I *have* heard from John, so whatever it is you think happened, I think there's just been a mistake."

Jim moved to the edge of the chair, his eyes wide open. "You've heard from him? When?"

"I had a text message late yesterday," I said, watching the

relief spill into Jim's face, the lines there softening, the frown that had draped his lips smoothing.

"Can I see?" he asked, holding his hand out for my phone.

"Well, it's personal," I said, holding tight to my phone and wondering why I'd said it was *personal*, since oddly, it was the least personal message he'd ever sent.

"Please, Nora, this really is a matter of life and death."

My heart began to race, my fingers to tremble. I clamped down hard on my lower lip and passed him the phone. I watched as he read, his eyes giving away nothing.

"He sent this late yesterday morning. You know that, right?"

I nodded, afraid to speak, afraid to move, afraid to breathe.

Jim passed the phone back to me. "Apparently, John flew to Tajikistan yesterday, a quick mission involving the Taliban and ISIS, or so I've been told, but we lost communication with him almost as soon as he landed and headed out. And then, we had word—"

"What do you mean? What mission? What's...?" And then in my mind's eye, I could see the gun in his bag, the dirt on his clothes, his frequent trips. "What's really going on? Tell me. I have to know everything."

Jim's shoulders slumped. "I guess you have a right to know, especially now. But I do have to have your word that whatever I tell you will remain between us, at least for now."

I nodded. I'd agree to anything just about now.

Jim cleared his throat, and I jumped up. "I'll get you a glass of water," I said, desperate to stall him, to keep whatever it was he was about to tell me, unspoken. If I never heard it, it couldn't be real.

He shook his head. "Sit down, Nora."

And I did, my fingers gripping the armrest, my heart in my mouth. "Go on, I'm ready."

"You probably had some suspicions that John was not exactly your average ambassador, right?"

I smiled in reply. That much I knew.

"The truth is—he's not really an ambassador at all."

I sat up. This was a load of crap. I couldn't listen to this. "I was there—at his swearing-in. He is most definitely an ambassador. He may be young, but he's definitely the ambassador."

"You misunderstood me. What I meant was that this assignment with John as the ambassador is a cover. The post and his assignment are temporary."

"I knew that it was temporary. We talked about that. I understand that."

Jim sighed. "I guess I should start at the beginning. He's the ambassador in name only. He doesn't work for the State Department. He works for the *firm*, the CIA. This post is a cover."

"The CIA?"

Jim nodded solemnly. "He's worked there for twelve years. Went in right from law school, I'm told."

"But he does work for the State Department. I met him there—at a party."

"State's another cover—a lot of CIA employees are listed as State. That cover allows them more access to dicey spots. Everything the night you met him was for show. The promotion, everything. It provided the backstory for this assignment, and a seamless transition to this post. It was all planned, cookie crumbs along the way, for anyone checking John out."

"But if you know—how is it a cover?"

"All planned, Nora. That night you met him, all of it."

"All planned? But he met *me* that night. We fell in love, at least I know I did, and I thought John did. That wasn't planned." My heart pounded hard against my ribs. "Was it?"

My voice cracked, and I bit down hard on my lip to keep the tears at bay.

Jim leaned forward and patted my hand. "That much is true. He loved you."

And all I heard was the word *loved*—the past tense. My breath caught in my throat, and the glut of tears that I'd held back sprang from my eyes. "Loved?" I choked out. "Loved, not loves?"

Jim moved next to me on the couch, locking his eyes onto mine. "He's disappeared," he said, his voice quivering. He paused, took a deep breath, cleared his throat and continued. "And he's presumed dead."

CHAPTER THIRTY-ONE

My heart stopped, my lungs felt as though the air had been knocked out of me, and I could almost feel the blood pooling in the center of my brain as all activity there ceased, save for one lonely thought—he was wrong. John couldn't be dead. It was only twenty-four hours since he'd turned to me.

I love you, he'd said. And if I concentrated, I could still feel his kiss, taste his lips, the touch of his hand on my skin. He wasn't dead. I would've felt it somehow, I know I would, and we had plans. We had—Jim draped his arms around me, but I pulled away and jumped to my feet. "You're wrong. I'd know it if he was gone. I'd feel it here." I banged my chest. "And I don't. I don't feel it, not at all. So, just tell me what happened. Or, what you think happened."

Jim chewed on his lower lip. "You know about the surge in terrorist activity worldwide, and the uptick in Russian arms dealings and threats of war, yes?"

I sank back into the couch and nodded though I wasn't sure I did know.

"His assignment here had to do with that. And just recently, with a direct threat to the embassy here."

My thoughts were racing and suddenly one thing made sense. "Is that what happened to Emily Somerfield? A terrorist? Is that why no one talks about her? To keep it quiet?"

"I..." He took a minute and shook his head. "No. And let me say first that you've never been in danger, not for a minute, but things are heating up, and John had planned to send you home soon."

I swallowed the hard lump in my throat.

"He was based here because it allowed him quick access to other hot spots—Iran, Syria, Pakistan, Afghanistan. The list, sad to say, is almost endless."

"But why did he bring *me* here? And why was he named ambassador if he was just going to travel and spy? Couldn't he—?"

Jim shook his head. "He was named ambassador because that diplomatic passport allowed him to glide in and out of countries pretty much unchecked. No second looks, no questions, no searches. He's a U.S. ambassador. End of story. And he was here because this is a relatively safe place, a country that barely gets a second look. Polite citizens, polite king, even the military coup here was pretty civil as coups go. And John had put his foot down. He didn't want to leave you again. Said he'd had enough. He'd met you, and he wanted a new assignment. This seemed tailor-made for him. He was here for fact-finding. Identify some people and sites, then call it a day. But almost from the first, things changed, and they changed quickly, almost too quickly for him to keep up with. He'd received information that arms were coming through Bangkok, and from here, on to arms dealers. And then everything seemed to explode, literally. Weapons that he'd traced showed up as part of a terrorist assault plan in Europe, and when it seemed clear that a Russian arms dealer was involved, we knew John had to be involved."

"But why John? Why not someone else?"

"You know of course that he speaks Russian?"

I shook my head. I didn't know. But Jim didn't seem to notice my confusion. He kept right on talking.

"And that was important. The CIA needed a Russian speaker to get unfiltered information as quickly as possible. This assignment was made for him. And with weapons slipping right through Bangkok, the higher-ups decided this embassy post for John was the best option. And for me as well—I'm with State, but I've been here. I know Thailand, maybe better than anyone, and they assigned me to assist John for this mission, so someone here could be his backup."

My head was spinning. "So, John's a spy? And he speaks Russian? With all of the mystery, I've been worried that there was another woman, another wife even."

Jim smiled weakly and patted my hand. "I had my own suspicions once, not about that, but we were sure we had a mole in the office. The Russian weapons dealers were always just one step ahead of us, and I began to think it was John, but of course that was nonsense."

"But I'm his wife. Why couldn't he just tell me what he really did?"

"That's just it. He couldn't tell you. Men go to their graves with that secret. It goes along with the job. *Wrap your lies in layers of truth*—a rule to live by for those in the business, or even the periphery. And it's a rule that even I can't break—at least not under normal circumstances. I couldn't tell my wife what I sometimes do either, and I suppose that's partly why we divorced. Too many secrets, and too much time apart. But John loved you. He was ready to give this up for you."

"Stop," I shouted. "Stop referring to him in the past tense." I rubbed my forehead and tried to think what to do, what to say, what to ask.

"I'm sorry, Nora. He was a good man, and it's killing me to tell you all of this. But I'm just trying to face the truth, the reality that we have. That's all."

"Tell me what happened yesterday, or today, or whenever it was when he disappeared."

"I don't know much. The CIA doesn't tell me everything, but I have been told there was a message that an arms deal was about to go down with a terrorist leader we've been tracking, and a Russian arms dealer. The story was that they were both hiding in plain sight in a small village, no protection, no guards, nothing. John went to confirm that. That's all. Just to confirm."

"Where is this village?"

He shrugged. "I don't know. I don't have clearance for that."

"And he went yesterday morning? Why John? Why not you or Dave, or someone else?" I didn't care if I sounded selfish. I didn't love *him or Dave*. I loved John.

"I'm not sure. I'm not CIA, just backup on this mission, so they wouldn't have sent me anyway. Dave is based in Pakistan. When I got into the office yesterday, I learned John had gone. You're right—it probably should have been someone else, but I guess it hadn't seemed like a big deal. It was a confirmation trip and that was it. The CIA's usual MO is to identify, infiltrate, collect intel, confirm it all and then fix, but that wasn't the plan today. It was apparently to confirm only."

"I don't understand."

"The agency identifies a problem or a person, they infiltrate to get what they need, and then they pinpoint or confirm the location, and then fix it, which means they go in and eliminate, or sometimes take the person into custody, and erase the problem. I know it sounds effortless and easy, but I'm sure it's not. It never is. Bin Laden is a perfect example. And that took years."

"But how did John disappear? And where?" My voice was calm and steady, but every other inch of me was screaming. This wasn't happening.

Jim pulled something from his pocket and rolled it around in his hand. "I don't have all the details. I was told he arrived at his first destination in Tajikistan, and was headed, in a small convoy, to the *border*. The only border we're interested in there is the one with Afghanistan. I don't know if that's where he was actually headed, and the agency doesn't even know if he made it. They lost contact. There was a report of an explosion, and that's it. No word, no clues."

I drew a sharp breath and tried to focus on what he was saying. I bit back my tears and swallowed the panic bubbling up in my throat. "Why would he go to fucking Afghanistan? I thought we were out of there. And why are you here talking to me? Why aren't you out there looking for John? And why the hell are you telling me he's dead? Jesus Christ!" I ran my hands through my hair and turned away to hide my fear.

"We're still trying to confirm that John actually went on the mission in the first place. Now, it seems no one's sure who sent him or where. It's murky as hell, but this was delivered to the embassy today. Have a look."

I turned back and saw, lying in the open palm of Jim's outstretched hand a smooth piece of lapis, the piece that was identical to mine. It was John's, his good luck charm. I was sure.

The air was suddenly sucked out of the room, and out of my lungs.

And I knew—the worst had happened.

CHAPTER THIRTY-TWO

I closed my eyes, and tried to imagine John—bleeding, maybe wounded, but not dead. But try as I might, I couldn't see him. I couldn't see him at all. I snapped my eyes open and reached for the lapis, running my fingers over the surface.

Jim held his hand out to take it back, but I held on tight and shook my head. "It's John's good luck charm. I'll just keep it for him." I curled my hand tight around the stone.

A sudden twitch distorted his right eye, and he blinked before finally reaching up to rub it away. "I guess that's okay," he said, his hand placed protectively over his eye.

The world—my world at least—was ending. Tears rimmed my eyes as I looked at him. I couldn't imagine my life without John, and so I wouldn't. "Please find him," I whispered. "Don't give up."

"We're not giving up. There's a team on the ground. John is my friend. I have no intention of giving up."

I nodded, grateful for that at least. "What can I do? There must be something."

"There is, actually. We do need your help. On the admittedly remote chance," he said, "that John's alive, we want to confuse his captors, so we're going to go on as though he's fine. I'd like you to stay in the house, no trips, no shopping. If anyone asks, we're going to say that John's sick, you too, and you're both stuck at home. I'm going to announce at the office that John will be out sick for a few days. If anyone calls—make something up—a stomach bug, whatever, and say that you and John are both down with it. Think you can do that?"

I nodded. "But I want to be involved. I want to do something."

"In time, Nora. For now, I need to have a look in his closet—see if there's anything there that might help."

I nodded. "You know where it is."

I heard his footsteps track down the hall, and then I heard the familiar sound of drawers being opened and closed, and hangers clanging, but I didn't care. I didn't care at all. I drew my knees up and rested my head there, the sound of my breathing and the whoosh of blood rushing through my veins blocking out all other sound. It couldn't be. I'd waited a lifetime for John. He couldn't be gone. I cried then, my shoulders heaving with the misery of it. I needed my mother, or Kelly, or both. I needed someone to hold me, and I wanted it to be John. Later, much later, it seemed, I felt a hand on my shoulder, and I opened my eyes.

Jim knelt before me. "I'm going to leave for a while, but I'll be back. Will you be okay?"

I could only nod. "Can I call anyone? I just need to talk to someone."

He shook his head. "I'm sorry, Nora. No one can know anything. If there's even a tiny chance that he's alive, that someone's holding him, we can't have any word leaked out. If all seems routine, we can confuse whoever's involved, and that might be someone right under our nose. But we need you to make this work. Understand?"

I didn't understand anything, but I nodded agreement.

"Okay, I'll be back later. Don't answer your phone; don't make any calls and stay off the internet. Think you can do that?"

"Yes," I whispered. I listened as Jim's footfalls padded down the stairs and out the front door. When I knew he was gone, I pulled myself up and walked to our bedroom, and I stood there for a minute trying to make sense of it all. But there was no sense to be made of it. Still clinging to John's lapis, I reached for my purse, my fingers fishing inside for my matching piece. When I felt the familiar smoothness, I curled my fingers around it, pulled it out and held it tight with John's piece, in the palm of my hand.

I threw myself onto the bed, onto John's side, and I grabbed his pillow and curled myself around it. And then I took a long, slow breath inhaling his scent, the sweet musk of spicy soap and aftershave. I remembered it all—the way his body felt when I slid my hands over the taut muscles of his back, the way he pulled me into the curve of his shoulder, and the sizzling feel of him inside of me. I knew the way his body swayed with mine, I knew the sound of his contented sigh, and the rasp of his exasperated one. I knew him better than I'd known any other man; at least I thought I did. I ran my hand along the depression in the mattress his body had created, and then I wept for John and myself and everything we might have lost.

I don't know how long I stayed like that, but I lay there rocking back and forth, the movement and the weight of John's pillow soothing me. I don't know how I fell asleep, but I did, and I dreamed that John was with me, that it was his body I was holding so tightly, and when I woke, I turned to look for him.

"John?" I called. The sound echoed back to me, and then I remembered—he was missing and presumed dead. I clutched the lapis, and I wept again and again until I heard a soft tapping at the bedroom door.

"Nora?" Jim said softly. "Are you okay?"

I sat up, placed the lapis in my pocket, and wiped my eyes and then my nose on my sleeve. I got up, pulled open the door, and shook my head. "No, unless you're here to tell me he's fine."

A small crease appeared in his brow, and I didn't need him to speak, but he did. "No word, yet. I just stopped back to leave his car here. I've left word at the gate for the house staff that you're both sick and they should just take a few days off."

I was about to say that Chai and the gardener had gone away, so I was alone already, but something stopped me, and I struggled to pay attention to what he was saying.

"But if, for any reason, someone gets past the front gate, just say that you're not well and you don't want them to come down with anything. Can you do that?"

My brain felt numb, but I'd do whatever he told me to do. I nodded and turned to shut the door.

"One more thing. You're sure he took his phone yesterday?"

I was about to nod again when I remembered. "No, I had to drop it off. He'd left it here."

"Did he call and ask you to bring it down?"

I shook my head. "No, I found it here. I called his office, but I only got voicemail, so I called Mae. I met her outside the embassy, and I gave his phone to her." I paused. "Is that important? I mean, he did text me."

"I'm a little concerned about the timeline. I feel as though I'm missing something." He scratched his head. "What about what he wrote? Or how he wrote it? Was that typical?"

I smiled for the first time since Jim had arrived this morning. "Well, he usually started off his texts with *hey, babe*. And he's never signed *best*. It's always been *love, John*. So, it was different, and at first, I was confused, but he was in a hurry, right? So, he just forgot, I figured."

The crease in Jim's forehead deepened, but he only sighed. "Okay, Nora. I'll be back later."

I crawled back into bed, reached for my phone and opened John's message once again. It *was* odd. Even if he knew I'd gone to Bān, he still would have called me *babe* and signed off with *love*. Though maybe he was in a hurry and asked someone else to send it. But I didn't really think he'd have someone else send me a message and sign his name. I sat up straight. The more I read his message, the less sense it made. I wondered if he still had his phone with him, and if Jim had already tried to call him.

I scrolled down to John's number, hit *call* and sat back, my fingers holding the phone tight to my ear. I heard the ring again and again, a distant echo snaking through the line. I gripped the phone tighter willing him to answer, but he didn't. When his voicemail asked me to leave a message, I hesitated, and then I hung up.

Jim had been clear—no phone calls, no internet, nothing.

CHAPTER THIRTY-THREE

I spent the day in bed, waiting for Jim to call or come back. At three o'clock, I decided to take a shower, get dressed and go downstairs. Maybe a cup of coffee and something to eat would clear my fuzzy brain and help me understand what was going on. I threw back the covers and padded to the bathroom, pulling my tee-shirt up and over my head as I went, and stubbed my toe on his duffel bag, probably knocked there accidentally by Jim. I reached down to put it away, but it was heavier than I remembered. Curious, I peered inside.

And my eyes opened wider. I could see maps, a GPS device, cellphones, what looked like a walkie-talkie, an iPad, and stuffed at the bottom—a bulletproof vest. I ran my hand across the hard surface. This was meant to protect him, to bring him home to me, but maybe he had another. Maybe this was only a spare. With that hopeful thought rushing through my mind, I pulled the vest up and out, and there, almost hidden underneath—was the stash of cocktail napkins grown larger than the last time I'd seen them.

I reached for the napkin that sat on top. Marked with the stain of someone's glass, it held a series of scrawls—numbers and letters—a phone number maybe? I picked up my own phone and dialed the series of symbols, and nothing happened. Not enough, or maybe too many, numbers and letters. I reached for the next napkin, so flimsy it crumbled in my hand. I tried to piece it together—a puzzle to be solved, but again, the letters and symbols meant nothing. The next napkin had only a word, or maybe it was a name. *Yut* was written across the napkin, the letters as tidy and flowing as a schoolteacher's. And though that word seemed faintly familiar, I couldn't place why, but my brain was still a jumble of worry and disconnected thoughts. It would come to me. I just had to wait. There were three more napkins, all with—at least to me—illegible and meaningless codes.

I slid down the wall and knelt there, laying the napkins end to end on the floor. The secret of everything—of where he was, of how to get to him—was in there, I could just feel it. I went through them all once more, but again—it was like trying to decipher Greek. I wondered if Jim had even seen these, and I got it into my head that he hadn't. I picked up my phone and called him. I listened as it rang again and again. When his voicemail instructed me to leave a message, I hung up. I'd just tell him when he came back.

I tried to think straight—to hold on to one clear thought, but I was struggling. I wondered if this was how breakdowns began. And then, as I sat there, the wires in my brain came alive, and I could almost hear them crackling as I realized that Emily had cocktail napkins with gibberish written on them, and John had the same. And even if they held different messages, the result was the same. Both had disappeared without a trace. My mouth went dry. I scampered to my feet, and raced to Emily's room, the new key dangling there, just as Mae had written in her note. I turned the knob and pushed the door open.

And I froze.

The room had been ransacked—the bedcovers and linen

pulled from the bed and thrown to the floor, the nightstands' drawers pulled open, and I tried desperately to remember when the locksmith had come. Was it only yesterday that Mae had left the cheery note that he'd finally been here? But who could have done this? I was the only who had access to the house. Anyone else would have to go by the guards. And Mae was with the locksmith, which seemed to rule her out. Who—?" And then I knew.

It was Chai—sweet, hardworking never-to be-suspected Chai, and the old gardener, and their secret gate. It had to be. Maybe they'd come back to the house. My stomach twisted with the thought. But why wouldn't they just use a hairpin and get into that room and take the money before they left? I couldn't wrap my head around this. Jim had been in the hallway alone too. And the noises I'd heard, crazy as it seemed, might have been him searching this room, instead of John's closet. And Mae —could she have stayed behind and looked for the things she'd said she'd left behind? But I didn't have the luxury of time to work it all out. I needed Emily's cocktail napkins. I'd tell Jim later about the room. All I cared about just then was finding John.

I stepped over the debris that covered the floor, and went into the sitting room. It was as much in disarray as the bedroom had been. The chair cushions had been upended, the wooden trunk open wide, its contents strewn about, Emily's DVDs, and books and iPad on the floor. I bent down to look—the trunk contained only one box and I pulled it out and opened it, a sigh spilling from my lips. The cocktail napkins were undisturbed. I looked again, my eyes searching for the box with the money. I knelt on the floor, my eyes and then fingers scouring through the mess, but it was gone. Without a trace. I didn't even have proof that the money had been here.

As dusk settled over Bangkok, Jim finally arrived, chicken

soup in hand. "I asked a secretary to pick this up for you and John. Setting the scene and all." He glanced at the container. "Smells pretty good." He sniffed over the soup and headed into the kitchen where he promptly took down a bowl, dumped half the soup in and placed it into the microwave. "Two minutes?"

I nodded. I didn't care about the damn soup. Burn it, for all it mattered. "What about John? Is there any word?"

He shook his head and punched in the cooking time on the microwave. "I'm not staying. I'll be heading to the Afghanistan–Pakistan border to find John, but I need you to maintain our cover. If anyone calls—and people will—or they'll drop by, just say you're both sick. No visitors allowed, etcetera, etcetera."

"Can I come with you?"

"I know you want to, but you can't. You'd only be in the way. I'll keep you posted."

"But I'm going crazy already here alone, not knowing what's happening. If you leave, I'll be all alone. Please, promise to call at least once a day." The microwave beeped, and I almost jumped out of my skin.

Jim rested his hand on my shoulder. "I know this is tough, but I'll give you the advice we give the new guys—stay strong, keep your head down and your mouth shut, and you'll be okay."

At that moment, with those words—he sounded just like John, and I held back a small laugh that turned into a huge sob, and then another bout of tears. "Please find him," I sniffled.

Jim wrapped his arms around me. "I'll do my best, honey. And remember—stay in, no calls, nothing. Watch a little TV. That'll get your mind off things. As soon as I know anything, I'll call." He reached into his pocket and pulled out an iPhone. "I'll call on this phone. You can use this one for limited calls, okay? Don't give the number out." He handed me the phone.

I took the phone with both hands and held on tight. "Does John know this number?"

"It's his work phone, the one he uses on the road. He knows it by heart."

I blinked away the veil of tears that covered my eyes.

Jim turned, and in one fluid movement, he pulled the soup from the microwave, set it on the table, pulled out a chair, and slid open the utensil drawer. He found a spoon and handed it to me. "Now eat. John will be mad as hell if he thinks I haven't taken care of you."

It was the first hopeful thing he'd said. *John will...* I grabbed a paper towel and swiped it across my eyes. "Thanks, Jim." I sat in front of the soup and watched as Jim turned to leave. Suddenly, all of my fears came rushing back, and I jumped up to block his way. "Please bring him back," I whispered. "Tell him I love him."

He gripped my shoulders and looked straight into my eyes. "I'll tell him. You don't have to worry about that. And I bet wherever he is, he's fighting to get back to you." He kissed my forehead. "I'll call first chance I get."

And then he was gone, the front door banging shut behind him and I realized I hadn't mentioned Emily's room or the money or anything. I sat down to the soup, picked up the spoon, and tried to eat, but all I could manage was a few swallows. I poured a glass of soda and sipped at it before emptying both into the sink. My mother always said if you're too sick to eat, at least drink some ginger ale, and here I was halfway around the world following her advice. I sank back to the table and dropped my head onto my arms. God, I missed her, and Kelly.

And John. Most of all, John.

CHAPTER THIRTY-FOUR

ut. I fell asleep trying to connect why that name or place or code, whatever it was, sparked something in my brain, but the thought was as elusive as... I woke in a blanket of sweat and tears, and when the fog of sleep cleared my head, only one thought remained. *John was missing and presumed dead.* There was no one-minute delay, no grace period in my realization that my world was falling apart. I ran my hands through my hair, climbed from the bed, and trekked to the bathroom where I took a shower, threw on a tee-shirt and sweats, and caught my reflection in the mirror. My skin was sallow, my eyes sunken, my hair dull—I looked sick. If anyone did stop by—it would be easy to convince them I was.

On the way back to my room, I saw the cocktail napkins still fanned out on the floor where I'd left them. I pulled one up, and there it was, that word—*Yut.* And suddenly it was clear—he was the man who'd approached me at Ban. He was somehow connected to all of this, or he knew something. I was sure of it.

And with that certainty running in my veins, I padded downstairs and brewed some coffee. But with my first swallow, I felt the burn as it spun through the raw emptiness of my stomach. I couldn't remember when I'd last eaten, but I knew I should. The refrigerator offered up the rice and chicken that I'd been unable to face after Bān —a place and people whose memory I'd all but forgotten. I ate without tasting, without the pleasure good food had always provided. My only goal was to fill the emptiness in my stomach. The emptiness in my heart was another matter altogether. John had been missing for forty-eight hours.

I somehow plowed through the morning, made my bed, did a laundry, ironed John's shirts, and tried to forget. Everything.

The house phone—which I'd never realized actually worked—rang at one in the afternoon. I jumped, afraid to answer, afraid not to. Finally, I braced myself and raced for the office. "Hello."

"Mrs. Fielding?"

The voice and accent were unfamiliar, and I hesitated, afraid that it was bad news.

"Mrs. Fielding? This is Doctor Worcester. The embassy asked me to call. Said you and the ambassador were both ill."

"Oh, of course. I'm sorry, and yes, we are sick, Doctor. A cold or maybe the flu."

"Would you like me to make a visit? I can come to your residence."

"No, no, we'll be okay, but thanks for calling."

"If you change your mind, let me know, and in the meantime—I'm sure you know the drill—fluids, rest and Tylenol, though here it's called paracetamol."

I thanked him again, and hung up, a fresh wash of tears stinging my eyes. How I wished that Tylenol, fluids and rest could make everything better. Since I couldn't make any calls, or use the internet, I went back to my closet and pulled out our wedding album. And I sat, and looked, and remembered. Like everyone's wedding photos, these showed a happy couple in the first hours of a brand-new life. What they didn't show were the secrets that would threaten everything I thought we had. I put them away. I needed to take my mind off of whatever was happening.

I turned on the television, so I'd have some background noise—happy chatter—to keep me company and keep my brain occupied. But it didn't work. I couldn't get John off my mind, and then I realized—I didn't want to get him off my mind. What I wanted was to wrap my brain around this. There had to be something I could do. Something. Anything.

I went back to the closet and sat in front of John's duffel bag. I examined the cocktail napkins again, but the numbers and letters and symbols might as well have been written in a foreign language—they still meant nothing to me. I pulled out the GPS device, the cellphones, and the other electronic gadgets. I wasn't a tech-wizard, but I was no dummy either. The cellphones seemed brand new. I didn't need a password to get in, but once I was in, there was nothing there—no calls, no emails, no apps. Ditto for the GPS which was still wrapped in cellophane. The iPad, however, offered up some information. John must have used this in the past, for the desktop display featured apps, email addresses, documents, photos, a contact list. I scrolled through it all, lingering over the pictures of our wedding before moving on to his contact list. My name was there, a small star drawn next to it, and I smiled. There were other names and numbers—women, men, familiar names, foreign names, and others—like *Black Ice*—that were likely codes.

In *Documents*, I found notes he'd written, some in a foreign language. Russian, maybe? He had folders organized by country, some by terrorist group—ISIS, Taliban and Al-Qaeda all had their own folder—and all seemed to offer up clues, hints, and even roadmaps, to what he'd been doing. My eyes were glued to the pages.

ISIS (Islamic State of Iraq and Syria):

Probably began in 1999 in Iraq under various names, pledged allegiance to Al-Qaeda in 2003; made gains to control Al Anbar, Nineveh, Kirkuk and other Iraqi provinces. Expanded into Syria in 2011—took control of some rebel areas; Al-Qaeda cut ties with ISIS in 2014. Expanded into Libya—and…

Taliban:

Founded in 1994, took control of Afghanistan in 1996. They are a fundamental religious group using the Koran to pound the nation into complete submission. Men and women were publicly executed for crimes both large and small. They were overrun by U.S. Forces in 2001 but they emerged again and wrested control from the U.S. backed government in August of 2021 as the U.S. Forces evacuated the country.

I read another page about Al-Qaeda and by then my brain was spinning. I knew they were all evil. There'd been plenty of stories on the news about how these groups murdered civilians, journalists and aid workers. But right now, I didn't care about their history. I just wanted to know if they had John, and, if they did, how to get him back. I went back to the iPad's Home Screen, and through his photos until I found a folder labeled *Afghanistan*. And there, I hit the jackpot. Hundreds of aerial and satellite images told the story far better than his words had. There were pictures of villages abandoned or bombed into dust, babies alone and crying, and children covered in grime and looking not so different from the refugees in Bān except for one thing—the Afghans all wore expressions of terror. The women and children cowering as Taliban towered over them, rifles in hand. And my heart broke for those poor souls but burst with pride at what John had been involved in when he was *at work*. If only I'd known. I'd fallen in love with a real-life American hero.

John had scrawled descriptions underneath some of the photos and he'd starred the ones of a village called Garm Chesma, nestled along the border with Pakistan. There were images of thousands of refugees fleeing Afghanistan and crossing into Pakistan. Was that where he was? But Jim said he'd maybe gone to Tajikistan to cross over into Afghanistan, and it was there they'd lost all contact with him, but now— seeing these images for myself, losing contact didn't seem so out of the ordinary. But the direction was all wrong. I pulled up John's section on maps and found Tajikistan to the north and Garm Chesma to the east and in Pakistan. Why fly north into Tajikistan when the border crossing he'd starred was on the Pakistan border? I sat back on my heels and shook my head. I was lost. Even the city names were almost unpronounceable to me. I abandoned the maps and pored through his contact list searching for Tajik or Afghan names though I wasn't sure how I'd know which was which.

I ran my finger down the list and stopped at *Jim*. There were several numbers by his name and one of those was the one he'd given me. As I scrolled further, the names were replaced by initials—R.F., A.L., C.M., E.H., and on and on. At the moment, it was meaningless to me. But I wasn't about to give up. I pulled out one of the new cellphones, plugged it in to charge, and dialed my own cellphone to see if it would work, and if it did, what the number of this new phone was. I heard the familiar buzz of my cell and I retrieved it from my nightstand. There was no number for the call—just a series of zeroes. I answered the phone to be sure it was the cellphone, and it was. And I was almost giddy. I had an untraceable phone to use.

I looked again at John's contact list and decided to start at the bottom. Those would likely be his newest contacts. I dialed the first and got nothing—not even a ring at the other end. I tried the next number, and got a ring, but nothing else—no answer, no person, no voicemail. The same happened with the next three numbers.

And then my own phone rang, and I froze. I picked it up. It was Mae. "Hello," I answered, trying to sound sick. I forced myself to cough.

"I just heard the news, you poor thing. Are you okay? What can I do?"

Her voice was filled with worry, too much worry for just a sick call. And I hesitated and wondered if she knew about John. "It's just a cold," I answered, sniffling. "John's sick too, but the doctor told us to rest and take Tylenol. I hope everything's okay with you."

There was a long pause, too long, I thought, but then she sneezed.

"Oh, gosh, sorry. I hate when I know I'm going to sneeze. Do you need anything? Can I stop by for a visit?"

"No," I answered too quickly. "We don't want anyone else to get sick, and you sound under the weather already. Thanks for calling though." I hung up before she could say anything else.

I turned back to the phone and the contact list and tried the next few numbers and came up with nothing. And then, I began to cry.

CHAPTER THIRTY-FIVE

Even with John's iPad and contact list, I didn't know any more than I did yesterday. There was still no word from Jim, and I was going crazy here all alone imagining the worst. I had to get out, maybe go for a walk, do something, anything, to clear my head and figure this out. I took a quick shower, slipped into pants and a tee-shirt, pocketed some money and my cellphone, grabbed my keys, and opened the front door. And stood there. Where could I go? We were supposed to be sick, housebound. I couldn't very well climb into my car and drive away. I heaved a long sigh, shut the door, walked to the kitchen and sat, my elbows on the table, my chin resting on my hands while I tried to think.

And then I remembered—Chai's secret path that led to the street. I jumped up. I could go to the Madrid—and maybe learn something. I wasn't sure what I was after, but if John *worked* from there sometimes, there had to be a clue. It was worth a try. I opened the back door and peered out. The garden was empty. I stepped outside and hurried through the garden to the secret path. I turned again to be sure no one was watching, and then I slipped onto the path and out to the gate. I carefully undid the latch, set it aside so that I could get back in, and followed the alley to Soi Ruam, where I breathed a deep sigh of relief. If I was going to help find John, it wouldn't be from the house, it would be from out here. I hailed a taxi—grateful that this wasn't my first time doing that in Bangkok—and sat back.

"The Madrid," I said.

The driver turned to get a better look at me. "Madrid?" he asked, his eyes crinkling.

When we pulled up, I paid him in *bhat*, and stepped into the bar, my eyes wincing from the sudden dark. I stayed there, by the entrance, for just a minute. If I wanted to get a look, see who was here, I had to disappear into the crowd, and so I did. I ordered a glass of wine and slid onto a stool at the end of the bar, where I was hidden by a metal post, and the sign for the emergency exit. I hunched my shoulders down as though that would help me be less conspicuous and then I sipped my wine and waited.

And as I sipped, my eyes searched the bar for any sign of the woman I'd seen with John, or for anything that might seem important to my search, but there was no one familiar, nothing that seemed out of the ordinary, though I wasn't sure anymore what was ordinary and what wasn't. Just as I was about to give up and leave, the door opened, and Renée entered. I slumped down on the stool and raised my glass to my lips and watched as she turned and held the door for her companion—Mae.

I almost choked on my wine. I covered my mouth and coughed into my sleeve so I wouldn't attract attention. I hadn't realized they were friends, but it made sense, I supposed. Mae had introduced me to Lisa and Renée after all. They sat near the entrance, ordered drinks and looked around. And just in time, I bent down as if to retrieve something I'd dropped. I counted to twenty, and raised my head carefully, but already they were engrossed in conversation, oblivious to everyone else in the bar. That in itself seemed unusual for Renée who'd always seemed to be on the prowl for men. Whatever they were doing, I knew I had to get out of there before they decided to use the bathroom which was right behind me. I counted out my *bhats*, slipped them under the glass, and followed the sign for the emergency exit. I leaned against the heavy door and had a quick look, and when I was pretty sure there were no alarms attached, I pushed down on the bar and stepped into an alley.

It was dusk already, the thick fog that precedes the rain, settling over everything. I made my way back to the street and caught a taxi back to Soi Ruam. I slipped in through the gate, latched it behind me, and walked back into the house, the deep quiet there somehow unsettling. I turned on the lights as I made my way upstairs, and there I clicked on the television. At least that would provide some life in the house. I checked the phones —still no messages. I was about to make myself a cup of tea when the doorbell rang. I froze. I pulled on my sweats and mussed up my hair. If I was sick, I had to look the part. The bell rang again. Maybe it was Jim with news. I flew down the stairs, pulled open the door, and my shoulders sagged. It was the guard on duty out front.

"Sorry to bother you, ma'am," he said. "But this came for you." He held up one of those padded manila envelopes and passed it to me before turning to go. "We're right out front if you need anything."

I nodded, thanked him, took the envelope and closed the door. I was about to throw the envelope on the hall table when I noticed it was addressed to me in John's handwriting. I tore at the seal, and a bag of Twizzlers fell to the floor. A note fluttered behind it. I picked it up and read:

```
Hey, babe, Just found these in the
airport in Dubai of all places. Knew
```

you'd forgive me for going away again if
you had these. On to the NWFP and then
home to you. See you soon! Love, John

I held tight to his note, retrieved the bag of candy from the floor and sank onto the stairs where I sat and let myself just cry —for John, for me, for everything. When I could bear to read it again, I did, and then I checked the envelope. He'd sent it two days ago, probably right before he disappeared. I wiped away my tears and ran upstairs. I'd check a map, that's what I'd do— find out where Dubai actually was. And to do that, I'd have to defy Jim and log onto the internet, but I was determined to help find John. Once I'd logged on, and searched maps, I traced my finger along the route. Dubai seemed out of the way if you were headed to Tajikistan or Pakistan, but maybe it was the only flight available. I looked up Garm Chesma and paused. It was in Pakistan—*the lawless Northwestern Frontier Province, the NWFP*—Wikipedia said. This didn't make sense. It didn't make sense at all. Why go to Dubai at all?

A lizard slithered by, its tongue darting out in search of insects to snare. It seemed a frightening metaphor for whatever was happening with John. But I knew I couldn't think that way. I wouldn't give up. I began to pace and tried to think. I cursed Jim for not calling and poured myself a glass of wine. I was missing something important. I was sure of it. I sank onto the couch.

CHAPTER THIRTY-SIX

I t's strange how you can adapt to even the most hideous of things. How everything can change in the blink of an eye, how your soul can absorb the blows, and free you of that unrelenting first terror, allowing you to adjust and continue putting one foot in front of the other. Already, I was adapting—my pulse was steady, my breathing regular, my eyes clear. I'd made it through the last few days. But incredibly, I was exhausted, every muscle felt knotted and tight, as though I'd run a marathon. I knew I had to sleep to clear my head and soothe my aching muscles. Only then could I figure out what I had to do. I placed the bag of Twizzlers and the cellphones on the nightstand, and slid into bed, the crisp coolness of the sheets the perfect salve for my body and mind so desperate for comfort. I pulled the covers up and over my head, blocking out everything but the welcome nothingness of sleep.

I woke early, the remnants of last night's fog seeping in through the half-open shutters. I rubbed the sleep from my eyes and stretched before reaching instinctively for John, my hands and then my eyes searching the room. And then the events of the last few days came tumbling back to my brain until there was room for nothing else.

John had been missing for seventy-two hours.

I reached for the phones—my own, the one Jim had left, and the new one from the trunk, but all were empty of messages. I rose, splashed water on my face, threw on my jeans and a shirt, and headed down for coffee. If I tried to establish a routine, I could keep going.

My phone buzzed. It was Renée. "Hello, *mon cheri*, so sorry to be late getting back to you, but you called me?"

The morning fog seemed to have settled in my brain. Had I called her and forgotten? Damn, had she seen me at the Madrid? "Uhh, I—"

"Probably forgot already. It was a few days ago. Late afternoon. You didn't leave a message, but I thought—"

And then I remembered—I'd called the day I'd gone to Bān and seen the place where little Suu lives. It seemed like a million years ago now. "I'd gone to Bān. I found Suu, and the dump where she lives, and I just wanted to talk."

"So, how is today? You are free?"

"No, John and I are still sick with some bug or other. We're both just staying in."

There was a long pause, and I could have sworn she was speaking with someone. "You sound busy," I said. "I won't keep you."

She laughed. "Ahh, so I am. But I'm going to Bān myself today—to deliver some things. I thought perhaps you might come with me, help me. *Oui?*"

Bān and little Suu—I'd almost forgotten them in the last few days. "I would like to, any other time, but I don't—" John's last words spun into my brain—"*Stay away from Bān. There are some issues there.*"

"Please say yes."

"Not today," I said. "I don't want to leave John."

An hour later, the gate guard buzzed to let me know that Renée was here. "I'll come out," I said, wishing she'd just leave.

When I opened the gate, I saw her, hanging out of the car flirting with the young Marine.

"Hello, *mon cheri*," she shouted. "Tell this handsome young man to let me in."

Afraid to make a scene, I nodded. "It's okay. Just for a minute though."

When the gate was opened, Renée pulled into the driveway and jumped out. She kissed both my cheeks her hand lingering there, her eyes crinkled. "You don't look well, Nora. You really are sick?"

I sniffled a little in answer.

"But you cannot just stay in. The sun is out—for now at least. Come to Bān, get some fresh air, and help me with this." She pointed to a pile of boxes stashed in the rear of the SUV. "Supplies," she said. "I have to deliver them alone. Lisa is still in London."

I shook my head. "I can't leave. Sorry."

She locked her eyes firmly onto mine. "What is it?"

"John's still feeling pretty lousy. I don't want to leave him here alone." I turned my gaze toward the house. "We've both been sick with the flu, and I'm just still feeling blaah, you know?"

"*Blaah?*" Renée mimicked me and she laughed. She brushed a stray hair behind my ear. "It is more than that, I think. I can see the worry in your eyes. Your husband?"

"Just that he's sick." I couldn't hide my tone—I knew I sounded sad, and I was. I probably shouldn't have said anything. I felt ready to burst into tears, and I sniffled to emphasize my sickliness.

"I think it is more than what you say."

I shook my head. "It's nothing," I answered.

"Ahh, but it is. I can read your emotions."

I sighed, but didn't say a word, and Renée continued as though I was waiting for her to go on when I was really wishing she'd just leave.

"You are hiding something. It is your skin that gives you away, the way you get little bumps on your arm when something is wrong, or the splotch of red on your cheeks, or even the way the little hairs on the back of your neck stand. You see, it is always someone's skin that gives them away."

I shrugged in reply and rubbed at my arms. I didn't see any bumps.

"I think I know what is going on," she whispered, her voice soft, but her tone determined.

This time, tiny goose bumps really did sprout along my arms, and a rush of heat burned my cheeks. My hand fluttered there to hide the evidence that she could so clearly read.

"I know your husband." She folded her arms and leaned back against her car.

I looked at her questioningly. I wouldn't say a thing. It was bad enough that I'd come out to speak with her.

"At the Madrid, when I saw your photo, and I pretended that maybe I knew him, well—I'm telling you now—I *do* know him. I know who he is and what he does."

I felt the blood drain from my face.

"You don't have to say a word," she continued. "When you said the man in the picture was a friend of your husband's, I knew you were lying."

I took a deep breath and looked her straight in the eye. "I didn't have any reaction that I remember."

"Ahh, *mon cheri*. You only thought you didn't. And even if I weren't an expert at deciphering looks and gazes, I would have known he was your husband. Your eyes sparkled, your pupils dilated, and a tiny smile danced on your lips. And I knew—you loved this man, and I wondered how much you knew about him and his work, and if maybe you weren't involved in his work, too. You see my dilemma?"

"What do you mean?"

"I know your husband well. We've worked together. I'm with MI6—the British intelligence agency. Surely, you've heard of them?"

I nodded.

"I didn't know that the John I knew was the ambassador here—but when I saw the photo and then your reaction, I knew exactly who he was, and I wondered what he was up to here in Thailand."

I kept my gaze steady. I wouldn't confirm or deny anything. Let her think what she wanted. And besides, if she was a spy too, what was she doing working with an aid group? As if she could read my mind, she spoke up, intersecting my thoughts.

"So, you have a dilemma of your own. Trust me or not? *Oui?* I think you should trust me. You don't know who else you can trust right now. Am I correct?"

I nodded. That much was true. I tried to remember if she'd met John at the embassy reception, the one that Mae had arranged. But he hadn't been there. He'd left on another trip.

"Do you want to tell me what's going on?"

I shook my head. "Not right now."

She heaved an exasperated sigh, climbed back into her car, and started it up. "You will call me when you decide you need help. *Oui?*" She began to back up, and then suddenly stopped and leaned out of the window. "There is an old Thai saying —*bad luck never comes alone.* Remember that and let me know when you want my help."

I bit back my tears. What the hell had I been thinking coming out to speak with her? Nothing was as it seemed. I patted my pocket, all three phones safely there—on vibration—in case there was word. And I prayed that Jim would call.

CHAPTER THIRTY-SEVEN

Once inside, I pulled out the phones, and laid them out, turning the sound back on and the volume to high. And when the phone that Jim had left rang, I jumped and snatched it up. "Jim? Is there any word?"

"Nothing yet."

My sigh heaved through the line.

"That's not bad, Nora. In fact, it might be good. How about you? How are you holding up?"

And this time, I remembered—everything—the cocktail napkins with their codes, the man at Bān and John's warning that last morning, and finally—I told him about Renée. "Do you know her, too?" I asked.

There was a long pause. "What's her name again?"

"Renée François, and she said she knew John, that she worked with MI6. A spy, I guess."

"Really?"

"Yes, do you know her?"

"Never heard of her. Never heard John say anything either. No more contact, okay? And stay away from Bān. Can you do that?"

And that reminded me—and I told him about seeing Renée and Mae at the Madrid.

He let out a long noisy breath before speaking again. "Shit," he muttered. "I'll be back later today or tomorrow. We'll talk, and I'll have a look at the napkins. In the meantime, just stay put. We'll figure this out."

I closed my eyes and silently thanked the gods for that bit of hope. I puttered around the house, got on the internet and looked up NWFP again, and when I was engrossed in that, the house phone rang and I picked it up. "Hello," I said, my voice hopeful that this was good news.

"Mrs. Fielding?" an unfamiliar voice with an unrecognizable accent asked.

"Yes," I said, wondering if it was too late to hang up.

"I've been trying to speak with you. I'm the man who approached you at Bân."

I could hear my own sharp intake of breath, and I moved to hang up, but he'd anticipated my move.

"Don't hang up. Please. Just listen first, and then hang up if you must."

I closed my eyes and listened as he spoke. The man with the evil eyes had a lot to say, and I wasn't sure if any of it was true.

"I'm from Pakistan investigating a weapons shipment for terrorists. I was assigned to track the weapons from Bangkok. I've only just been given your husband's contact information. We're working on the same deal, just using different sources. I know he's away right now in Pakistan," he said.

He had my full attention at *Pakistan*. Maybe he did know something. It couldn't hurt to listen.

"Al-Qaeda and ISIS have extended into Pakistan and India and elsewhere, and they're doing it through the refugee camps along the Myanmar border. Do you follow that?"

"Not really. Why there?"

"Because they can get guns and equipment from Indonesia through the camps. The stuff comes through Customs in Bangkok, gets a stamp for an aid group, and then slides right on through to the camps, and from there—to the terrorists. We've only just identified Bān as one of the transit camps."

"But I've been there. I didn't see any terrorist movement."

"Oh, but you did. You were right in the middle of it."

"What are you talking about?"

"A member of the aid group you work with is handling the deliveries."

"That's crazy."

"No, it isn't. I'm watching the French woman deliver the equipment now."

The acid in my stomach began to churn. I knew I was in way over my head, but I still wanted to trust Renée. At least I *knew* her, and I believed her story that she was one of the spies, the good guys. She said she knew John. "She's delivering medical supplies to the camp. I saw her today. And I saw the supplies."

"And she wanted you to go with her, right?"

"Well—"

"And you said no, because John is in Pakistan, and you were told to stay away from Bān."

He'd finished my sentence for me, except that he said John was in Pakistan. "How do you know where he is?"

"Because I'm involved in the same investigation."

"But you tried to speak with me last month. What was that all about?"

"Naiveté, that's what that was. I knew who you were, I'd seen that newspaper photo, so I knew you were probably reliable. I just wanted your husband to contact my own agency —the Pakistan Intelligence Service."

"Everyone's connected here, huh," I said, thinking of Renée and MI6. "So, what are you working on with John?"

"I'm not working with him yet. But we've been working on the same supply route. Russian money and suppliers bring the weapons from Indonesia to Bangkok, through the refugee camps, on to Pakistan, Afghanistan and India. It's been a long process, but I think we're about to have a big break. I just need help in tracking this French woman and her boxes of supplies. I'm pretty sure she'll head back to Bangkok. I need someone there to follow her."

He paused and I could hear his long, tired sigh snake through the phone.

"I don't understand why you've chased me down. Why not just call John weeks ago?"

"No cell service out here, the satellites were down. Nothing works in the jungle the way it's supposed to."

"But you're calling me *now*."

"I'm on the other side of the camp, and I'm connected to a Thai military satellite. They've stepped up their presence here, but of course, they don't give a second glance to the aid workers, and that allows free rein to those among them who are here for the wrong reasons."

"Why can't you just tell the Thai military then? I mean, if they're right there—"

"Because everything will just blow up. It would be like sending out a red flag to the terrorists to change their route. We'd lose all of our work. We just have to wait and watch. And it's important that Renée be watched in Bangkok. Understand?"

I harrumphed loudly. Though Renée's eyes may have been piercing, this was the man with the decidedly evil gaze. And then I caught myself. Had I thought they were evil before Renée had mentioned that?

"I'll send you proof—pictures of the weapons and of your

friend. I have to document everything, so I'm staying right here. I'm only calling to ask you to let John know that it's Renée François and the other aid worker, they're the ones working out of ISIS Iran, and here with a small lead team. That's all—just tell him that. He'll know what to do."

"That's *all*? If it's true—it seems pretty important. If you really do know him, why can't you just call him yourself?"

"I've tried. His phone is turned off."

"What about Jim? Did you call him?"

"Jim? No, I don't know that name, but if you trust him, just pass on my information and tell them both that Yut with Pakistan's Intelligence Service called. *Please*. Just do that. Nothing else, just that. It's important."

And then he hung up, or we were disconnected, or something. Either way, I was left with the phone in my hand, and more questions swirling through my brain. I tried calling John's cellphone, and this time, just as Yut had said—it was turned off.

Jim couldn't get here fast enough.

CHAPTER THIRTY-EIGHT

Exhausted, I'd fallen asleep and woke to a funny crackling sound—like static from the television. I opened my eyes and reached for the clicker, only to realize that the television wasn't even on. I checked the cellphones, but they were quiet too. The noise persisted, and my confusion deepened. I pulled back the covers and rose in search of the incessant hissing sound. It seemed to be coming from the closet, so I headed there, and as soon as I stepped through the door, the crackling sound increased, and I turned instinctively toward it. John's duffel bag, it was coming from the bag. Alarmed, I stepped back. Was it one of the weapons? A bomb?

My heart pounded in my chest, and I hesitated, afraid to investigate, afraid not to. Cement blocks might have been weighted to my feet as I stood there immobile, my heart pounding, the hair on the back of my neck—just as Renée had said—standing up. And it was the thought that Renée was convinced she knew me so well that finally propelled me forward. I bent and unzipped the bag, and the hissing sound almost exploded in my ears. I jumped back and waited. And when nothing happened, I inched forward and peered inside once again, and there on top of the pile of weapons and gadgets was the walkie-talkie I'd seen. I lifted it gently and listened as it sputtered and crackled, the heat of it warming my hand. I held it tight to my ear praying for John's voice to leak through the static, but the only sound that came through was the crackling hiss. I inspected the radio, pressing buttons and changing channels until I lost everything, and the radio went quiet. The sudden silence descended around me like a tomb. Frantic, I pressed the buttons again trying to undo whatever damage I'd done, and when the hissing resumed, I breathed a sigh of relief. Someone was trying to reach John, or maybe even me. I prayed that the batteries would hold out until I could show Jim.

I was squatting there when a phone rang, and I raced for the nightstand. Jim's cellphone was lit up and, almost breathless, I answered it. "Hello?"

"Hey, Nora, you okay? You sound out of breath."

My head was spinning with the possibilities the crackling walkie-talkie presented, but I was becoming a quick study in keeping secrets. "I have a lot to show you. Are you on your way?"

"Twenty minutes. Do you have coffee?"

I scurried to the kitchen, turned on the coffeemaker and went back upstairs to shower and dress. I couldn't remember when I'd last washed. My hair was heavy with grease and my skin shiny with perspiration. It suddenly occurred to me that John would be coming home, and I needed to be clean when he did. I felt almost giddy as I stepped into the warm spray and lathered up, washing away not just the build-up of grime, but the build-up of fear as well.

By the time the doorbell rang, I was dressed and determined to find John. I handed Jim a cup of coffee and led him to the trunk where I showed him the still crackling radio first.

His eyes grew wide as he held it. He fiddled with the

buttons, pressed one, and spoke. "Bravo echo calling J.F., bravo echo calling J.F." He released the button and stared intently at the radio as if willing a reply.

"What does—?"

He shook his head and placed his finger over his lips. And I was quiet, save for the pounding of my heart. A tinny, far away voice broke through the static, but the words were broken up, and finally they were lost again in the sputter and hiss of the radio. Jim toyed with it again and spoke into it, but this time— there was nothing. He laid it down and turned to me.

"Sorry about that—bravo echo is Bangkok Embassy. Old-fashioned codes and outdated radios, but we use an encrypted channel. It's reliable as hell, and almost impossible to scramble and hack. John and I still use these." He tapped the radio. "And maybe—"

My heart fluttered in my chest, and my hands flew to my mouth. "John? Do you think it was John?"

For the first time since John had gone missing, Jim smiled. "Could be."

And then I remembered. "A man named Yut called," I said quickly, afraid I'd forget if I didn't just blurt it out. "I'm sorry to interrupt, but he said he's with Pakistan's intelligence agency, and to tell you and John that it's Renée, that she's the one delivering weapons."

"Renée François? The one you mentioned? The aid worker?"

"Yes. He said she was delivering weapons to Bān. But she stopped here on her way out and I saw the boxes. I'm no expert, but I don't think they held weapons. I've seen those supply crates piled up at the camp. And besides, she said she works with MI6, the British—"

"Shit," he said. "I know who MI6 is, and I can tell you they don't have any French women on their roster. They barely tolerate Americans; no way they hired a French woman." He raked his hand though his hair. "Where does she live? Do you know?"

I shook my head.

"Do you have her cell number?"

I grabbed my phone and watched as he copied it down.

"What's going on?" I asked, but he didn't seem to hear me. He'd pulled out a small laptop and was typing furiously. When he hit *send* and turned back to me, his face was pinched.

"The cocktail napkins?" he asked, all attempts at composure gone.

I laid them out and watched as he studied them, his brow furrowed, his gaze intent. Finally, he laughed and held one up. "Did you notice this one?"

I looked closer and saw the logo of the Capitol Hilton, the place we'd met a hundred years ago. A tear sprang to my eyes, and I reached for the napkin. He'd scrawled Nora across the back and written my cell number. "That's odd—I'm pretty sure he just put my number into his phone."

"That napkin, my dear, was his insurance. A vital lesson in our business—always have a backup, and for us—cocktail napkins carry a lot of information. Indispensable."

I shook my head in confusion. "I don't get it."

"That's just it—no one ever does. We do a lot of work out in the open where we can blend in and meet our contacts, our sources, without attracting attention. A crowded bar is a great place to do that. People drink too much, and they forget what they see, and sometimes what they say."

"But—"

"The cocktail napkin? Perfect method for passing information. Even if it's intercepted, people don't pay attention. They throw them out, allowing us to continue on. Deals have been made, secrets uncovered, and lives saved because of these little bits of paper. John always joked that if terrorists and dictators really wanted to end clandestine communication, they should just outlaw cocktail napkins. But dictators and thugs don't seem to understand the value, and we're not about to clue them in."

I watched as he laid out the napkins and went through everything again.

After an eternity, he leaned back and sighed. "I'm going to the embassy. I'll check John's desk and see if there's anything there."

I reached for the package of Twizzlers and the note from John and passed them to Jim. "These arrived yesterday."

Jim held the package and laughed. "He's been looking for these for months."

"Look at the note. It says he was in Dubai, and on his way to the NWFP. But, why Dubai?"

"Central location. Easy to get into and out of. He probably had to pick something up or meet someone before continuing on. It's not unusual. He could get to Pakistan or Tajikistan easily from there."

"But would a man who's approaching a life and death assignment be looking for these?" I held up the candy.

"I hear you. His searching for candy makes it seem as though he was approaching this as any other mission, and that gives me hope."

There, Jim had said it—that elusive word—hope, and I latched right onto it.

"I'm going to get a move on," he said. "And I want you to stay put and hold on to this."

He handed the radio to me and gave me a quick lesson on how it worked. "That button is the squelch button—it will suppress the static you hear when we're on, but not getting any transmission."

"How did the radio just turn on? It was in John's duffel bag when it started."

"You likely hit a button when you first found it, and when it began to pick up something, the static grew until you followed it."

"Was it John?"

"Maybe. We use a silent channel and transmit only when necessary. I can't think of anyone else who'd be on this frequency, but I can't be sure."

And the tiny glimmer of hope simmering in my heart, grew. "He's been gone before and didn't call me at all. I didn't know anything until he arrived home. Is it possible he's just doing his job, and doesn't know about this mess?"

"It's entirely possible." Jim collected the documents and napkins and placed everything back in the bag. "Do you know how to use a gun?"

He said it so matter-of-factly, I almost fainted. I swallowed hard and shook my head.

"Never mind then," he said. "There's not enough time for a lesson." He pulled the zipper on the duffel bag and stood.

"Hold on to the radio, and the phones. Don't answer anything unless it's from me. Understood?"

And then he was gone, the door banging shut after him.

CHAPTER THIRTY-NINE

I stared at the radio and the phones for what seemed like hours, willing them to make noise, any noise. But the silence was deafening until the rain began in earnest, the crash of thunder drowning out everything. I held the phones and radio close, my eyes searching for what my ears might miss. And finally, it happened. Jim's phone lit up once again, and my fingers trembled as I hit *answer*. "Hello?" I shouted to be heard.

"Are you okay?" His words were garbled, our connection broken up.

A burst of thunder interrupted him, and I couldn't make out what he was saying.

"Get out," he finally said. "Get out of the house. Hide in the garden, somewhere. Renée's on her way, and her plan is to get you. Take the phones and radio and run."

I paused, unable to even process what he was saying.

"Get out now. Call me when you're outside. Don't go through the front gate. Renée's there right now trying to convince the soldiers to let her in."

And then, in the quiet between booms of thunder, I heard the gate intercom squawking, and I understood. "I'm leaving," I whispered into the phone, and raced down the stairs, and out through the kitchen, holding tight to the phones and radio. Once outside, I held them close to my chest to keep them dry. I slowed as I traced the tree to the secret path and blessed Chai for showing me this route as I slipped in between the sopping wet branches and shrubs and stopped. Should I stay right here? Jim hadn't said, and I wasn't sure what to do. And then I heard voices, Renée's among them. Her tone was light, and I knew she was flirting with the guard.

"She's been ill," I heard her say. "She asked me to check on her."

He mumbled something in reply, but I couldn't make it out.

"The ambassador will be so grateful that you let me in," she said, and I watched as the exterior lights came on, cutting through the rain and fog and intersecting the hidden path. He'd let her into the house. It would only be a matter of minutes before she realized I was gone.

A bead of sweat trickled along my neck, and my pulse quickened. The birds, the insects, the rustling trees, all of it, ground to a halt as if the world was ending. What the hell was I going to do now? I held my breath and moved back further. And waited. A flash of wind and rain rustled through the trees, and I shivered. The air seemed charged—as though lightning were hovering in the trees just waiting to strike. Something brushed my cheek, and I froze, my eyes wide open, my body stiff with fear. And then it brushed me again and I saw the source—a swaying palm frond. I exhaled and backed away.

And then the radio came to life—a series of beeps and then noises and then static. And in the midst of that, I heard Renée.

"Nora? Is that you? Where are you? You are in danger! Do you understand?"

Her voice was moving closer. She was just outside the path. The radio crackled, and I turned and ran along the path, finally unlatching the gate and emerging onto Soi Ruam, the road busy with evening traffic, headlights dancing in the street's puddles. From there, I ran. I turned right, and then right again and finally back onto Wireless Road, and then I stopped. I could see the embassy's gates from there. I called Jim.

"Nora, where are you?" he said, his voice high-pitched and nervous.

"On Wireless Road, about a block up from the embassy."

"How did you—? Never mind. Are you safe where you are?"

"For now, but I'm out in the open. Renée's at the house. She knows I'm not there. She'll be looking for me."

"I'll come to you. Start walking toward the embassy, but as much as you can—stay in the open so I can see you."

I began to answer when the radio started up again, a series of beeps followed by more static.

"Has it been going off?"

"Yes," I said, heading toward the embassy. "But it's just the beeps and then the static again. Does that mean anything?"

"I don't think so. Keep talking. I'm leaving through the front gate. Can you see me?"

He waved, and I waved back, and in that fleeting instant, a gunshot rang out, and instinctively, I ducked. Jim turned back toward the embassy and raised his right hand—a gun firmly placed there. He began firing at someone, and the gunfire drowned out all other sound. Jim jerked back, and I watched in horror as he dropped to the ground and lay there unmoving. I stopped dead, but only for a millisecond. I knew that whoever had shot him was looking for me, and if their eyes had followed his wave, they already knew where I was standing. I darted behind a car, and then the next one and the one after that until I was finally back on Soi Ruam, safe, but only momentarily. I heard the shriek of alarms and sirens fill the air, and I knew help was coming for Jim, but not for me. I wasn't sure where to go, or who I could or couldn't trust. I retraced my steps back to the hidden gate and lingered there trying to decide if I should go inside, or—my cellphone rang, and my heart stopped. It was Jim.

"Jim?" I cried out. "Are you okay?"

There was a long pause. "Nora? Is that you?"

The voice was familiar, the tone puzzled, and it took my brain a minute to process who this was. And then my heart fluttered. It was John. "Oh my God, where are you? Are you all right?" But he didn't answer. All that came through was background noise—people shouting, sirens blaring, horns beeping. "John!" I shouted, afraid he hadn't heard me.

"Nora, I'm outside the embassy. I hit redial on Jim's cell. Was he talking to you just now?"

I began to cry. "He'd told me to get out of the house. I was coming to the embassy. I saw him go down." A loud sob shook my shoulders. "Is he okay?"

"Where are you now?"

I told him and he told me to wait, not to move, but I couldn't wait another minute. I started to walk and then run, back to the embassy. Just as I turned onto Wireless Road again, I saw him, his hands gripping the steering wheel of a U.S. government SUV, his eyes scouring the road. The beams of his headlights bounced off of the lingering rain puddles in the street, and I ran out in front of him, waving my arms frantically. When he saw me, he skidded to a halt and jumped out, his arms around me so quickly, I barely had time to kiss him hello. The radio and phones fell from my hands and landed on the street with a loud clatter. But John didn't seem to notice, and I didn't care.

He held me closer than seemed possible, and I melted into him, allowing the curves and angles and strength of him to give me comfort. I held on tight, his body pressed into mine, and for the first time in days, I thought that things would be okay.

He let go of me long enough to cup my face in his hands and

kiss me. Then he pulled me close once again and I ran my finger along the cool shiny band of gold that circled his ring finger.

And the terror and fear of the last few days slipped away.

But I shouldn't have let it slip so quickly from my mind. Things were still unsettled. I just didn't know that then.

CHAPTER FORTY

John tried to send me home. He promised that he'd be there soon. But I'd heard that more times than I cared to remember. I wasn't going anywhere until I learned what was going on. He finally relented and led me past the phalanx of armed guards, policemen and Marines, and into the relative quiet of his office. But my thoughts were still spinning, and the next hours were a blur of questions, and nods and murmured conversations. Harried men spoke into radios and phones, and typed into laptops, and I could only watch. I wasn't one of them. They had to fix this, whatever *this* was. I saw Renée in the crush of men with earpieces and guns and she smiled and nodded before turning to John who was in the middle of it all. I sat in his leather chair and once they turned to me, I recounted the events of the last few days starting at the beginning.

"Jim said you were missing and presumed dead, and I—" I could hardly speak through my tears and sniffles, and John wrapped me in his arms, and urged me to go on. And I did. I stammered out everything, and men took notes and listened intently. "And as I turned onto Wireless Road, I saw Jim, he was coming to get me, and then I heard gunfire, and I saw him turn to shoot, and that's when he went down. How is he?" I asked, tears streaking my face. "No one's said anything. Is he okay?"

John clenched his jaw and shook his head. "He's dead." He paused and leaned forward, brushing my lips with his.

I felt a heavy weight press the air out of my lungs. "Oh God, no," I whispered.

"I'm sorry, Nora, but you might as well know the truth. Jim, my friend, my lifeline in the business, was likely a double agent. He's been using Bān as a transit point for his arms deals. The weapons were stored in UNHCR crates. And when they passed through Bangkok with the UNHCR logo, they avoided Customs inspections. They were simply waved through. It was brilliant, really. And almost foolproof."

"But how could he...? And... what about Renée?"

John's eyes grazed the room searching for her, but she had slipped out. "She's with MI6 and she was here posing as a UN auditor to follow the trail. I just learned she was here, by the way, but I know her, and more importantly, I trust her. The insider at the camp was Lisa Bates. Do you know her?"

Lisa? "She's away," I finally said.

"Away as in pulled in for questioning. She's the one who pointed the finger at Jim. She had no idea that Renée was there to follow her. She bought her UN cover story. Renée intercepted one of those UNHCR crates at Bān a few weeks ago and found the weapons and money, and then she went to the airport and watched as Lisa and Jim signed for the crates at Customs. She was just pulling it all together and had made plans to take Jim into custody when she noted how taken you were with Lisa and Bān and she was worried that you'd be unwittingly tricked into assisting them. She had to move fast. She arranged for Lisa to be called back to London where MI6 arrested her and she spilled the whole story."

"Why couldn't Renée just tell me?"

"She couldn't risk it. She'd already figured out that you had no idea what I really did. She was afraid you'd unknowingly tip Jim and the others off."

"Did you know she was working on this? And if you did, why couldn't you tell me?"

"I was working on the arms destination angle; Renée was working on origination. Perfect example of the right hand not knowing what the left is doing. The CIA and MI6 weren't working together on this until yesterday when we got word. Damned bureaucracy. We should have been working this together."

"I still don't understand. Who's behind this?"

"We aren't sure yet if it's ISIS or Al-Qaeda or the Taliban, or a new group, but Lisa was definitely targeting you. She hoped to trick you into delivering arms to Bân, and through you, she could blackmail me to close the loop on any potential problems."

A chill went through me. "Emily Somerfield, the last ambassador's wife, the one who went missing, she worked with Lisa at Bân. And when I asked Lisa about that, she denied it. Could Emily have been involved?"

"I don't think so. I don't think we were aware of that, but we'll definitely push Lisa on that information."

"So, what happened?"

"We were closing in on the whole operation. I was in Garm Chesma on the Pakistan–Afghanistan border, the distribution point of the weapons. We'd taken those men into custody, and I was on my way home. That's when I learned that Jim was involved, and he was at the office trying to destroy any evidence. He apparently planned to just take off."

"But he's been helping me. He's been—"

He leaned toward me and took my hands in both of his. "It seems he's been selling arms and any weapon you can imagine.

He had us all fooled, right up until yesterday. Renée confronted him today and he panicked. He called you almost immediately after she left the embassy to warn you to get out. He called because he'd learned that I'd just arrived back in Bangkok. He was surrounded by people who'd been watching him. He may have been the one who planted the story about my being in Tajikistan. He knew all along where I was, and he knew too that everything was unraveling. We think his initial plan was to get you on his side, to draw you in and use you as proof that he was still with us, that the weapon deals were part of his own investigation."

"But he..."

"I never disappeared. He was supposed to tell you I'd be back in a day or two. I'm sorry you were caught up in this mess."

"But he was trying to find you. I'm sure of it."

He paused to take a deep breath and rubbed my arm. "We've known for some time that there was a mole in the office. We just didn't know who it was."

And I told him that Jim once thought it might be him. He only shrugged in reply.

"I didn't even know you spoke Russian. There's still so much I don't know."

"I speak just enough to get by. *Ya lyublyu tebya*—that's Russian for I love you. That's all you really need to know, isn't it?"

But it wasn't, and I didn't answer. I needed to know everything, starting with Jim. I wasn't entirely convinced that he was a bad guy. He'd been so good to me, and I still had no idea what had really happened out there on Wireless Road. "Someone shot at Jim. Who—?"

John squirmed in his seat, and I realized how hard this must be for him. I reached out and stroked his arm. "You don't have to tell me," I whispered.

"His gun was drawn, his finger on the trigger. He meant to use it. The guards were afraid he was going after you, to kill you or take you hostage. They had no choice."

I swallowed the fierce lump in my throat. It was hard for me to believe that Jim would have hurt me, but I'd never know for sure. This was not a life I could even pretend to understand, and here I was, right smack in the middle of it, trying to figure it all out. "But—" I shook my head. "Never mind."

"Tell me," he said.

"There's so much, I'm not even sure where to start or who to trust. I saw Renée with Mae a few days ago. They were deep in conversation. I'd given Mae your phone, and everything seemed to fall apart after that. Is she a part of this, too?"

He shook his head. "We don't think so. And the phone? The one you gave to her? I had just left for Dubai en route to Pakistan, didn't even know I'd forgotten it. She left it on my desk. Maybe, Jim saw it there and sent that text to you and—" He shook his head and sighed.

"But Jim had questions about that text. He didn't seem to know anything about it."

"He was acting. It's part of what we do."

I blinked away a tear, and wondered—was *John* acting now? I pushed those thoughts away. What I needed was answers. "I just don't understand any of this."

"And I never thought you'd have to. It's my fault that you were even in that position. I'm so sorry, Nora. I'd never do anything to endanger you. You know that, don't you?"

A well of tears gathered in his eyes, and I brushed them away. And then I remembered Yut's name neatly printed on one of the cocktail napkins and I asked John. "Is he one of them or does he work with you?"

A shadow fell over John's face. "We're not sure. I do know a man named Yut and it does seem that Pakistan has been investigating this as well, but I don't have any information that this Yut was involved. Renée's working on that. He may be exactly who he says he is."

"What about Bān? The refugees, the people who live in the dumps. What happens to them?"

"Things will probably be better for them. We've literally just figured out that Bān was the transit point. We'd thought the arms were going through a nearby village and when that didn't pan out, we thought maybe it was the dump. It seemed like a possibility. But those places will be okay. Well, as okay as they ever are."

"But Lisa's gone and Renée, well she never really worked there. Who'll manage it now?"

"The UN has people there. And more on the way."

And suddenly, the men who'd been taking notes and typing on computer keyboards, slipped out leaving just John and me. I sighed and worked the kink out of my neck. "Why couldn't you tell me about your job? Even in Boston or DC, why couldn't you just tell me the truth?"

John's face crumpled. "Nora, I couldn't say anything. It's part of being in the firm, we're in so deep that no one can know. Most spouses go to their graves thinking their husband or wife is with USAID or State. It's how we keep ourselves and the people we love safe. And I do love you. More than you know."

"I know that you love me, but I don't understand why you couldn't have said *something*."

"I couldn't, and I never thought I'd have to. I thought that Thailand would be safe. I could do my thing from here and you'd be happy. That's what I thought. I swear, Nora. We chose Thailand as our base of operations because it is so safe. Christ, even their military coup was relatively calm. And Bangkok gave me a great jumping off point. It allowed me quick access to Pakistan, Afghanistan, Iran, even Yemen."

I was still confused, angry even, but I had to admit—my curiosity was piqued. "But why be an ambassador? Why not just be a spy? Pose as an assistant to somebody, or something? Isn't it better to be the little guy that no one watches? The guy that follows the ambassador?"

"That's just it – the little guys, the assistants *are* watched. Everyone knows they're the ones doing the real work, gathering the information, setting events in motion. Ambassadors are usually figureheads. They do a few receptions and that's it. Foreign governments do long, hard checks on the ambassador's staff. Ambassadors are assumed—for the most part, don't go quoting me—anyway, they're assumed to be all fluff and no substance. They get a wider reach and no one really knows who they are. But the reality is—as the ambassador, I can do more, have a bigger impact, and with my ID and diplomatic passport, I can go anywhere, and there's no record. I'm more invisible now than I ever was before."

That was precisely what Jim had said. And I brushed away a tear as I remembered his kindness to me. John pulled me into his arms once again. I covered his lips with my hand. I didn't want to hear anything else. I couldn't even process what I'd already heard.

"Can we just go home?" I whispered.

CHAPTER FORTY-ONE

But, at home, I fell apart, my memories of Jim still fresh and still painful. I didn't believe, not for one second, that he'd intended to hurt me. I didn't care what John said. He hadn't been there. And even Lisa—I couldn't see her as a terrorist either. And the more I thought about Jim's death, and how close John and I had come to that same fate, the more anxious I became until I just collapsed in a heap in John's arms. He called the embassy doctor who showed up armed with a syringe full of something and a bottle of Xanax, which turned out to be better for what ails you than wine. I fell asleep curled up next to John, and when I woke, his arms still tight around me, we made love, or maybe love wasn't involved at all, maybe it was just a frantic re-affirming of life, of everything we'd almost lost. When he touched me, my nerves, raw from everything that had happened, seemed to explode in a torrent of desperate, throbbing pleasure that left me as sore and satisfied as the first time I'd had sex.

When we finally crawled out of bed to shower, I hesitated, acutely aware of how much had changed in the last twenty-four hours. For starters—there was Jim. And now there wasn't. I closed my eyes and sat on the edge of the bed just rocking back and forth, a stream of tears running from my eyes. John helped me to the shower where he tenderly washed away the sweat and grime and sadness that covered me like a second skin. And then he draped my robe around me and brought me hot tea and Xanax to help me through the day. And through the haze that the Xanax offered, all of his explanations made sense. I was still sad. I just wasn't hysterical. But when the effects wore off, my doubts and questions bubbled back to the surface. "What about Emily Somerfield? There was money hidden in a trunk in her room."

"We've been looking into it. Jim was the only one who could have ransacked that room and taken the money. He's probably the one who left the money there and then took the key to keep his secret safe. Lisa's been talking more as well. Apparently, Emily had discovered what was going on at Bân and Lisa thinks she might have been killed but insists she doesn't know anything else."

A shudder ran along my spine. "Have they found Emily?"

"They're still looking." And as he held me tighter by the minute, he asked what we should do.

"Go back home," I said without a second thought. "I can get my job back at Bain and Worth and you can get a job as a lawyer. We'll be fine."

John smiled and said he had too many years in to just up and quit, but that he'd apply for a transfer. But we all know how that goes. He worked for the government, and the government moves slow as molasses, as my mother would say, so though he put in a request asking to be transferred immediately. The only reply he received was polite and almost dismissive: *"Your request is under advisement."*

And, though I still peppered him with questions about what I came to call *the incident*, his answers seemed vague and not quite what I was looking for. Then I remembered how, early in our relationship, I'd looked up the State Department on the internet to try to figure out what it was John really did there, but all I'd found were meaningless platitudes and ideas, and I thought that's what he was giving me now. And maybe, he wasn't being purposefully evasive, maybe it was just so ingrained, he couldn't even see it.

But he was still trying hard to make me happy, and the first thing he did was to move his damn duffel bag and guns to his office in the embassy, and though he spent hours and hours holed up there each day, he came home to me each night. And sometimes he arrived home with bad news—Lisa had escaped while she was en route to a court appearance and the last shipment of weapons had inexplicably slipped through Bān and on to an unknown group. Though a worldwide watch had been issued for Lisa, she was still at large. Though I found it hard to believe, John said she posed a real threat to us.

And then Chai and Patiwat returned, and I was effusive in my welcome hugging her thin body close. "Is everything okay with Patiwat and his family?"

Her eyes teared up and she shook her head.

I gripped her bony shoulders, almost relieved to get involved in someone else's problems. "Can I help?"

"I don't think so, Miss. His granddaughter disappeared many months ago. No one will help. No one believes him."

"Tell me," I said, sinking into a chair in the kitchen. "Maybe I can help."

And she told me the child had disappeared with Emily Somerfield. "They'd gone out together one day and neither ever returned."

An icy finger ran along my spine. How could I say that Emily, and the child too, might be dead? So, I nodded and said I'd speak with John. And Chai turned back to her table and began to clean her space with a steady, practiced hand. I crept away, embarrassed that I was as helpless as she.

Finally, John came home with good news. "Bān has been cleared by the Thai military," he said one morning. "It looks like they'll need all the help they can get. You interested?"

And I smiled at the possibilities that Bān offered. "Only if you'll come with me—at least once. You can see for yourself how the dump dwellers really live and what the camp's really like, maybe then you'll see that a little help out there will go a long way. And before we leave Bangkok, maybe we can put some kind of plan in place."

He leaned close and brushed my lips with his. "Deal."

And the next day, when it seemed the rainy season was surely over, John and I headed out to Bān on sun-splashed, bone-dry roads. "I can't wait for you to meet Suu. You'll understand how I feel when you meet her and see the children in the garbage dump."

John squeezed my hand, his mind somewhere else, but his eyes firmly on the road. When we pulled into Bān, a small crowd surrounded us, and they followed us to the little clinic where I poked my head in to say hello. Nath sat alone, entering information into the patient roster.

"Hello," I said, stepping inside.

He jumped up and bowed, and I bowed in turn and introduced John.

"I'm hoping to get back here more often but I wanted to show my husband around if that's okay?" Nath nodded and we headed out with a crowd of children at our heels. I showed John the camp, the small play area, the main road that wound through the center, and I watched as he took it all in. But we weren't done yet.

"Dump next," I said, steering him back to the car. We drove to the area where I'd spotted Suu, the place we'd slipped through to the dump, and I had John park the car so I could get out and look around, and while I was hemming and hawing—was it right here, or maybe there—Suu appeared like a tiny angel, and took my hand, and I melted all over again.

I knelt down to hug her, and she kissed my cheek and patted my hand. When I called John over, she turned abruptly, a scowl on her face. She looked ready to run, but I grabbed her hand.

"No," I said, one hand over my heart, the other pointing to John. "I love him, my husband. Understand?" But she didn't and her scowl deepened as she tried to pull away from me.

"Kids," John said. "Maybe when we have our own, they'll like me better."

And with those words, a small thrill passed through me. Suu pulled at my hand, snapping me back to attention, but I held on tight, and pointed through the woods. "Take us, please?" I whispered, this time my hand on her heart. She understood that at least, then smiled and tugged at my hand and we followed the path through the trees and out to the dump. I could hear John behind us, his breathing speeding up, a cough catching in his throat as the breeze carried the scent of the dump to us. We came through the clearing and out into the heaps of garbage, and I could hear the sharp intake of breath that meant John was seeing it all just as I had not so long ago. He caught up to us and placed his hand on my back. I turned to see him shaking his head.

"Incredible," he whispered, his eyes scanning the trash, and the people who lived among it.

Little Suu watched him warily and finally flashed a shy smile, taking it back quickly when she saw his gaze fall back to her. I squeezed her hand tighter. Damn, I loved this kid. I caught John's eye and inclined my head to Suu. He smiled, and I knew she'd had him at hello. We followed her around, John watching intently as she showed us the place she called home.

John finally sighed. "We need to come back with an interpreter and plans to make changes. No one, least of all little children, should live like this. This is one thing we can work on. You were right. I should have come out here long ago."

And, with those words, I knew I'd love him forever. I passed him my iPhone. "Will you take a photo of Suu and me?" I pulled her close and she leaned into me smiling as John snapped away.

He passed my phone back and grew serious. "Maybe we should be searching here for Emily Somerfield. She worked here. She knew what was going on. The Thai police should have looked more closely out here, but we definitely will." His gaze tracked the enormous expanse of the dump, the endless piles of trash. He ran his fingers through his hair and shook his head sadly. "Jesus, awful to think she might be out here, but we need to move quickly."

I hugged little Suu and we drove back to Bangkok, talking all the way about possibilities and plans. Well, I was talking, John's mood had darkened, his thoughts on Emily and perhaps Jim.

I was upstairs changing when I heard a loud wail from downstairs. *Chai*, I thought instantly. *She's cut off a finger*. I took the stairs two at a time and stopped cold. Chai was holding my phone, tears streaming down her face, her fingers trembling, her screams gone silent.

I'd left my phone there on the entry table, the photo of Suu and I my new background photo. I reached for the phone and she pulled it away. "What is it? Do you need to call someone?"

"Where did you get this?" she cried.

"I don't know what you're talking about," I said, afraid that she'd somehow lost her mind.

She held the phone out. "This girl is Patiwat's granddaughter! Where is she?"

And she began to scream loudly again. Soon a guard was knocking at the door to check on me. I reassured him that I was okay and turned back to Chai and explained how I'd met Suu and where she was. Chai crumpled to the floor in a heap. It took some time for each of us to understand the other's story. It turned out that Emily Somerfield had spent time with the little girl, whose name really was Suu, and she'd taken her along the last time she'd gone to Bân. Neither of them had ever returned and when Patiwat went and tried to report the child as missing, the police dismissed him. He tried to speak to the last ambassador, to plead for help, but the poor man was grief-stricken and desperate to find his wife. Chai and Patiwat looked everywhere but it was as though Suu had vanished into thin air.

I called John with the news and we four headed out the next morning in search of little Suu. When she spied the car from the safety of the jungle, she came running towards us, and when her grandfather stepped out of the car, she threw herself into his arms. My own heart burst with joy at the sight of the two of them holding tight to each other, tears of joy streaming from their eyes.

And I knew, if I did nothing else worthwhile in my life, this moment would be enough for me.

CHAPTER FORTY-TWO

I learned that little Suu had been trying to tell me all along who she was. She'd believed that Emily had sent me there to get her and bring her home, and each time I left, she'd cried. It broke my heart to hear that, but she was home now. And that gave me some peace. Still, there was so much more to do at Bān. And I was ready.

It took another week before John received his reply about his transfer. Apparently, the State Department really liked John—which came as no surprise to me—and they wanted him to stay on as the ambassador—for real. No CIA work, he said, just a straightforward diplomatic assignment. And when he asked me what I thought, I almost didn't have to think about it. "We can live out in the open? Go to events? And have dinners? Get Suu into a school that can help her?"

"All of that and more," he replied.

So, together, we said yes to the offer. And when I called my mother to tell her the news, that John was the ambassador, there was a long pause.

"Well, dear, I already know that."

I laughed so hard I cried.

And then Mae was assigned to help me out two or three days a week and Chai was assigned to us full-time. And with Suu at her side, she donned her apron, cleaned out the refrigerator, and tsk-tsked at the state of the kitchen. "All I can find here is soup and old vegetables and rice." She wrinkled her nose, shook her head and drew up a shopping list.

Mae called with a head full of ideas. "I think we should arrange a luncheon, give you a chance to meet some of the important local officials, and we should have a dinner to reintroduce you as the ambassador's wife. And then, of course, we'll be invited to cut ribbons and speak at Bangkok events." Then she arrived with a bright smile spread across her face, and a notebook in her hands. She jotted everything down as we spoke. "We'll need to shop again, I think," she finally said, and nodded to herself as if I wasn't even there.

And Elizabeth Miller, the Canadian ambassador's wife called. "Oh, my dear, we heard about the trouble at the embassy, and we've been so worried for you. A few of us would like to take you out for a glass of wine. What do you think?"

And all I could do was smile in reply. It seemed if you were really an ambassador's wife, life would never be dull, and people would be lining up to take care of you.

The next days were a flurry of activity—John was busy at the office arranging a search of the dump and trying to wrap the investigation up, Mae was working on arranging official events and appearances, and I was busy being—well—the ambassador's wife and trying to forget the events of the last month while enrolling little Suu in a school in Bangkok. Things were working out after all.

And then the news came, Emily Somerfield had been found. She'd been murdered, her body stuffed into one of those wooden UNHCR crates and left at the dump. Her devastated husband arrived to claim the body. The diplomats and wives all attended a short service and extended their sympathies. I suggested that we dedicate a new garden to her and the wives all nodded agreement. And just like that, Emily was forgotten again by most everyone. Except by me. When I promised her husband that I would continue her work at Bān, he gripped my hand and smiled through a veil of tears.

John was out of the spy business, but the memory of Jim still haunted me. I still had questions and doubts, but I buried them —and all of my old suspicions—away.

Then one evening, I came upon John shouting into the phone in a foreign language. Russian? "Renée?" he shouted. "*Nyet, nyet.*"

And even I knew that word was Russian for no. I coughed, and he turned and said something into the phone before hanging up.

"Hey, babe, I didn't see you," he said sheepishly, the silver flecks in his blue eyes dancing in the dim light.

"What was that all about?" I asked warily, praying he wasn't back in the spy business.

"Nothing," he said, pulling me onto his lap. "Just wrapping things up. Nothing more."

And I smiled because I sensed I was supposed to. He kissed me then, a deep soulful, passionate kiss.

"So, how's the ambassador's wife?" he asked playfully as he unbuttoned my blouse.

This time, I smiled for real. I was the ambassador's wife after all, wasn't I? And I loved my husband whose favorite color I'd learned was blue, his favorite book anything historical.

And just as I leaned in, his phone rang. "I have to take this," he said, pulling away.

I stood up and walked away, reminding myself that here I was—still just thirty-five—and the ambassador's wife at last.

And then I stopped, and as I listened, John's voice dropped to a whisper. And I wondered—was I really?

THE END

ACKNOWLEDGEMENTS

I am enormously grateful to Cynthia Manson, my incredible agent and even better friend, for her extraordinary guidance, her cherished friendship and her unshakable faith in my ability to craft a story. I am more grateful than a simple "thank you" can ever convey.

To Betsy Reavley, Tara Lyons, Shirley Khan, Hannah Deuce, Katia Allen and the wonderful team at Bloodhound Books, thank you. I am enormously grateful to be a part of the extraordinary Bloodhound family.

To my family and friends, who've always believed in me, my gratitude is endless.

And finally, to my readers, I want to say a huge thank you for choosing to read *The Ambassador's Wife*. If you did enjoy it and want to keep up to date with all my latest releases, please visit my website: www.robertagately.com. There, you can sign up for emails to learn about releases, giveaways, etc. Your email address will never be shared, and you can unsubscribe at any time.

ABOUT THE AUTHOR

Roberta Gately, a nurse, former aid worker and author, lives in Boston where she continues to write and work as a nurse. She has written for several nursing journals including *The Journal of Emergency Nursing* as well as a series of articles for the *BBC World News Online* and the *Huffington Post*.

ALSO BY ROBERTA GATELY

Lipstick in Afghanistan

The Bracelet

Footprints in the Dust

Dead Girl Walking

The Frozen Girl

Her Mother's Cry

A NOTE FROM THE PUBLISHER

Thank you for reading this book. If you enjoyed it please do consider leaving a review on Amazon to help others find it too.

We hate typos. All of our books have been rigorously edited and proofread, but sometimes mistakes do slip through. If you have spotted a typo, please do let us know and we can get it amended within hours.

info@bloodhoundbooks.com

www.ingramcontent.com/pod-product-compliance
Lightning Source LLC
Chambersburg PA
CBHW040217170726

48295CB00014B/705